THE DAMAGED PICKUP TRUCKERAR

ABHINAND.T

Contents

ABOUT THE AUTHOR

Abhinand.T

Abhinand.T (born November 7,1999, Kerala) a newly risen Indian novelist, known for his science-fiction trilogy of novels called The Pillscape Trilogy published in the year 2024, which includes, 'The Accidental Ventures of Kiran' 'The Damaged Pickup Truckerar' and 'The Flambopian Escapade'. The whole trilogy discusses the hypothetical situation that if we human beings were some puppets of one massive invisible force ready to conduct one merciless mission on the entire Universe! And what if this force possessed magical powers, and had control over scientific knowledge, time, consciousness, nature etc. His other works include the Philosophical drama "The Forgotten Sacred Essence: An offering to Humanity" and the Horror drama "The Garlic farm Graveyard is Not the Reason!" both published in Malayalam and English language, in the year 2025.

The second son of Mr Thulasi C and Mrs Sudha, has an elder brother AravindT. Abhinand earned his graduate degree in

Malayalam literature, and his post graduate degree in English literature, both from Kerala University. He successfully achieved the certificate of UGC NET in English literature, which is an exam conducted in India to determine the qualification for Assistant professor in Indian universities and colleges.

He is passionate about writing, which encouraged him to become a full-time writer, specialized in existential philosophy. He is against the Alienation, Escapism and Selfishness widespread across the post-modern world, a major theme of his writings.

PREFACE

The second part of 'Pillscape Trilogy' but serves as a Prequel to the first part 'The Accidental Ventures of Kiran'. Ok, let me introduce you all to my work;

Human beings believe in Universal laws. For example; people strongly believe that by working hard and smarter, they can achieve anything they want, because they try-hard to believe in the principle 'The World has more Greatness than Evil'. Is this true? I want to test that theory. 'Soul of Fiction', I invoke you to create a plot, to let me find more about that theory. (someone whispers "done") Great, now all I need is to create a character who knows driving, and must place him in one of the long driving jobs... I created Larry. Welcome Larry. "Hi, where am I?" Larry spoke. I can't answer any of your questions because I don't care, just take that way and... the stage is all yours. Get out!

The bell has rung! Sound of bags rustling filled the class. Giggy has taken out a textbook from her drawer, it has a nature-themed cover page, she looks excited. Random teacher walked in, "Good morning teacher, may God bless you" said the whole class. The teacher is busy dusting the board and the chair, "Good morning class" she finally said. She is also carrying the same textbook Giggy has in front. "Open page number 56, read the story silently" she said and moved to the open window, and started scrolling through her phone. The whole class turned into a swarm of bees, and Giggy encouraged me to take a look at the story titled "FAMILY GENIUS". With nothing else to do, I started reading the story.

"—Once upon a time, there lived a colony of Ants, called the CENSI, and their King 'Tan', and his most trusted administrator Rick, who was the most intelligent ant lived there. Rick invented various weapons and defences to counter enemies and won many wars. Rick then started conducting research on the structure of their Ant colony situated near the rocky mountain, and for some reason, none of the members knew how it came into existence. Rick was uncomfortable living with not-so intelligent Ants, especially the King who had no interest in anything other than to celebrate made-up festivals, and to organise feasts. Rick was very frustrated with the King's attitude for not embracing the power of Ant brain, and for spreading laziness around the whole Ant colony!

Rick, with his genius mind, deciphered some of the hidden construction secrets, and decided to build an individual sized home near the riverbank. Rick left the Ant colony, his wife and two kids, reached the riverbank. He asked permission from the river for taking some of its muddy flesh, but the river ordered Rick to decorate his riverbank with plants and trees in return. Rick roamed inside the distant forest, and collected as many seeds as possible, spread them around the riverbank. The seeds started to sprout within a day, and the river happily granted Rick what he wanted.

Rick then went to meet one lonely plant, and that was me, he requested me to give some of my tiny sticks. But I made Rick agree to one condition; Rick must narrate a story for each stick he takes from my body, and he must build the structure next to me.

Rick collected at least fifteen tiny sticks from my body; he had to visit his ant colony friends to gather stories. About one year later, Rick finally achieved his dream; built in the shape of a match box, had four compartments inside, and one strong ceiling. He felt tremendous pride and was eager to show his achievement to his friends and family. They all became shocked to see the structure, praised Rick for the rest of the day. The King was amazed by the beauty of it, ordered his subjects to start building more of those buildings. Rick was delighted and taught others about the techniques. With more hands working, built several other buildings within a month, covering most of the riverbank. Each Ant family received their own house, and started to live happily, completely abandoning the Ant colony.

One year later, things started to get more complex. No more festivals were celebrated, no more war meetings were held, no more family gatherings, no more marriages. And most importantly, all the ant members were forced to collect food individually, sharing was ceased to exit. Even the King had trouble getting food on his table, had to roam around the forest like a beggar. In the meantime, the weak enemy clan 'SICEN' started to plot against Rick's clan. They saw the King's condition and knowing they had no weapons anymore, SICEN enacted their plan slowly. At first, they secretly ambushed males who were collecting food from the jungle. Rick saw that but kept the information secretly inside his mind. Rick started to prepare his family and his house for the upcoming danger.

Rick noticed his neighbouring buildings getting filled with weapons such as twig spears, dirt ball slingers, leaf shields, tiny rock throwing trebuchets etc. Rick went to the Ant King's building, but he could only find his decayed corpse. Rick was traumatized, he ran back, realised that the whole territory was under attack by the enemies. He surfed back to his house, Rick was shivering, his wife already loaded up every weapon they had, and started shooting it across the map, had no care whatsoever whether the shots hit any of the neighbours or not. Rick had something hidden under the floor, it was 'used stapler pins' that he collected from the river stream when he was building the structure. Rick took his mighty weapon and waited for the enemies.

The door started to shake violently, and Rick could feel the violent knocks on the door indeed hitting his chest. Rick screamed for alliance, but all he could find was the neighbour Ant looking out of his window, holding a tiny slingshot, but he kept observing the events at Rick's house, without taking any action, and finally he closed the window. Rick's family was butchered mercilessly, but the enemy clan spared half of the 'CENSI' inhabitants. A month after the assaults, I have grown so long, could see the decaying corpses of Rick and his family. And now, after ten or more years, the buildings are no more! The river has reclaimed all its stolen piece of earth. Meanwhile, I keep looking at the sunrise and sunset, waiting for the arrival of a new genius Ant member from the Ant colony—"

That's an interesting story for sure. I looked around, guess I finished reading first. With nothing else to do now, started contemplating on my current situation! Did I dream all that old life or Have I been put back into my younger life, kind of a time travel thing! ... "How is the story, class?" teacher asked. (Unclear chattering's) "Ok, now who can tell me about the moral of the story?" teacher asked. I have almost raised my hands but decided against it because am lazy to elaborate my findings. I would have raised my hands if I knew how to answer within a single sentence. Some of the students poured their findings, but not worth mentioning here. Finally, the teacher stepped to the centre of the class and offered her explanation; "Wars are dangerous, it destroys peace, say no to Wars"

I

Predictions by an Astrologer

The World is a Zoo of different living and non-living things. Humans rule the animal kingdom due to their highly advanced reasoning skills. You might be wondering why I am saying these philosophical blabbering's. Well, my name is Larry and I am one unemployed man, but I am not one lazy stack of flesh. I have started to pen my life into a well-polished book, gifted by my best friend Alan for my birthday, even though I have neither wished nor gifted him anything for his own birthday. Ok, now I will tell you why I started writing this thing... Who am I kidding, right? Sorry to trick you guys, I am too lazy to write, I am using a voice recorder that has a storage of five gigabytes! And this thing can transform my voice into written Pdf file also. Ok, back to the narration — For the past few months, my life has been a pile of some routine actions. When I was fired from my job, things turned tricky and out of hand. Now I want my painful existence to be heard by the world, I believe it is always great to read about other people's sufferings and to offer useless pity comments.

I have a wife, Susan and five children, three girls and two boys. I have to feed them all, we live in a poor neighbourhood, and I was one of the few people who earned something. I was working at the office around the corner of the 22-dh street, filled forms for over seven months, but the intervention of pesky computer brain made me lose my job. Even though I didn't like the job, the low payment was enough to supply food on the table for my gigantic family. No! It's not what you think, I have no brother or sister, my parents died ten years ago. To be honest, my parents had a small pension money that kept us running smooth for the long past years, but now I lost all my savings and earnings all together. Oh, again I got carried away talking about my sweet parents, sorry readers! What I meant with the phrase 'gigantic family' is that I have three daughters and two sons.

My wife's mother lives with us, resulting in a total of eight stomachs to fill in. No! I didn't want five children; it was all an accident. No! Not an accident, you know, right? Well, I should elaborate then, no problem. Me and my wife Susan belong to the love marriage category that is so underrated in our place, I guess it should be underrated. She was working at the bank, I don't know what made her fall in love with me, it is true that I tried to lure her into my love trap, but all I was looking for was definitely not love but money and sex. Luckily, I had a handsome physique and bright skin back then. The most striking incident occurred one month after our marriage.

She quit her job! I mean, who would ever think of that? In a world filled with slogans of women empowerment, my wife elected to abandon her hard-earned job and became a full-time housewife. Well, now I realise why she did that, she doesn't have to cook anything just because I have no means to buy anything to cook. The five pesky little things keep screaming for food all day and night, it is not possible to satisfy their hunger even with a truck full of food, then how can they remain silent! Normally, I go to the dilapidated farm where papaya and cabbage grow, pick some of them along with some leaves and stems, boil all in one pot and serves hot, without any seasoning, its taste relies on the random leaves and stems.

But today, the farm is not on my side. Some cruel animals have taken control of it, not to mention my unsympathetic rich neighbour who destroys a large portion of the farm with his heavy collection of guns for fun. I forgot to tell you guys that he owns the farm. I went to the farm early and picked some leaves and stems, boiled it while praying for some miracle to happen to at least make the thing a little eatable. I am sure that there is no poisonous stuff inside my brewery now, such kind of luck will never bless me. Unfortunately, the brew doesn't even satisfy one's olfactory senses, Susan started cursing me for being a big lump of mud. I can't remember how many times she cursed me repeatedly.

I have noticed her regular use of the statement "Why you are being a big fat piece of nothing, I dreamed of a bright luxurious future, and you gave me this dull crap life, I wish I never met you". Normally, I remain silent throughout her pounding me down the ground with words, sometimes offer her fake promises that I can't even recollect myself. But I can recollect the luxurious parties happening inside the compound of my rich neighbour, he has never invited me to any of his functions. I always wonder why he does not offer me any help; I know I am being ridiculous to ask for someone else's money, but the fact of the matter is that he burns through a lot of money to conduct one single party, out of his three hundred parties all year.

I am sure that a single bottle of rum served during his parties will grant my family a whole year of food. Ok, I must stop condemning others for not helping me, great. I wish my mother-in-law would die quickly to ease the hunger tension. I don't like her at all; she always suggests me to sell one of my daughters to some pervert man. I have my doubts that she was once a prostitute. She regularly points out my wife's attractive traits that she can use to make a good career in prostitution. Susan thinks about it heavily but for some reason she gets back down from the thought. My rich neighbour stares at my wife every time he drives by our house.

Things are getting very tricky; I must find some source of income from somewhere. "Damn you AI" I say this out loud routinely. If the AI didn't interfere my work, my life would have been ok. They say they develop this pesky artificial brain to reduce the burden of human beings, but my burdens have become twice bigger now, and they have no answers for my problems. What! We need money to live! If they want to replace human beings with metal brains, they should give a good amount every month for the rest of our lives. Is that too much to ask for? Who cares really? ... One day, Susan took me to see an astrologer, she believes that he will be able to help me. But how? I don't understand the point, am not a believer of these kinds of fellows. How can anyone be able to tell us about our future and our problems?

Let's put it this way, the people who seek help from these astrologers shall be having some problems in their lives, and then these astrologers burn it more and suggest some absurd remedy! Whatever! I went with Susan, and she led me into a two-story building, freshly painted, two sport cars parked inside the open garage, two beefy dogs that keep barking constantly. We went inside; the waiting area is filled with visitors. (laughs silently) He has a fancy name; 'Sosobretris' After waiting two hours, he called us in. We sat on a good, cushioned chair, and he is sitting on a royal chair, like the ones described in Kingly legends. He is holding a pack of cards, and he keeps shuffling it aggressively enough to drop some of them on the ground accidentally. To help him, I bent down to pick two cards.

Before stabbing them back into the deck, I took a quick peek. The first card was the picture of a hanged man... No, I believe he was still struggling to catch his breath, there was a crowd surrounding him, cheering. The second card was the portrait of some male God, may be Zeus... I don't know for sure, but he was holding a golden sword. Sosobretris is staring at me angrily, and then he spread out the deck in front of me, asked me to pick four cards and never peek at them. I did so, and he ordered me to give him the four cards. He laughed slightly and showed us the first card.

Card One — Prometheus chained to a big boulder, with vultures feasting on his chest — He explained that I will forever be chained.

Am not surprised with his prediction, I mean, it is a universal fact. Clutching on to universal facts is a technique used by these people. He noticed my 'I don't care' smile and started to elaborate on what he mentioned, "You will become part of a plan of action that will destroy every bit of peace and happiness of yours. You will undergo unimaginable transformation, suffer intolerable amount of pain. And just like Prometheus gave fire to humanity, you will succeed in handing over the world something of higher value, with the cost of your life" Am still not moved by his fancy narration. He then shows the second card out of the four.

Card Two — A red diamond placed into melted gold — Yes, it is what I said, can see melted gold scattered across the diamond. His expression changed to amazement, started to describe the thing; "You will make uncountable amount of money, and have the blessing to hold even the rarest of earth jewels, but no matter how much you gain, you will never be able to make use of the wealth" Once again, not surprised! Most of the people are good at gathering wealth, but only a few will make happiness out of it. Another universal fact! Again, he noticed my 'I don't care' expression, he started to elaborate; "You think am toying with you or something! Do you have any idea about this diamond? It is the rarest piece of jewel existing in earth, only one of them has been found in centuries of digging. It is what you will be able to hold on to, at some point in your life..."

"I must get some museum job then" I muttered, but he heard it clearly. "You will be this diamond's sole owner but won't be able to receive any benefits from it" he said in a mocking tone. Anyway, he then picks up the third card, and before showing it, he asked "Are you by any chance, work as a driver" "NO" I said. Finally, Susan has decided to speak up something "No sir, he once worked as a tourist bus driver, it was two years back" He flipped the card slowly and showed us;

Card three — One man sitting on a beach alone, a shipwreck drawn next to him — "Crusoe..." I said proudly. He just completely ignored my proposal and started explaining what it really is; "The picture of Odysseus, the man who went on plenty of voyages, and was stranded on a boat for two decades. It means that you will also be send to multiple journeys, captaining a crew and lead an adventurous life, and might get stranded in nowhere for the rest of your life" For the third time, am still not surprised or scared. At this point, I have a feeling that this astro-man is pounding me hard with his grudge for insulting him first. "How can anyone suffer these many troubles? Does not make any sense bro" I said. He looks very angry, flipped the fourth and final card, it is ...

Card Four — The Dinosaur! — (Grrrr). He didn't enjoy my funny sound expression. He explained; "You will earn many of the power badges with your skills and bravery, and reign supreme in every territory you shall be assigned on to. You will be fearless and cause property damage. But at the end, you will go extinct early, without leaving any mark on the table" Damn! What is the need for him to end such a good narration with a bomb. (Farts hard) "It was me, for your payment and was specially crafted for only you, freak, feel free to curse me, fool" I said proudly. Susan takes a hundred dollar bill out of her handbag and stretched out her hand towards him. I grabbed her hand and dragged her out of the room with me; she is still holding that hundred. We went out of his house, called a taxi and reached home. Ignored her curses for my bad behaviour and took a short nap. After a few hours, heard a knock at the door.

It is Alan, my best friend who visits me every month, and he always notify me about a lot of illegal job vacancies. I don't know what he is expecting from me with his monthly visits. I am hoping for some good news today from Alan.

Alan: 'Hey man, good news'

Me: 'Are you asking me or telling me?'

Alan: 'Stop joking man! I have received news about a cheap sale of a pickup truck for eight hundred dollars!'

Me: 'Good deal, but I don't have a single penny'

Alan: 'I know, another good news incoming. There is one job offer as a delivery guy, you will receive six hundred dollars per delivery, only costs around hundred dollars' worth of fuel. I have collected money for two deliveries, now you can buy the pickup truck for eight hundred, fuel for two hundred and spend the last hundred lavishly'

Me: 'Oh, you poor thing, you should attend some first-grade class, you moron. I will be left with two hundred at the end'

Alan: (laughs) 'I will take a hundred as my commission, you dummy!'

Me: 'Nice! I feel something weird about this contract, give me more details on this delivery thing?'

Alan: 'Don't worry my man, if it relieves your doubts, the delivery company is "DM Chocolust industries", happy?'

Me: 'I have heard about them, the big fat factory that has hundreds of guards standing outside, carrying rifles, my rich neighbour always orders chocolate from them, I have seen big metal boxes loaded on mini trucks aiming towards his house'

Alan: 'Keep in mind that you have to sign a document stating that you have no problem with taking this risky job, and even if you die, the company holds no responsibility'

Me: 'I believe this company is fond of rich people who would kill anyone for fun, I am not feeling good about this contract'

Alan: 'You have past that phase where you can take your life decisions carefully, come with me next Monday'

After Alan left, my wife started cursing me for stealing her gold chain. I promise I have never touched the thing, but she still accuses me for it. The chain theft issue has made a rumble inside the house that resulted in her signing a contract with a local prostitution company. After searching the whole house, still I can't find the gold thing that she accused me of stealing. I highly doubt that she was lying about the gold thing just to satisfy her dream job opportunity. The first day of her new job turned out to be a good one surprisingly. Susan was very happy to describe her only client of the day.

She said "The best day of my life, finally I have found some form of satisfaction in my boring ridiculous life. I had my fears about huge beastly men who take pleasure in beating women's flesh all around, but I was matched with a rich man who was completely alone and had no friends to share company with. We spent six hours straight talking, cuddling, drinking. He explained that he spent all his life trying to grind money to attract success and a good life, but when he achieved a significant amount of wealth enough to satisfy two generations of his family, he realised that he didn't have any needs other than the universal call of hunger inside his gut.

Unfortunately, his wife is a gold digger who has never offered any emotional support or children to uphold his family. Thus, he started to spend all his earnings on poor prostitutes like me." Even though I enquired her about the sex part, she didn't offer any reply, but she restarted her accusation of me stealing her gold chain that she claims having worth over five hundred dollars. I have clarified her gold chain accusation by looking at a photo we took at a marriage ceremony, she had that thing for real. I have shifted my accusations to my five kids and my good for nothing mother-in-law.

I forgot to tell you guys about my five kids. Three girls and two boys, the girls are named as G1 (10), G2 (12) and G3 (14). The boys are named similarly as B1 (13), B2 (14). Looks like a modern mathematical problem, isn't it? I can't make a judgement on who stole the gold thing. Girls are universally praised for their love for shiny objects, and boys are universally praised for their use of drugs and other weird things. I have decided to analyse all of them, but can't find anything suspicious, Poor kids! Now there is no need for any further investigation, the grainy sack of nothing-in-law thing must be the cat.

Before I can spy on her, an ambulance siren is heard. The ambulance stopped at the front; an attender called out my name. He ordered me to take the person out of the backseat. I went near the backseat, and my wife is lying unconscious under the seat. After taking her to the bed, the ambulance driver screamed out for us to pay him two hundred dollars, but I have decided to remain inside. Luckily, he beat my mother-in-law and took something valuable from her for his payment. She cursed me for not defending her, I became enraged and threw the garbage bag to her face. After a few hours, my wife started to regain her consciousness. She started to narrate what has happened.

Susan narrates, "I went to the building today and was expecting the rich man I met yesterday, but unfortunately, I was matched with a big muscular man who was ten times bigger than me. He didn't wait for any conversation, quickly jumped on top of me and ripped off all my clothes with one swish movement with his left hand, he hugged me tightly to the point that my eyes bulged out of its socket, then threw me to the ground and jumped over me one more time, luckily, I lost my consciousness after that." The most shocking thing she revealed is that she wrongly accused me of stealing her gold chain because, she has found it inside the wardrobe today.

Finally, Monday has arrived. Alan and I made our way to a junkyard. I am not enjoying the disgusting premises; the junkyard is full of filthy mess. Larry went inside of an isolated building surrounded by the large mess. In the meantime, I have started to look around the mess. I believe there exists a famous saying that by looking at the waste, one can identify one's personality. I am surprised seeing good quality chairs, electronic appliances, furniture etc. Sadly, there is one big fat camera spying on a pole, analysing each step made by me.

It is quite ironical to think that anything, regardless of its condition, earn the title "junk" when it is thrown into this junk shop. During my exploration, I made the worst mistake possible by opening one shiny refrigerator, it is filled with decayed meats and fluids. The disgusting smell covered the whole planet it seemed. Luckily, the owner has no problem with the smell, and he guided me to my coveted prize, the pickup truck. Sadly, it is stabbed inside a big pit of waste, and it is pulled out with a massive machine. This thing is a big piece of rust swallowed by dust, the owner ordered his workers to clean the thing, and without hesitation, they pushed the rusty king into a pool of blue liquid.

Larry is missing, the owner then escorted me to the isolated building. I have settled the payment of seven hundred and fifty dollars. "It is all yours" he said after handing me the keys. The keys are designed like a coiled snake. After waiting for almost an hour, the pickup truck is pulled out of the pool of liquid, still retains its rusty king title, but it has some eye-catching colours on it. It looks like a rainbow painted on top of the truck; the junkshop worker made it clear that the rainbow pattern was caused by the oil sewage inside the pool. He asked me to start the thing and get out of there, but I am worried whether it turn on or worst, blow up.

After turning the key for some time, the pickup truck started with a furious jump. Out of nowhere, Alan entered the truck and signalled me to pedal the accelerator hard. This truck has the tightest gear and pedal system; it requires one special workout just to press the pedals. I have somehow managed to reach my house, but my legs and hands are in serious pain. The pickup truck is my only source to get money and support my family. Soon, I received a big contract from the famous marble company N&N, but I disagreed to deliver the stock to a very distant place because they have offered only fifty dollars per delivery. I am very concerned about the high delivery payment offered by the chocolate factory, for sure it won't cost a hundred for fuelling both deliveries.

My wife has no problem with me going for such a long trip with my not good pickup truck. On the day before departure, I have checked my truck for many hours, filled all types of oils, loaded an extra two tires. My only prayer is that the engine be good, since I have no idea how an engine works. At dinner, my children kissed me. I became emotional, because I have a feeling that my trip will get interrupted. I have even thought of abandoning the contract, but Susan has encouraged me to proceed with the trip. She always remembers me about the struggles of our life, because she believes that those words are the true motivation for any man out there.

The weather is also not in favour of me, it is snowing and I know that most of the well-equipped trucks will struggle during such weather conditions, and my truck does not even perform good at perfect weather. I laid on the bed, and after a few hours, I was drowned in deep thoughts and fear, while Susan kept snoring beside me. After a few hours of sleep, I made my way to the chocolate factory.

II

First Breakdown

The chocolate factory looks like one military outpost, there are two entrances to pass through, and at each of them, several guards stare right into our eyes, ready to shoot at any time. Luckily, I have managed to surpass the two entrances. Someone hand signalled me to take the vehicle to the backside; while driving the truck around, I have noticed some shoes and dresses spread across one spot. At the backside, one huge metal box, the size of four refrigerators, is waiting for my pickup truck. With the help of some machinery, they have mounted the box into the cargo bed of my pickup truck, squeaky noises sprouted up as expected.

One of the gunmen slapped on the truck's door and ordered me to get out of the vehicle. He then signalled me to go and meet a man sitting inside a cubicle. I walked up to the cubicle, filled the form handed out by the man, and then he handed a strange document about the instructions that I have to follow. The first page is a route map, what appeared strange is that the route map is prepared cunningly to avoid every police check post. I asked him if I can use the good roads, but he said "No". The next page contained the rules that I must follow while delivering the thing;

Do not try to open the package

Delivery must be done within the estimated time

Do not stop the vehicle at any point before reaching the destination

In the case of an attack, use the rifles attached to the box.

If the alarm sound is heard, replace the oxygen bottle with a new one provided with the box.

Empty out the waste box if necessary.

What! Does chocolate need oxygen? I don't know, but what I do know is the fact that I must complete the delivery mission at any cost. Quickly memorized all the routes and started the engine, it is almost night, must deliver it before morning. I have been stepping on the accelerator pedal for some time, but still, it moves at the speed of forty kilometres per hour. The off-road routes are very painful to get through, especially when you have a vehicle that makes you jump on smooth roads. Surprisingly, there are sign boards here and there inside the dense forest. Felt like my spinal cord getting ripped off, and thus exited the forest path, switched to the smooth road.

I regret my decision immediately; sirens of police vehicles encircled me. I am getting frightened and confused at the same time. Why do I have to fear the police officers? It is only a chocolate box. But what I fear is that what if it isn't what I think it is. Sure enough, the police vehicles have overtaken my snail pro max pickup truck, luckily, I switched routes and entered the forest route again, the police vehicles have lost track of me. In the middle of the forest, I have decided to stop the vehicle and analyse the big chocolate box carefully, but I can't open it even with my hardest pull.

After taking a short nap, unfortunately, the night turned morning. I became scared and checked the instructions again. I can see melted chocolate dripping out of the big box, and one big green alarm is blinking heavily. After going through the instruction manual, I have found that the oxygen levels have depleted inside the box, and as a result, the inside of the box has started to heat up, and it made the chocolate to melt slightly. Before getting too much late, I have managed to reach the destination by seven o' clock sharp. It is another factory without a name.

Like the previous one, this place also has many guards equipped with rifles. They let me in; after reaching the backside of the facility, a big man came over to investigate the box, he is not happy with my delayed delivery. He ordered me to visit the cubicle inside the facility. I moved my way to the cubicle, and suddenly, noticed some shiny fantasy dresses arranged closely on one corner, alongside the dress there are high heel shoes, bracelets, ornaments, blonde wigs, artificial flowers also. I entered the cubicle, an old man warmly welcomed me to have a seat, he introduced himself as Dany, we then engaged in a small talk.

Dany: 'Welcome Larry, how was your first delivery?'

Me: 'Sorry, I am a little late. The police chased me throughout the path... Why did they chase me?'

Dany: 'I don't know, why are you late?'

Me: 'I told you already!'

Dany: 'As per the rules, you must take punishment for breaking one. Either you pay three hundred dollars fine or work inside this factory for three days'

Me: 'I don't have any money on me, so number two it is'

Dany summoned two men; they escorted me into the facility. I am tasked to fill up barrels of wax like thing, definitely not candle wax. The fragrance inside the hall is mesmerizing, I have noticed that some of the workers are pouring perfume into the wax barrels before sealing it fully. The facility has offered me a luxurious meal consisting of roasted meats and chocolate desserts. In addition to all, they have given me the best room for stay. To be honest, I have taken a liking to my new job, but Dany has no interest to trap me inside this wax store job. After sharp three days, Dany kicked me out of the facility.

I drove to the chocolate factory again. Again, they put the big metal box inside the truck, but the destination is different than the previous one. My new destination is twice far away compared to my first one. I have no option left other than to obey what they decide. The hidden paths to my new destination are very rough, almost dipped my vehicle into a nearby river. At last, the second route ended at the front of a big mansion, with a lot of luxurious vehicles parked outside. The walls surrounding the mansion is for sure made from gold, each of the bricks has diamonds pressed all over it to give it a shiny appearance.

The security officer hand signalled me to enter the underground parking lot, and I did exactly what he ordered. The guards have taken out the box of chocolates, after a few minutes, two men dressed in rich robes approached the box, they opened the box by simply scanning their fingerprints. I am observing them closely, and noticed their facial expressions changed into a dog's face when it sees a bone on the ground. "Do you want some?" one of them asked me. "No, not a fan of chocolate" I replied. He laughed hard and went inside with his buddy.

I can see bright light emitting out of the building, have decided to enter the building. There are no security guards standing on the entrance, and after entering the big hall, I am shocked to see all kind of illegal activities hovering inside. A lot of naked men drinking and smoking vigorously, while molesting the frightened naked women sitting beside them. They look hopeless and scared at the same time, while some look already dead. I have noticed a strange looking device attached around these women's neck, that has one blue light blinking on it. I have taken one big sip of the free alcohol provided.

Even though the hall is fully air conditioned, the naked women are sweating hard, and the sweat has formed a glacier all around their body. The sight of these naked men harassing the women is insufferable. It is horrible to see how disgusting men can be. Some of the men are literally biting their meat grinding teeth straight into the smooth icy skin of the women, followed up by slapping them all around. Suddenly, a middle-aged woman grabbed my hand and dragged me into a nearby luxurious room. She is wearing a shiny golden robe, and she ordered me to undress myself. I have clarified her mistake of assuming me as a prostitute, but she is not listening to what I have justified.

She takes out her fat purse, picks out a handful of cash and throws it to me. "Need more?" she asked angrily. I am shocked to see that much money, thus, agreed to her offer, undressed myself and did all she wanted me to do to her. After few hours, I took leave from the building and stepped slowly to my truck, immediately one image left me speechless and made me stuck like a pillar. One of the naked women is lying unconscious on the ground, but she does not have the blue light collar around her neck, and her face is not visible because her head was blown out somehow. I have seen some movies that showcase the brutal ways to kill a human being, but never have I ever thought about seeing it in real life.

Now that's a thing to wonder about, don't you think? I mean, how does such brutal gore-some clippings provide pleasure and entertainment to human beings? "Why am I wondering about useless thoughts?" I thought myself. Have started the engine and then quickly went to my house, luckily, I was not followed by the police. After entering the house, I went inside my room and started counting the handful of cash that the lady blindly picked out from her fat purse. I have counted a total of six hundred dollars, and thus, decided to go for a small budget tour next day.

Susan and the kids are happy to hear my newest announcement, unfortunately the kids gloated about the tour thing to their grandmother. She became furious and started cursing all of us, she made her wish that all of us will be dead during our budget tour. We started our journey early morning, sadly the pickup truck didn't start first and it caused a few hours delay to our small journey. I am not feeling well because of the famous saying about bad luck associated with this kind of delay before a journey. Anyway, we moved quickly and reached our first and only destination "The mysterious mountains". The entry fee is only hundred dollars for a family.

I have experienced the biggest happiness seeing my five kids happily laugh around the green rockish place. Susan is not enjoying the scenes because of her still suffering from the beat down she received days ago. For some reason, I am not enjoying the beautiful scenery around me, Susan is with me all the time, I am feeling guilty for cheating my beloved wife. The kids are nowhere to be found, me and Susan sat on the grassy land, after a few hours the kids finally returned. We went inside a mid-setup restaurant after checking the price table thoroughly. Without letting the kids select any of the fancy dishes, I have ordered chicken noodle soup for all of us, and they don't have any issue with my uncanny behaviour.

After eating the delayed lunch, we started moving and entered an apple farm that has hundreds of apple trees, full of juicy apples bundled together. As expected, the kids have started climbing the trees, and they threw rocks to unbind the apple bundles, but they had poor aim. Unfortunately, some of their throws hit other people, resulting in me losing an additional fifty dollars to the injured people. I became angry and announced the end of our journey, slowly moved to the truck. Suddenly, a minivan accelerated towards us and stopped next to us, four masked people jumped out of the vehicle and grabbed my hands tightly, they tried to force me into their van.

Luckily, I have realised that I am stronger than the four masked guys, my strongest kicks and punches made them fall to the ground. Quickly, they retreated into their minivan and drove off. Susan assured that the masked guys are women, but I didn't notice anything womanly about them. Some random people suggested me to leave the place immediately for their safety because they fear some form of terrorist attack happening anytime soon. "I am not a terrorist" I said loudly, but no one listened. We all entered the truck, and it started without any delay this time. I have made sure no one followed us, but the unlucky thing occurred, my beloved truck stopped moving for some reason.

We are stranded in the middle of the forest way, and after walking for a few miles, one big mansion appeared within our sight. The mansion looks strange; it has no gate or walls. All I can see is the mansion decorated with bright lights. Suddenly, my eyes caught the dilapidated well on the left corner of the house, it doesn't have a pulley system or a grill on top. Moved closer to the well, have realised it is thrice wider than a normal well. The stony wall of the well is covered with bloodstains, even after noticing all these weird signs, I dared to take a peek. "Oh..." my voice has stuck inside my mouth, immediately backed off and stopped Susan from looking into it.

Like always, my kids climbed the stony well wall and stared at the contents inside, but they didn't express any reaction like I did. The mysterious well is full of dry and juicy bones. Before running away from there, the main door of the mansion has opened, an old woman stepped out and greeted us warmly, she then invited us into her mansion. We remained silent while staring at her nonstop. She introduced herself as Heltan, we strike up a conversation;

Heltan: 'Don't be afraid, come inside. It is my lucky day to have some visitors'

Me: 'The... Well thing... What is it?'

Heltan: 'Why surprised? You know, this is a forest area housing numerous animals that eat and get eaten anytime. Every day, my house front gets filled with half eaten animal carcasses, what should I do? I made one big ditch for all those souls'

Me: 'Why there isn't any smell then? What trick do you use?'

Heltan: 'I use magnesium zedmo... Enough with the questionings. Who are you guys?'

Me: 'We came to visit the "mysterious" mountain thing, and my truck has damaged. Do you know any mechanic? Help us!'

Heltan: 'Oh, you don't have to plead. It is your lucky day, I am a good mechanic, just give me some time. In the meantime, please take rest inside'

Heltan welcomed us into her giant mansion and then she went out to take a look at the truck. We are relaxing peacefully on the royal chairs spread out across the giant hall. Susan and the kids look excited to examine each corner of the mansion, and they left me alone in the hall. Something strange caught my eyes, it is a wall filled with framed photos of numerous people and families. I think she is a photographer or may be her family is too big. Another mysterious feeling breached into my head, it is about the people, I believe I met some of them personally a few months ago, but not sure completely. Heltan is slowly coming back to the mansion, she is not angry about my family's ransacking of her place.

Me: 'Sorry, they became excited. You should search us all before letting us go. Please!'

Heltan: 'Come on Larry, don't be ridiculous. I don't care about any of your worries, please do whatever you like inside my mansion, burn it down or flip it sideways, it is always nice to have some company'

Me: 'The truck, how is it? Start?'

Heltan: 'Sorry boy, the thing has broken its gear lever, and you must wait till morning to get the necessary supplies. Pick a room and erase all your worries there. Thanks for coming here'

Me: 'Thanks!'

Heltan pointed at a stairway in the corner of the hall. "Enjoy" she announced. I have followed her directions and finally reached the room compartment; the first thing came to my mind is "Don't judge a book by its cover", because the rooms are designed to equip only one individual. The rooms don't have any windows, furniture, appliances except for a tiny bed, and the rooms are fully air conditioned. Susan and the kids have already taken their own individual rooms. I took the room closer to Susan's, and when I entered the room, fresh silence crashes on me, completely making me unaware of what is happening outside. Luckily, Heltan knocked at the door to offer me a plastic bag full of exotic fruits, and I stuffed it all inside my starving belly. The cold air and the tiny smooth bed offered a peaceful few hours' sleep.

Suddenly, a gut feeling kicked inside me to search for Susan and the kids. The worst has happened, one of the boys is missing. We started searching for the boy around the mansion, including the underground basement covered with "Restricted Area" sign boards. The trail of steps led me to a big door that is left open slightly, blood is dripping out from underneath the door. Finally gained some confidence and entered the room, as expected the room is a cool place to store different type of meat. I have noticed some empty steel containers with fancy stickers on top of it. The unusual thing being, some of the cuts look big enough to confirm that they are not from any of the standard meat providers.

After inspecting the room further, my eyes caught the newly received meat that is hung on the ceiling, blood is dripping from it into a plastic bucket placed underneath. This meat is covered with a plastic wrapper, my curious brain made me peek a little into the plastic cover, realised it is a tiny human body without the head, my mind turned blank suddenly. Susan's voice coming from a distance jerked me back into reality. There is one more wrapped thing placed on top of a barrel, and it is my missing boy's decapitated head. Without wasting any more time, I took the plastic bag and ran to Susan and the kids, but the mansion is locked from outside.

Looking through the keyhole, I can see Heltan slowly making her way back to the mansion, she slowly climbed the steps. I have ordered my family to sit and act like nothing has happened. "What happened? Where is our son? What is that ball like thing in your hand?" Susan asked curiously. Heltan unlocked the door and came inside, surprised to see our presence in the main hall. Heltan requested us to wait while she went inside to take something. Without losing any minute, I took a peek inside the bag she was carrying, it is full of fruits. Heltan came back with a handbag, took out a camera and ordered us to stand together for a photo. I am prepared for the horrible things that will be following soon.

Heltan: 'Smile please... Wait, you entered the basement?'

Me: 'What basement? No!'

Heltan: 'Oh, don't worry about that, just asking!'

Me: 'You killed our son for meat, you old fat devil!'

Heltan: (laughs hard) 'It was not me; this mansion is haunted by satanic creatures; it was your mistake to let your kid wander around dangerous spots'

Susan is weeping hard with the kids, Heltan shouted at us to smile for the photo and took a random picture of our family. After taking the pic, she took a grenade from her handbag and aimed it at us. "Goodbye people, don't worry about your funerals, you will be buried in the richest mansion in the world, Ha" she proudly announced and then threw the grenade at us. Susan and the kids stood like statues, ready to accept their fate, but I threw the handbag at the flying grenade, thanks to my cricketing career, my throw hit the grenade, and it flicked to the corner, exploded. Before letting Heltan take another grenade, I jumped over her and dropped her to the ground, offered her some of my heavy fists.

We ran back to the pickup truck, luckily, it started somehow. Finally, we have reached our home. My mother-in-law is laughing hard looking at my frightened face, surprisingly, she hasn't noticed that one of the kids is missing. I opted not to bring in the bag of head, have lied to Susan that I will search for him tomorrow, because we all live by some promises and somehow it gives life purpose. At night, I have decided to take the next delivery from the chocolate factory, after getting ready for work, slowly walked to the truck, there are dogs surrounding the truck, and from inside the truck, a disgusting smell keeps coming out.

After a furious fight with the dogs, I entered the truck. The bag is getting wet with bloodstains and worms. Teardrops keep running down my face, but nothing can reverse the timeline, I know! I am planning to secretly bury my boy's head in the abandoned church, inside the dense forest, which I saw during one of my off-ride deliveries. When I reached the chocolate factory, one big hound, size of a baby elephant, red colour, yellow eyes, keep staring at my truck and started barking heavily. Luckily, the factory workers loaded the metal box of chocolate into my truck quickly. I kept the engine running the whole time to avoid yet another breakdown.

My new destination is marked at the other factory where I received the three-day labour punishment. First, I have to bury my kid's head, but before I could do that, police vehicles trapped me inside the forest, it looked like they knew I should be coming here. Hopelessly climbed down the truck and stood silent to announce the acceptance of my fate. Surprisingly, after searching the load, they didn't feel anything suspicious about it. Unfortunately, they started searching the driver's cabin and found the decapitated head of my kid. They handcuffed me, threw me into the police vehicle and drove off, leaving the truck in the middle of nowhere.

III

Bakery of Pastry

We have arrived at the police station, and before questioning me, offered some heavy boot kicks and slaps. I am chained in one dark cell; lights turned on suddenly. The doors are opened slowly, and one high ranking officer entered the room and started questioning me;

Me: 'The head... Where is it?'

Officer: 'Sorry, pesky street dogs! Anyway, how many have you killed?'

Me: 'No, I didn't kill anyone. The head belongs to my elder son; I was going to bury it inside the abandoned church'

Officer: 'So, he died naturally by plugging off his own damn head you say?' (laughs hard)

Me: 'Stop laughing you bastard, my son died because of you people, useless bags of mud'

(The officer kicks my chair down)

Officer: 'How dare you say that to my face. Explain you wretched dog!'

Me: 'I have lost my son to a cannibal old woman living near the mysterious mountain tourist spot, she has a big mansion with a hellish well full of flesh and blood, grenades in her handbag, killed over thousands of families all by herself with her seventy-ish old body, while you guys were haunting after my snail max pro truck that breaks-down for fun! Have you people any responsibility?'

Officer: (laughs) 'That is none of our business, why should we get involved in such dangerous matters? We have family just like you, you creepy dumb truck driver'

Me: 'Then why did you get into this job, you coward kitten?'

Officer: 'For the money you sicko' (laughs and leaves the cell)

Time is ticking down; I must complete my delivery task before morning. Luckily, the officer didn't lock up the cell or maybe it doesn't have a lock system. The policemen are sleeping peacefully on their desks. Slowly and cunningly, I made my steps and went outside, took an abandoned cycle placed near the entrance, pedalled hard into the forest. The pickup truck is still waiting for me, but bad for me, the delay has caused the chocolate box to melt and drip out of the container fully, the oxygen levels also turned low. After inserting the new oxygen tube, I heard some weird sounds coming from inside of the metal chocolate box.

The box is locked with a passcode; after checking the instruction manual, I have found the emergency passcode written in block letters, but a huge warning also written near the passcode column. I don't have the patience to read the thing, thus entered the passcode immediately into the metal box's screen. The box chamber is opened, strong smell of chocolate drilled into my nostrils, almost made me faint. Few minutes later, I have regained myself and my eyes witnessed the most disturbing image. Ok, that is a bit exaggerated, but the second most disturbing image my eyes have ever seen, because the first position is still owned by the bones and flesh room that I saw inside Heltan's basement.

Inside this metal box, there are six women standing, wearing a metal blindfold, they are tied to the walls except the door wall, with metal handcuffs, and yes, they are naked, but their bodies still hold the sign that they were flooded in frozen chocolate. The oxygen tube is attached to their nose, and this kept them alive when they were drowned inside the chocolate. Surprisingly, their mouth is not tied up, and they probably have eaten a lot of chocolate already. They look dead, but after touching one of them, I felt heat on their skin, sure they are not dead. On the door, there are different buttons labelled for different functions.

Again, I don't have any patience to read the functions of all of these buttons, except the one big red button with the word "Release" written on top of it, pressed it quickly, the metal handcuffs have opened and they are good to go but they are still standing there. Meanwhile, I received a call from the manager of the chocolate factory.

Manager: 'What did you do, circus clown! Who told you to release them?'

Me: 'Clown? What on earth are you freaks doing with these poor women, have you gone mad? Is this new flavour for candy or something? I will report this to the police?'

Manager: 'You betraying scoundrel! How dare you threaten us! Lost one child already, want to lose the other four plus the wife'

Me: 'What! Oh, sorry sir, I was just joking with you. It was the police... caught me last night for some absurd reason... made me lose my precious duty time... led to the melting of chocolates, and the oxygen thing, sounds...'

Manager: 'No excuses you moron, just do what I say! Close the box immediately, take the delivery to some abandoned place, and wait for backup. It will take about five hours, do not let any of them escape'

Me: 'Yes sir. I will not let them move'

The manager cut the call, and I quickly climbed the truck and closed the metal box, took control of the truck and drove without any real destination. Because I have become a wanted man, I should be more careful or my whole family will be erased off from the books. Luckily, I have found one dilapidated building, parked my truck safely beside a wall compartment. I am exhausted from the surprise events, went inside the building to take a short nap. The building appears to be some kind of party pub, it has the dancing poles, alcohol station but sadly the bottles are all empty without even the smell! It has a few rooms with dusty beds and chairs.

I chose the big bed with twenty pillows, inside one big room that has a lot of dusty mirrors covering its walls. The room might have been a place for group "meetings" for sure. After lying comfortably on the still smooth bed, I have entered the blank realm of sleep followed by the mysterious dreams, in which we have no control over the actions happening inside it. Definitely the oddest experience any human being will encounter in his lifetime... I had one horrible dream last night, it was me tied to a steel bed with invisible rope or something, and a cannibal man standing beside me, sharpening his knife.

He then proceeded to filet my flesh off the bone, slowly and smoothly, starting with the legs. I tried my best to move my body to break free, but I couldn't move an inch. It is the unique beauty of dreams; one cannot exert free will to change his fate just like the real world. And another peculiarity dreams have is that we cannot realise whether we are dreaming or not. Luckily, my fileting dream was an official dream, and when I woke up with horror still splashing around my face, I felt the presence of somebody inside the room. No! Not ghost. It is one of the naked women and she is sleeping on the corner of the large bed.

I dared not to wake her up, but my careful footsteps made her wake up quickly. She is not frightened to see me, but she has many questions to ask, not about me but about the whole chocolate thing and mostly "Where am I?" and "I want to see my parents". As you guys know, I don't have an answer for her genuine questions. She keeps asking me about when I will kill her! I am getting tortured left and right, left side with terrifying dreams and right side with the woman's blabbering's. She then left the room and went outside the pub like building.

The manager called me again, and I shared him my location. He reminded me to remove the box from direct sunlight, but I can't recall him mentioning about the sunlight thing last time. Quickly, I ran to the truck, and there are a lot of screams happening around the box, painful screams from inside and screaming for help by the one naked woman I met inside the pub. I have opened the box using the secret passcode, suddenly the outside woman kicked my stomach off and pushed me out of the truck. I am still conscious enough to see what she is doing, she has unlocked the women and gently escorted them into the pub.

I can only count five new women stepping out of the metal box, so the woman that I have met inside the pub has already escaped the box. I must put all of them inside the box or else my family will be in grave danger. I am scared to enter the pub again, because they might be plotting to eliminate me. I have decided to wait outside to make sure they won't escape the building. After an hour, one of the women approached me while raising her hands up to announce her surrender, a quick scan with my eyes assured that she is not carrying any hidden weapons. She is still naked! except for the brown patches made by the melted chocolate in which they were drowned earlier. She introduced herself as Merlin, and we have engaged in a conversation.

Merlin: 'What do you want from us? You sick animal!'

Me: 'I am just a chocolate delivery man, who are you and the others?'

Merlin: 'So, you say we ransacked your chocolate box to steal it, and then we were trapped inside it, huh!' (she wipes off some chocolate from her body and throws it to my face)

Me: 'Calm down girl, don't bully me. I am only a delivery man, father of five kids, if you have any issues, ask the chocolate factory officials, they will be here in an hour'

Merlin: 'An hour!'

Me: 'Do you want me to inform them to hurry up?'

Merlin: 'Are you toying with me or something? This is a joke? Look at me, you sicko, I am standing naked, in the middle of nowhere'

Me: 'Sorry dear, I don't know how you people entered this metal thing, how can I help you now?'

Merlin: 'Please help us escape from here, do not let them find us'

Me: 'Ok then, get the girls'

Merlin led them into the truck; they dropped the metal box. We moved quickly as possible, have no idea where we are going or what the fish is happening. Somehow, I have managed to find an abandoned house that has a scary feel. All the women jumped out of the truck, they ran inside the house without a second thought. Merlin is staying inside the truck with me, still naked. We cut down some of the biggest leaves we could find and gave it to the other women. They wore the leaf dress and started cleaning their newly found house like they own it.

Merlin explained to me that she was preparing for her journey to Xemland country to pursue PhD and was planning to settle there. Just two days before flight, her house was ransacked by a team of four masked men, tall and muscular, they kidnapped Merlin and after all that she regained consciousness a few hours before the chocolate barrier melted off. She has no idea where she is. I have already planted my suspicions on the chocolate factory being some kind of sex racket or human trafficking port, but I have no courage to take any action against them. Merlin requested me to inform the issue to the police station, and to buy something to eat for them.

I know I should not enter a police station, but I promised myself to do something about the matter. The pickup truck started smoothly this time, first I went to a market few kilometres away from the forest, bought some fruits and a big loaf of bread. Surprisingly, there is a police station nearby, I became nervous. Finally, I told one of the well-dressed gentlemen about the matter, but my instinct didn't allow me to reveal the exact location where the victims are staying. He calmed my nerves and asked me to stay inside the market while he transfers the information. He slowly made his way to the station, meanwhile I bought more loaves of bread.

While waiting for the man, I have noticed a bundle of chocolate bars stacked on the desk of one of the shops. The label on the bar says, "Chocolust" it is made by the factory that I have signed the delivery contract with. I bought one of the smallest packets and tried it, it tasted sweet and delicious. The shopkeeper remarked that it is the most selling chocolate bar in the world. I am shocked, made me think the worst way possible, did the factory people prepare some absurd recipe involving the flesh of human beings? Quickly,

I noticed the man coming out of the station, he is not alone, accompanied by a few police officers wearing a bunch of golden stars upon their shoulders.

I have decided not to appear before them because of my wanted status, but I have decided to eavesdrop the conversation between the man and the high-ranking officer.

Officer: 'Where is he?'

Man: 'I don't know, must be here somewhere. He was wearing a black shirt and black pant, a red ribbon tied to his left hand, no moustache or beard, white hair, muscular and tall. Go search him'

(The officer orders his troops to search for me, and they continued their ongoing talk)

Officer: 'Why didn't you bring him inside? You idiot!'

Man: 'I have tried, he didn't want to, how can I force someone into a police station? Don't worry, we will find him soon'

Officer: 'If we don't find him, he might cause trouble. We must eliminate him immediately'

I am literally shaking behind a bag of corn, moved sneakily into the truck and turned the key, as expected, it didn't start. Yes, I get surprised when my beloved truck thing starts in the first turn of the key. Unfortunately, the key is stuck and there is no way to get it out. I should surrender or try my best run to outrun them. When I looked out of the window, I saw one trooper ransacking the corn bags, ripping them off completely like he held grudge over them. A thought came to my small mind that how can they identify me? Only one of them knows my face, thus, I took off all my clothing except my underwear.

After slowly slipped out of the vehicle, moved carefully while maintaining a confident face by looking straight into people's eyes. I ran away from the market successfully, but the food supplies are still inside the truck and the truck itself I should worry about next. Walking down the road, I found a building and snuck my way into it through the narrow window. It is a storeroom for the whole market, am starving very hard. Immediately, my eyes caught the packages of Chocolust chocolates, there are thousands of them stacked in the left corner.

"Fulfil your lust with Chocolust, rich and creamy, sweet and bit salty, elixir from paradise" the description says. The witty thing made me laugh so much; I don't know why. Unwrapped few of the Chocolust package, luckily found a coupon inside one of the packs, it says, "Call me for real lust", and has a random phone number. Again, my curious mind provoked me to call the number as soon as possible, and I did, a woman picked up the phone and asked me for the code. "What code!" I asked. "Coupon code you stupid" she replied angrily. Yes, there is a strange code written on the coupon. It says, "Bakery of pastry", she then gave me directions to my prize.

Again, my pesky mind ordered me to get to the destination, but the skinny faces of the six women inside the abandoned building flashed to my mind and forced me to step out of the storeroom, made my way to the market to take my truck if it may start somehow. Luckily, none of the uniform boys is there, I entered the truck and turned the key, it started. "Whoo!" am excited. Quickly accelerated the thing to the abandoned building, night has arrived. Somehow, I have managed to reach the abandoned building, but there is no sign of the six women. When I entered the building, have realised it is not the building I am looking for.

There is someone lying on the ground, he looks familiar. It is the man whom I asked to inform the police officers. He was shot in the head and for sure dead. There is a gun next to his body. I took the gun and it is fully loaded except the bullet in his head. I have put the gun in my pocket for future action because of my current status. The dead body made me contemplate my current life situation, my family will be killed any moment, my death is confirmed too, and still, I am wandering around looking for some strange women. I walked back to the truck and drove to my house.

Unfortunately, I have reached the abandoned building where the six women stay. Yes, I did not plan to do so but the six of them were waiting outside looking for me, they have built a fire to get my attention. They are happy to see my truck; they stand very disciplined even though they are hearing the craziest hunger bells inside their guts. I gave them food, they ate it quickly and escorted me inside, led me to a big room that has a makeshift bed made of leaves. They pushed me onto the leaf bed and laid themselves around me, covered my entire body with their body heat.

I don't know whether they are intentionally offering me some form of sexual gratification for my services, or they are scared and need my presence like a father figure. If it is the second reason, I am ashamed of myself because their touch has made my bad side to kick up. I have started to contemplate on my life after buying the millionth hand piece of junk for a bargained price of seven hundred dollars. Human beings normally go after cheap stuff instead of good ones, and at the end we suffer for our own mistakes. I guess it is a universal truth.

I am thinking if it was all planned by the almighty God, maybe I am destined to bring peace and prosperity to the world by unmasking the biggest racket. The chocolate I ate while inside the market's storeroom is making me lose my balance. Slowly, my mind slipped out of the conscious realm, strangely some whining noises started to bother me... Quickly woke up... Where am I? I believe am in my bedroom of my family house. My good old bedroom that has a comfortable mattress and an office chair to circle around the room. My skin looks younger now, suddenly, the alarm is triggered, made me jump up. Surprisingly, I am not tired, I mean, what happened to my middle-aged tiredness? When I looked in the mirror, I have realised that my body has turned younger, back to my teenage years. WHAT!

IV
Lesson not Learned

Somebody knocked on my door; it is my mother. I am shocked, she hit me with a stick for not getting ready for college. "College! What!" I have no idea what is happening, there are two possible assumptions, maybe I am dreaming my past, or I was dreaming my future middle-aged self's struggles. I became ready and gathered the information about where to go from my college ID card. My sister is also readying to go to college, I believe she used to come with me. My memory appears to be tampered with my middle-aged self-future dream.

Surprisingly, I am happy to go to college even though I didn't enjoy my college time, but my weird dream of future has made me a new person somehow, it is like I have become a middle-aged man wrapped up with the skin of a youngster. Now that I know what I should do and don't do, I have a feeling that I will succeed in life and will not end up inside a junk pickup truck! I am enrolled in chemistry subject but have no interest in studying it, I wish I could change my subject. Anyway, I went to the hall. My father is reading the newspaper cunningly though he has no job and won't try to get one either. I believe I didn't have many interactions with my father because of him being a good for nothing fellow.

Like I mentioned, now I feel the urge to have a small talk with another middle-aged person. Strangely, I am not seeing my father as my father but a friend of mine. Me and my father engaged in a good morning conversation;

Me: 'Good morning... Dad'

Dad: 'Good morning son, why are you late?'

Me: 'Oh, I was very tired. You know, middle age problems!'

Dad: 'What! Remember what happened last week?'

Me: 'Susan was hammered by the beast, my little boy... Sorry, what happened last week, can't recall'

Dad: 'Susan, little boy?'

Me: 'Characters in a movie I watched last night'

Dad: 'Why are you being so lazy? Did you complete the syllabus or something!'

Me: 'You're the one to lecture me about laziness, huh!'

Dad: 'How dare you talk back to me, I will not come to your college today, deal it yourself'

Me: (laughs) 'I am scared...' (laughs again)

Father angrily walked away from the hall. "let's go" my sister said. I have no idea how we are going to college. We didn't have any vehicle except one rusty bicycle, and sure it won't be the answer I am looking for. "Why are you being weird? Only three minutes left for the bus" she said. Now that I learned about the transportation procedure, have started walking faster. Luckily, the bus stop is only a mile away, and the bus has not come yet. "What happened last week?" I asked my sister. "What are you talking about! There is nothing happened between me and Billy, we are just friends, stop harassing me brother" she said.

I am bewildered, then asked her again with more clarity "What happened last week, to me, father told me about something, parent teacher thing, what was that?". She laughed and accused me of using drugs that might have erased all my memory. Anyway, she has decided to answer my question clearly, she said I was caught for not attending the classes for over an entire month. "That's my boy" I thought. I am confused about why I was that much lazy, again asked my sister for answer. She explained that I have issues with some of the senior bullies, they have tortured me for not obeying their made-up laws.

She also mentioned that one of the bullies is the son of a famous politician. Out of nowhere, two buses stopped at the bus-stop the same time. I have entered the first bus because it is first, the bus took off quickly while the second one remained at the stop, unfortunately I can still see my sister waving at me from the bus-stop. Yes, I am in the wrong bus. The bus named 'Mandrake' moved swiftly, trying its best to never stop and praying for no one to call it. I have engaged in a war of words with the conductor, he is not winning the slightest, my younger tongue has learned so much old stuff, and it helped me win the battle fair and square. I made a loud shout to stop the bus and stepped out slowly.

While standing there without the slightest idea of where am I or how can I get to the college, someone approached me on a motor bike, he is staring at me angrily like I did something brutal to him. He gets closer to my side and started questioning me.

Him: 'What are you doing here?'

Me: 'Who are you, freak?'

Him: 'I am your principal, you dumb boy. Did you forget everything after wandering like a tramp for the past one month? If you don't like studying, then why did you enrol into this! why don't you just stay at home?'

Me: 'Do you own this college? Have you invested in me? No! Then why are you raising your voice against me'

Him: 'Lost all manners, I see. Get lost you idiot!' (starts engine)

Me: (takes out the key from his bike) 'Not so fast. Answer my questions first!'

Him: 'How dare you threaten me! I will show you who I am'

Me: (laughs) 'Show what? You really think you're some kind of powerful being? You dumb puppet, do you have any idea why I didn't attend any class last month?'

Him: 'You were lazy, it's a fact universally acknowledged'

Me: 'Are you acting dumb or born dumb! I know that you puppets have no power to even wipe your own... don't try to satisfy your cowardice issues on innocent people like me'

Him: 'Calm down dear, tell me your problems, I promise you my help'

Me: 'Don't worry about helping me, I know what to do. Take me to the college, as a favour'

The principal took me to the college; I have forgotten how it looked like. It is beautiful with a lot of plants and trees, I mean, a lot of overgrown grass and useless plants infesting on each part of the college surrounding, clear evidence of lack of maintenance and a true manifestation of the punch line "we don't give a damn". My skin turned reddish from contact with the long grass because it is hard to avoid them. Suddenly, a boy hit my shoulder and greeted me with the words "Morning Pal, to the movies?". I have no recollective evidence about this freak, but I believe I should moral police him and get him back to the good tracks.

Me: 'Why movies? Go to your class and study you fool!'

Him: 'What happened to you dawg! Me, fool?' (pushes me to the ground) 'apologize now you dummy'

I became enraged, jumped up and smashed his face away with my strong fist. He started bleeding, he scurried away. I can see my sister entering the college entrance, she didn't notice me. Luckily, one female student enquired about my last month whereabouts, she introduced herself as 'Giggy', she navigated me to my class and she also entered the class, she is my classmate! All the students are looking at me like I am a new student. "What are you looking at you clownish babies!" I said loudly. Giggy is smiling at me, and she made me sit next to her.

Suddenly, a teacher entered the class. She is carrying a bulky text and a stick. Her attention turned to me, made me stand up and poured out some lengthy questions that I didn't care to hear or answer at all. She became enraged and took me to the principal's office, the two conjoined and started accusing me for not listening to them. "Stop! What do you want from me? Give me some time to adjust with this place, stop trying to show off in front of me" I said proudly. They are again shocked to hear my brave replies. Without asking me any further questions, they dispersed their short meeting.

Me and the teacher returned to the class; she started to teach her subject that is chemistry. After drawing some weird symbols and writing some equations in a few minutes, without describing how they came into existence, she asked the most clichéd question ever asked in a class – "Have you any doubts?" – and as expected, none of the students has any issue with the thing she made on the board except me, I have started questioning her about each line she sketched, again she pulled the next clichéd answer available – "You should have learned the basics" – I am confused and again asked her for clarity regarding the matter.

"If I need to learn the basics, then why should I have to sit here watching this?" I asked. The teacher became angry and yelled at me to get out of the class. "Oh great, kicking out the student who wants more clarification, great teacher" I said and didn't move a little from my seat. I am not feeling any form of fear because inside my mind I see her as my younger daughter, I don't know why I feel like such. Maybe, all of that middle age stuff wasn't a dream, maybe I have time travelled into this timeline somehow. The teacher keeps yelling at me to get out of the class, but still I made no move. She left the class immediately and does not return before the bell rung.

After some time, a long bell is heard. Giggy is very happy hearing it; she asked me to join her to the movies. We went to the theatre, and she bought the tickets luckily, I have a feeling that she knows everything about me. We are seated in the back corner seat, which I didn't like that much because it is here the usual teenage hungers are satisfied. I feel ashamed to sit here because of my middle age personality that has risen somehow. I can only find teenage people inside. Giggy is not liking my strange behaviour, but I have managed to calm my older nerves. I have no interest to watch the romance movie that is playing in front of my eyes.

Thirty minutes later, Giggy has started holding my hands. She made her head rest upon my shoulder, then offered a kiss. I didn't feel any emotion in that kiss, instead am getting tired mentally. At the interval, I took leave from the theatre, but she also made her exit. "Sorry dear, I have a headache" I said. She calmed me and called a taxi for me. The taxi driver dropped me at my house, and he wants his fare that I don't have, but what I do have is a picture of the driver not wearing seatbelt while driving. My blackmail is successful, he left calmly.

I took a shower and planted myself on the bed for a short nap. My father wakes me up and he demands answers for my behaviour at school today. "It was nothing, the teacher wanted me to learn all by myself, if that is the case, then why should I have to go there" I said furiously. "Stop playing around like you are one old grandpa" Father asked me. He advised me not to raise my voice again in the class or else I shall get terminated from there. "Oh, so that's how I became a driver of the pickup truck" I murmured but somehow my father heard it. He left my room and returned after a few minutes. "Made an appointment with psychiatrist Bob, tomorrow, be ready morning" he said and left without hearing my response.

While wondering about what is happening and what should I do, found some love letters sent by Giggy. My phone is getting filled with messages from Giggy. I am surprised to find out that me and Giggy are in a relationship for the past six years! I mean, how can I not remember this stuff! How could I forget this kind of stuff even though something strange happened to my life timeline. I have started to contemplate on what I should do to know more about my current timeline. I do remember that my sister is studying philosophy and is having an affair with a senior boy who will cheat her soon.

I do remember that my father will kick me out of the house for some reason, which if I have to guess, for not studying properly. I do remember that my mother will get exhausted and die from doing multiple jobs to keep the family train running. I believe she is currently doing stitching, gardening, poultry farming, working as a part time cook and cleaner for our rich neighbours. Now that I know what will happen to my family, I must do my best to prevent the bad things from happening. Next morning, my father wakes me up early and he forcedly takes me to the psychiatrist guy who charges hundred dollars for a session.

Bob: 'Hello Larry, what is your problem?'

Me: 'I don't know Bob, I feel like I am stuck between two timelines'

Bob: 'What are the things you are watching recently besides porn?'

Me: 'I have watched a lot of superhero movies on television with my kids; I wonder if that has to do something about my current situation'

Bob: 'Your kids? Have you been playing any games recently?'

Me: 'No, I was busy riding my rusty pickup truck all around many undiscovered locations that you cannot find inside a map'

(Awkward silence)

Bob: 'Forget everything I just asked you, now tell me what happened at your college, to you?'

Me: 'I want to change my dull future, but the teachers were not co-operating with me, they didn't offer any help for me to grasp all of that weird use of English language'

Bob: 'Tell me about your unconventional behaviour recently'

Me: 'Why do I tell you? It is your job to tell me what is wrong with me. Tell me now!' (hits the desk hard)

Bob: 'Calm down boy, don't need to raise your voice. These kinds of emotional outbursts are common in teenagers. You will be alright soon. Take care'

Me: 'You charge hundred bucks for this! What kind of a creepy dumbass are you! Have you any other jobs? I don't feel any change whatsoever meeting you, do you know anything about this timeline thing? Of course you don't, now, give me one satisfying answer that is not found on the first page of an internet search'

Bob: 'It is just an age problem! Don't worry, teenagers like you should be after pretty girls. Have fun dear'

Me: 'What! You creepy fatso! I have never watched porn videos and didn't experience any lust towards anyone even though I have a girlfriend, explain that'

Bob: 'That's strange! You should visit a hospital as soon as possible'

Me: 'And? ...'

(Bob closes the door)

Bob: 'What is wrong with you freak? Don't you have any man parts?'

(I hit his face with fierce power, he fell to his chair, nose bleeds heavily)

Me: 'Listen you fake fatso, I know how people like you disgrace men like they are some kind of savage beasts with only one sole purpose in their lives, to satisfy their sexual lust. Men also want to succeed in their lives, and they also have a variety of dreams other than just the satisfaction of lust. As a father of five children, I know what lust really is, it is just a reminder for all beings to not let earth turn into a wasteland'

Bob: 'Have you gone mad! Get lost, I will refund your payment. Get lost now!'

Me and my father started walking home, he is happy that he didn't lose his hundred dollars but at the same time angry with me. Suddenly, he took a right turn and entered the supermarket. I am shocked to see him buying two Chocolust chocolate bars with the lucky hundred dollars. "Fifty dollars for a chocolate bar!" I exclaimed. "It is worth every penny, dear son" he said with a cheeky smile. For another surprise, Giggy is inside the market, and she came to meet us, she also knows about my early meeting with Bob. I have then realised that Giggy is our family friend and is somehow matched with my horoscope to marry me.

My father quickly unwrapped the chocolate bars, his face became dull after opening the first one, but an evil smile blossomed on his face when he opened the second one. He has found one of the coupons, handed the chocolate bars to me and Giggy each. "What is this coupon for?" I asked him. He replied that it is just a lottery and he quickly moved away from our sight, meanwhile Giggy ate the chocolate bar fully and has started eating mine. I am confused whether I will be married to Susan or not. To be honest, I don't like Giggy's attitude that much. She is always running after high marks in tests, holds pride for overtaking me in every academic test possible. I mean, what's up with that!

Giggy keeps pushing me to study better and aim for a great future. But what can happen if you push something that does not have wheels. Even though I don't like her academic hunger, I do enjoy her company. It is always a blessing to have a true friend by your side and be there for you anytime. None of my other classmates ever tried to have a conversation with me. My middle-aged mentality has forced me to call my classmates using the pseudonyms; son and daughter. Also, I have successfully stopped some fights happened inside the class, with my old age blunder-full phrases.

Even though I have no problem sitting inside a class full of younger students, the only problem I am faced with is the lab classes. During one of the lab exams in chemistry lab, I made a big mistake that I still don't know but the mistake caused one of the beakers getting destroyed completely. Everyone including the teacher started laughing at me, though the incident made no impact upon me, Giggy was embarrassed and became furious with my foolish behaviour. "Don't study to become a fool yourself, be better" she advised me. I don't like her attitude, turned angry and pushed her to the ground in a fit of rage. She became frightened and ran away from my presence then returned with an apology of her own.

I can't retrace how my relationship with Giggy will end, sure it won't happen that easily. I believe something terrible will happen when it happens finally, something terrible enough that makes one's memory about such an incident getting bottled inside forever, for that person's own safety and well-being. After the lab breaking incident, Giggy has started coming to my house more often, mostly to teach me about the exam syllabus. One day, due to a small headache, Giggy became unconscious and fell to the ground. Me and my father quickly took her to the nearest hospital.

V
Desires are Uncontrollable

The doctor examined her and made her go through a series of tests, maybe all of the tests available in the hospital, to make a total of two thousand dollars bill. Finally, the doctor revealed his findings, Giggy suffered a minor stroke because of her lack of sleep, I know she was studying hard in the nights, but I have never thought that studying could cause fatal damage. Doctor advised her to sleep at least seven hours every day for the rest of her life. I know she won't obey this command, but I have to make sure she gets enough sleep. The doctor suggested her to buy some kind of device that will track her sleep cycle regularly. Giggy is not interested to wear that thing on her hand, but my angry face made her wear it.

While looking at the street through the hospital windows, I have found a second-hand vehicle store that has a lot of vehicles parked aesthetically. What caught my attention is one pickup truck that looks exactly like my pickup truck, which I might have with me in the distant future, this one looks less rusty and has glossy painted body. I left the hospital and ran to the second-hand dealer shop, but the shocking thing occurred when I tried to enter the shop, some kind of invisible wall has prevented me from entering the shop. I am confused, after some time, I have realised that I can't enter any of the nearby buildings and shops in that lane.

After getting back to the hospital premises, I tried to enter one of the coffee shops but can't do that either. Again, something blocked me from entering the shop, and for another absurdity, I can't even see what is happening inside the shop. To find the reason, I have tried to enter different buildings, somehow, I can enter a few buildings and see what's happening there. To ease the absurd situation, I went back to the hospital. Giggy is not feeling well, not because of her bad health, but she is irritated that she wasted so much time in the hospital and couldn't study anything at all. I feel pity for her current state. I have decided to console her competitive mind using my experienced reasoning about the real world.

Me: 'What is your problem girl! do you want to get killed at this age?'

Her: 'I know you are not concerned about our future, but I can't drop my studies like you kind of did already. How are we going to live if both of us fail to achieve a successful job?'

Me: 'Point taken. But your body need sleep to recover, I am sure you know it better, you will score good marks even if you miss a few hours of study every day. Be confident'

Her: 'Few hours every day will add up to a total of thousand hours every year, how about that?'

Me: 'Stop being stupid, just do what the doctor said, even if you fail to secure the "success" job, I will take care of you myself'

Her: 'I don't want to settle inside a low budget life; I want to live my dream life. Please don't force me to wear this thing'

Me: 'If you are this much concerned about your studies, why did you take me to the movies?'

Her: 'I don't want to study the whole day; I want to have fun also. I always make sure to compensate my wasted hours with my sleep hours'

Me: 'I don't want to hear any excuse from you, I will be monitoring your sleep hours from now on, your new device is connected to my phone, sleep seven hours per day or I will break up with you'

Her: 'Don't say that... How can you forget me! All these years we have been together, and finally you said those cursed words to me'

Me: 'Don't get upset, dear, I love you, and am very concerned about your health, I mean, you would have died when you had that mini stroke earlier'

Her: 'Ok, I will not disappoint you!'

Giggy is finally discharged after two more days; her anxiety is getting worse. After two more days, I have noticed that she has started her new sleep routine. I am still concerned about the invisible wall thing that denied me access. I made enquiries to my father about the issue, but he called me a madman. Next morning, I made my way to the hospital and discussed the issue with the doctor, but he announced that he can't say anything without me taking a series of lab tests, thus I left the hospital. Before going home, I tried to enter the shops again, but still, it is not doable. Finally, I threw a medium sized stone into the shop, the stone has disappeared.

While wondering what to do, someone grabbed my throat. His forehead is bleeding slightly, realised what I have done. He slapped my cheeks off my face. Shockingly, with each of his slaps, I can see the dilapidated pub in which me and the six naked women were staying, the future timeline. The man keeps hitting me, finally he threw me into a sewer and left. I was bathed in dirty sewage water, somehow managed to reach my house. After taking a long shower, I have decided to investigate further on my timeline thing. Giggy is doing fantastic with her new device.

I have decided to embark a journey to my old self's place. I woke up early and took a bus to the railway station, without telling anyone. I took a sleeper class ticket to the place and took a short nap, the train has finally reached 'Dunnbir', I believe I have never gone past this stop in my current timeline. Suddenly, I was transferred back to the station, can't enter the train no matter how hard I tried to break the invisible wall. People are murmuring about my stupid behaviour, as they walked through the invisible wall easily. Suddenly, my eyes caught two people sitting on the platform bench, eating local food and having casual talks. My eyes turned watery and my veins electrocuted, they are Alan and his sister Susan, my future beloved wife. I can't stop staring at her, Alan got up and approached me to have a conversation.

Alan: 'Stop staring at her, you pervert little boy!'

Me: 'Stop joking with me man, how are you?'

Alan: 'What! Do I know you freak? Who are you?'

Me: 'It's me Larry, your sister's... Future husband?'

Alan: (hits me in the face and pushes me down to the ground) 'Get your head out of here or else...'

Susan: 'Hold on brother, he looks familiar, aren't you the lazy brother of Jane?'

Me: 'Yes, it is me. Before you ask for clarification about my previous words, I must add that I am not feeling good lately, my mind is not stable, please don't mind me'

Susan: 'Wait... Hold on!'

I didn't obey her commands, just walked away and bought my return ticket to home. I have decided to visit Giggy's house to see how she is doing. She is studying inside her room, not wearing the device. "Where is the sleep monitor thing?" I asked. "It's charging, don't worry" she said calmly. As expected, I found the device attached to her younger brother's hand, who is only fifteen years old and is not studious like Giggy. "What is wrong with you?" I asked. Without hearing any of her weird replies, I moved out of her house and went to my house. I pledged myself to not have any connection with Giggy ever like one good teenager will do in such a situation.

Now, my sole focus is to save my mother and sister, maybe doing such a thing will alter my struggle-some future. First thing on my 'to do list' is to convince my poor sister about her dangerous blind love towards Billy, even though I used to believe that he is a great caring person. Jane is not taking my advice seriously; she also called me a madman for talking about the timeline absurdity. I have even tried to threaten her by telling mother and father about the matter, but she has no issues with that, because my parents love Billy! I changed my attention to Billy, tried to convince him to either leave my sister or treat her with love and respect instead of lust and betrayal.

"Don't worry brother, I will never make your sister weep, I have no intention to do anything lusty" he said happily. Somehow, I was brainwashed by his calmer attitude, and it made my first mission fail. My sister announced her pregnancy, and for sure Billy has already left the country. I know I couldn't have done anything since they were dating for two years now. I tried my best to console my sister "Don't worry dear, we will do an abortion secretly, I will arrange the doctor, stay calm". She is not interested in my advice, pushed me to the ground and jumped out of the first-floor window.

I have the feeling that I can never change my boring future, and I will suffer the worst mother-in-law all by myself. For two weeks, I haven't talked to Giggy, but Susan became a regular visitor of my house. She is very hurt because of Jane's fate. Giggy made her visit finally, she is furious after seeing Susan with me, she left immediately. I am not concerned about Giggy anymore; my next objective is to save my mother from her cruel fate. I requested Susan to help me; she agreed to have a talk with my father about the issue. Susan revealed that she has suffered the same fate, her father was also one useless drunkard who let his own wife die from exhaustion, her mother did multiple jobs along with regular gifts from her husband in the form of beating!

Me: 'Father, I can't let mother lose this way!'

Father: 'Has she been studying something? Very good then, she will win the exam, I have faith in her'

Me: 'She has no faith in you, how can you let her suffer this way?'

Father: 'She didn't complain anything to me, don't put words in my mouth, go and study well, get a job you lazy sloth!'

Susan: 'Uncle, Larry's mother is experiencing muscle aches and headaches regularly because of her weariness due to her decades of over-work and her old age, you must take the income wheel from her hand and take care of your family'

Father: 'Oh, I would really love to take her income wheel; she hides her income in a wheel thing? Interesting'

Me: 'It's a figure of speech, you idiot. Now get some job and provide for your bloody family from now on, let the poor bird rest'

Father: 'How dare you insult me in front of this strange woman! If you want me to provide for you two, think again. You are a strong boy, why don't you take the whatever wheel she was talking about earlier'

Me: 'I have my studies to do, don't you know?'

Father: (laughs) 'I have received a call recently from your principal. You have been scoring single digits in all your exams. You are my blood, the blood that cannot dilute the alphabetical massacre found in academic texts'

Me: 'Point taken!'

Even though my father made a valid point about my academic career, I have decided to never give up. Susan also encouraged me to study hard; she offered her help in the form of lectures done by herself, even though she is a pre-graduation student. Susan is also very enthusiastic about science subjects. Finally, I went to the college after three weeks of absence, and it is time for the industrial visit. It is exciting to spend some time somewhere other than the four-wall cubicle. I have found that Giggy is not present in the class since our break-up, I believe she is studying in her house and for sure not worried about me.

Unfortunately, Giggy made excuse from the industrial visit trip. I am not worried about her weird decision. I believe she made her decision only because of the fear of losing "quality hours" of study. Anyway, me and my classmates have arrived at the college at four o clock in the early morning, teachers have started to curse the foggy atmosphere, finally the tourist bus has arrived. The trip has started, sadly the trip is only one day! We have reached our destination within two hours of travel. I am in complete shock! The chocolate factory it is! The 'Chocolust' chocolate bar factory that traps and supplies naked women.

It is very big and has numerous guards surrounding the factory. The factory looks new; I can smell the smooth paint fragrance. One masked man approached us and introduced himself as 'Fig C', he is appointed to guide us throughout the factory. Fig C made us follow him to the chocolate mixing chamber, but my eyes are fixed on a door with a 'Do not enter' sign board. Because I know what to expect behind that door, I tried to sneak into that door, but the invisible wall again made me stop before I could try to enter that door. I have tried to break away from the main group numerous times, but all my efforts were stopped by the invisible wall block.

Finally, we have reached the chocolate mixing setup, it is a big metal container that is spinning rapidly. Nothing impressive, my classmates have started taking notes on the chemical solutions mixed with the chocolate to make it not turn hard. Currently they have been working hard to find a solution for making the chocolate more refreshing, and they have made a plan that is to make air pockets inside each chocolate drop, then filling them with pure oxygen. "Very impressive, why does anyone need oxygen from a chocolate bar? There is plenty of oxygen available everywhere" I said. The masked man didn't like my question; he ignored me and continued his parade.

The next stop looks magical, it is like a barrack full of weapons made with chocolate, different types of nuts, vanilla, strawberry etc. I took a chocolate grenade and pulled out the candy stick pin, it exploded right away, the nuts inside the grenade were shot into all nearby students, some of the nuts managed to penetrate their skin, making a small amount of bloodshed. The teachers took this opportunity and insulted me in front of the whole class. "Yours truly..." I said to my crowd and moved to the next section of weapons. There is a rifle sitting proudly on its stand, went closer to it, took it and started shooting the grenades and other chocolaty explosives, made a big mess of chocolate all around the place and on everyone there.

I am escorted out of the factory and ordered to stay inside the bus for the rest of the trip. I am happy for doing so, and while taking a long nap on the large back seat, one of my classmates returned to the bus to take some medicine for something. "What happened?" I asked him, he replied that there are some issues happening inside the factory. Students have started to experience dizziness and loss of breath after eating some chocolate bars, the authority clarified that the students are in such a state because of their blood sugar level spike. The trip is put to an end immediately, all the students have returned to the bus except five students who have become unconscious, and they are staying inside the factory for better treatment.

After a few more days, the factory announced the death of the five students, and surprisingly, none of the other students or the teachers have any interest in questioning the factory people. "What do they want with the lives of five male students?" the teacher asked me. I am confused about what to do, Susan came to meet me. I have described to her about the dangers hidden inside the chocolate factory, but she is also in favour of my teacher's opinion. "Don't worry Larry, they were boys" she said. Another strange thing happened is the news that there won't be any funeral service for the five dead students because, the factory claims to have done that already by themselves.

Again, no one found anything suspicious about the weird news. Luckily, Susan has noticed the suspicious air circulating around. She promised me to help me, and she has started collecting data about the factory thing. She has found that there were several deaths happened inside the factory over many years. Apparently, the factory is listed as a tourist destination, and all the "mysterious" deaths happened inside the factory are labelled as accidental deaths. And the factory has always conducted the funerals for the dead victims all by themselves.

I have made a report on the strange events associated with the factory, and innocent Susan has advised me to go to the nearby police station. But I know it can lead to more problems, thus decided to post my findings on social media platform with the hashtag #Chocolust. Shockingly, the moment I clicked the post it online button, the post was taken down by the internet immediately, and my account is terminated. Susan believes that some kind of error has caused it, but I strongly believe that I know what happened and thus, decided to meet Giggy to discuss the matter further. Susan accompanied me to Giggy's house, and surprisingly she is wearing the sleep monitor device.

Me: 'Hello dear, how have you been?'

Giggy: 'Who is this?' (points her finger at Susan)

Susan: 'I am Susan, Larry's friend'

Me: 'We need your help; can you find out the materials inside this' (hands over a Chocolust chocolate bar)

Giggy: (reads the ingredients chart written on the cover) 'Chocolate, nuts, sugar, oil...'

Susan: 'No, No, what he meant is to find the hidden ingredients and chemicals inside this bar'

Giggy: 'How can I do that? I am not a scientist!'

Me: 'Listen, you studylust girl, just find out the chemical solutions and the mysteries present inside this chocolate bar'

Giggy: 'What makes you think that I have knowledge of chemistry?'

Me: 'Because that is what you have been studying while sacrificing your own life'

Giggy: 'Wrong! I am not studying for my graduation; I am not stupid to do that. I am studying for government service exams instead'

Me: (sighs) 'Just put this thing under your microscope and look!'

Giggy: 'Fine'

Giggy carefully observes the Chocolust chocolate bar under the microscope. She feels something strange, and tells me to buy one different chocolate bar, I bought one from the nearby store. Giggy puts the new bar under the microscope and found that it is different than the world famous Chocolust bar. Giggy explains that she has found blood cells on the Chocolust bar, and she is sure about her findings. Giggy takes her phone to inform the food and safety department about the issue, but I stopped her from doing so. "I will do it myself" I said.

"I am happy that you found someone prettier than me" Giggy said. I am not concerned about her teenage emotions, left her house quickly and went to a store to buy more Chocolust bars with the tour money I have saved. Susan and I ate them together, and luckily from one of the bars, I found the strange coupon with the call me number. I remember calling the number in my future timeline, carefully dialled the number. A woman picked up the phone and ordered me to "Tell the code". Susan found the code written in small font, it says, "Desires are uncontrollable". The woman gave me directions to a location.

VI

All because of Gluttony

I am eager to find my unclaimed prize; Susan has no idea about the whole prize thing. Alone, I took the bus to the location, luckily it is in the middle of the city. I have found the building 'DX residency' mentioned by the woman. Again, the invisible wall prevented me from entering the building, but I have promised myself to not return without knowing the prize that awaits me. Yes, I know what to expect, but I have to confirm that it is what it really is. I called the woman again and told the code, requested her to take my prize out of the building, if possible, but she cursed me and hung up the phone.

I have decided to send an imposter of me, chose one middle aged man, bribed him to enter the building and visit room twenty-four, tell the code and claim the prize. He entered the building slowly, fifteen minutes later, he returned empty handed. He thanked me and returned my bribe. I have confirmed my assumptions regarding the prize, and asked him, "Is she pretty?". "She is very pretty, young and skinny" he replied. I bought a small toy from the store and convinced Susan that it is the prize, and she believed it instantly. Susan has another news to share; Giggy has called Susan for some help. Giggy said she has a fever and wants Susan to get her notebook back that she forgot to take back from her tuition class.

Susan has started walking to the tuition class alone, but me also joined her and we both took a bus to the place. It is inside a hotel building, luckily no invisible wall popped out in front of me. Susan and me slowly walked into the building and climbed upstairs to the room number mentioned by Giggy. Knocked on the door three times, one middle aged man opened the door and welcomed us inside. I can't remember him, but he seems to know me and my academics. He handed me Giggy's book, but the book contained only rough notes and time-pass art, and for another thing, only ten pages are used in total.

We left the room and walked straight to the elevator. Out of nowhere, a masked man jumped out of the next room, he is holding a machete and is aiming it at Susan. Luckily, me being an experienced teenager, I grabbed his arm fearlessly, but he broke my hold and stabbed Susan on her forearm, somehow, I have managed to kick him to the ground, and he lost his machete. Random people came to help us; with no other choice, he ran fast to the elevator and entered the already opened elevator. Quickly it went down, but I have spotted one circuit breaker and turned it off.

The elevator has stopped mid-way, and police have arrived to catch the criminal. He is taken to the police station, while Susan is taken to the hospital nearby. Luckily, her forearm wound is not that serious and has been discharged after a couple of days. I have received a call from the police station, and it is about the criminal, he has confessed the truth about who sent him to assassinate Susan. As you might have guessed, it is Giggy! She hired a local criminal to kill Susan and to make a cut on my legs for some reason. Police have registered case against her, but I have managed to get them cancel the case.

Before I can go to Giggy's house and ask her about the intentions regarding her brutal plan, Giggy's suicidal news have arrived. When I reached her house, police handed me her suicide note, because of her mentioning me inside the letter. It says,

The death of an innocent studious girl

"I have decided to put an end to my boring life. I know that a lot of people are confronted with the problems that I have faced, and most of them have gone through their problems easily, while a few like me, are tripped hard and fell face first to the metal pole specially designed for us. I have a problem, my careless attitude towards human emotions and friendships. Now that my big mistake has taken hold of my life, I have realised how pathetic my life has been. My only form of emotional support was Larry, and finally he has taken away by one pretty girl. The world has made me a machine that has its solo existence circling around the acts of reading and learning unwanted things for the need of securing a living inside this unsympathetic world. While filling up my knowledge bank, my stubborn self; cut loose the metal bond with dear Larry. Is my hard-earned knowledge not enough to make good decisions! They say knowledge is power, is this the power that I wanted? The power to hire an assassin to eliminate an innocent girl! I believe, my sin has bypassed every form of mercy that exists inside this Universe, suicide is my only option. I am dead-hausted from my daily studies, but none of that helped me during my decision-making process. Goodbye Larry, Goodbye Susan. Forgive me!"

I feel pity for her and became guilt conscious. Before I can see her one last time, my vision has bleached and I have started to shake vigorously.

(Whining noises)

"Wake up" someone screamed in my ears, finally I have my vision back, I am back inside the dilapidated pub, not the abandoned house! "Where was I?" I asked the six women. "Here!" they said. They are starving again, Merlin asked me to help them somehow. But 'Somehow' can't be used to make payments, and I have no cash left. Merlin made a weird smile, which I believe is an indication of something uncanny about to happen. Merlin asked me to drop her in the town area, maybe she has money with her; I thought.

I dropped her in a small town, a few kilometres away from the forest. "Go and check on the others, I will be back in sometime" she said. I am confused what is she cooking inside her mind "It is dangerous to walk through the forest; I will stay here for you" I said. But she forced me to go and protect the five women inside the pub. Finally, I did what she said, the five women are sitting around the fire setup. They ran towards my truck the moment I have entered the premises. "Sorry ladies, Merlin will be back soon with the food, wait!" I spoke. They all turned back to the fire except one who stands in front of me. She introduced herself as Susan.

Susan: 'Hi Sir, can you please take me home. I will give you anything in return for your service'

Me: 'Sorry to disappoint you dear, I am not sure if I will be able to return home somehow'

Susan: 'Where did you take Merlin to?'

Me: 'Don't worry about her, I dropped her in the town, she promised me that she will be back soon with food for us all'

Susan: 'Do you have any idea about the Chocolust thing?'

Me: 'I don't know much, but I do know that it is not just a factory'

Susan: 'I am a private detective, and I was assigned to investigate a missing case'

Me: 'It is them for sure... Do I know you? I think I have seen you somewhere. My name is Larry'

Susan: 'Oh Larry, I remember you but don't know for sure! I have been swimming inside drugs lately and it decayed my memories. But still, I believe my name has something to do with you'

Me: 'Susan is my wife's name!'

Susan: 'Oh, my real name was Kaitlyn and then received the name Susan by some weird means I believe'

Me: 'Yes, I remember that part but don't know what was I doing then? Shouldn't be anything associated with intelligence for sure' (Laughs) 'What are your findings about the factory?'

Susan: 'I have observed their delivery locations, found that they transport numerous deliveries to the toy shop factory. From there, the boxes are supplied to mega mansions owned by super rich people. I was caught when I tried to infiltrate the Choco factory'

Me: 'What about the other four women, you know them? Why did they put naked women inside chocolate containers?'

Susan: 'I don't know why they do such a thing, but from my research I have found that hundreds of women, aged between fifteen and thirty are missing, there is no investigation going on either'

Me: 'What about their families? I mean, they cannot remain silent in such a situation... right!'

Susan: 'They can do nothing, after studying the data of last ten years, I found that the lost women are labelled as killed in other countries, by accident'

Our conversation is interrupted by the arrival of a motorcycle; we became scared and quickly went inside the pub. It is Merlin accompanied by a big muscular man. The man looks like a criminal because of the wounds on his face, thick beard and moustache. Merlin happily escorted him into the big bedroom, she started to caress and kiss him, followed by stripping off her leaf clothes and stripping him slowly as well. She then started to massage his back and during this she took a pocketknife from his jacket, pushed it hard into his skull multiple times. She has already seen me looking through the door that has a lot of holes on it. She then started to loot the man thoroughly.

Merlin hand-signalled me to join the strip search, but her face turned dull after finding no cash on him. "Dirty beggar bit**" she said. I calmed her and went out to the forest to find something edible to provide the women. Luckily, I found a dead rabbit and some plum fruits, happily walked to the pub. The aroma of cooking meat caught my nostrils attention, it is coming from the pub. I thought maybe Susan went hunting and caught something in my absence. But my assumptions are wrong, the cooking meat belongs to the motorcycle man. You know what I am going to say, yes, the man has been butchered and placed over the fire, they took oil from the motorcycle and increased the rage of the fire tremendously.

"Come Larry, eat some sweet meat" Susan announced. I have realised that they have drunk a lot of the rum bottles tied around the motorcycle. Merlin took the plum fruits, crushed and added it to the cooked meat platter, she handed me a leaf plate filled with cooked male human meat marinated in plum juice. "Not bad than eating a dead rabbit" I thought, took my first bite, luckily the meat is overcooked heavily, and it helped to not feel any gut reflex. Merlin and the others happily consumed the meat without any guilt. Unfortunately, the pile of waste attracted some hungry predators that forced us to stay hidden inside the pub.

Susan has started her investigation on the four anonymous women. I have already told her about Merlin, the other four women described how they were entrapped inside the Choco box. Just like Merlin, they were also preparing to go abroad for better "lifestyle". One day, they were kidnapped and taken into the chocolate factory, washed like a car, and then put inside a freezer for some time before they were dropped inside the metal box, and then put one big pipe down their throat for oxygen, filled the whole box with chocolate. I have also mentioned her about the 'code to claim prize' reward offered by the factory.

Susan already knows about the prize thing, and she explained that — "I have once bought so many Chocolust bars to find one coupon, and found one in the tenth bar, called the number to claim the prize. I lied to the code lady that I was a male, went to the location mentioned by the code lady. I was disguised as a man and entered the building to collect my prize. Before entering the room, some masked guys searched me. Inside the prize room, a young woman was waiting for me, and she was wearing a metal collar around her neck. I observed the room closely and moved closer to the woman sitting on the bed. "I am all yours" she said happily, but I could see nervous sweat flowing down her forehead and eyes.

"What is your name?" I asked her but she repeated the phrase "I am all yours". She started to play with her eyes, meanwhile I was observing the spots she pointed to with her eyes. Those spots were filled with microphones and one big telescreen disguised as a television. My detective brain cooked up a wise idea to fool the hidden spies around us. I found a spot that was not covered by the telescreen but there was one big microphone hidden behind a flower vase. I started to act fake romance with her, and somehow managed to roll her to my newly found spot. Wrote a note with my hidden pen and pocketbook and made her read it.

We then rolled back to our normal position to avoid getting caught. "Your turn" I said. She then happily played alongside me and rolled down to the spot repeatedly, and with each trip to the same spot, she managed to write a full page. I hid the note in my hidden pocket and left the building happily. I went home and sat comfortably on my chair, calmly read the note.

Name Polly. 25.

Trapped last year.

During Chocolust factory tour.

Family held hostage, killed sister.

Automatic guns inside the building.

Went through multiple abortions.

Save my family. Please sir.

Address- JV apartment room 45. Bee road 56.

Help!!!

Without wasting little time, I went to the address mentioned in the note. There was no sign of violence, I simply entered the building. The family greeted me happily and there were no signs of a hidden microphone or a telescreen. I made up a lie that I was a high-ranking income tax official, showed my fake ID, started my small investigation. They looked very innocent enough to not look at my ID; I found out that Polly's sister was alive! Her family was never threatened. My eyes caught the sight of Polly's photo hung on the wall, brightened with a low voltage LED rice light. Yes, they were stuck inside the belief that Polly was already dead from a building collapse in some foreign country.

I enquired about Polly's whereabouts before she went to the anonymous country. Her father answered that she received a job offer from some factory, she went to an interview conducted in a random location and then after a week, they received a handwritten letter from Polly narrating about her newly found freedom and wealth because of her new high paying job, and she announced her breaking ties with her family. "Can I see that letter?" I asked, without questioning, they handed me a framed letter. The first look of the letter guaranteed me that it was not written by Polly, confirmed it by comparing with Polly's note.

"She was given full freedom and had no financial issues ever; I still don't know what she was talking about in that piece" Polly's mother said. "Did you try to bring her body back here for funeral stuff?" I asked. They revealed that they tried and all their attempts ended, when the anonymous country demanded a hefty amount. After lunch, I took leave from there. Since then, I haven't received any opportunity to meet Polly or find one of the coupons" – Susan ends her narration. We stayed inside the pub for a whole day because of the wild animals' presence.

Things are getting harder again with all of us starving again! Merlin again took me to the mini town and asked me to return to the pub. I have decided to see what she is doing now even though I know what she will do. I hid my truck next to a makeshift shop and shoplifted a whole bag of potatoes, luckily, no one noticed my theft. Merlin has started talking to a young muscular man, and within a few minutes, the young man called a taxi and both he and Merlin started their journey to the pub. I sneakily followed them and as expected they have entered the dilapidated pub premises. Merlin and the young man went inside quickly.

Because I know what to expect from Merlin, am getting guilt stricken for not stopping the death of an innocent young man. Suddenly, something else caught my attention. The taxi driver has started to examine the metal chocolate box that is hidden inside the door-less storeroom attached to the pub. The driver tried to open the thing with a passcode of his own, and it unlocked without any drama. He takes out his phone and started dialling someone, I am getting frightened, revved the engine high and rammed into the storeroom, hitting the man hard. He fell to the ground unconscious, bleeding from his nose.

Luckily, he didn't get the time to click the dial button. I took his phone and started scrolling through his gallery to see if it has anything about the factory thing. His gallery is empty except for two pictures taken today, and both pics are taken from the toy shop factory. In the first photo, he is holding a princess's dress and her fancy innerwear. In the second photo, he is holding hands with a young woman who is wearing one fantasy outfit. Her face gives the impression that she was being forced into the whole pic thing. Suddenly, I heard a big scream from the pub. "I failed!" I thought and ran inside to see what I knew my eyes would see.

The young man was brutally killed with the sharp pocketknife she used to kill her previous victim. "Everyone, please help me butcher this pig!" Merlin announced proudly. I am standing shocked and took a closer look at the young man. He looks like a teenager; his helpless eyes are staring at me while his wide-open mouth cursing me. He was stabbed multiple times in his stomach. "How could you!" I asked Merlin. She didn't hear my words; she is busy butchering the poor son. She happily cut out his man part and claimed it belongs to the wild animals growling outside, and she threw it out of the window, but her bad aim caused it to hit the wall instead, creating a filthy mess.

Me: 'STOP THIS NONSENSE!'

Merlin: 'What happened? Where is that driver guy, is he gone?'

Me: 'He is dead, happy?'

Merlin: 'Take his body here or else the wild beasts will eat him'

Me: 'Oh, don't worry about the wild beasts, one heartless beast with a bloody brain is standing tall here, I want to address that thing'

Susan: (picks up and throws the man part out of the window) 'Sorry, I am very hungry'

Merlin: 'Oh, don't worry about her, she will be alright'

Me: (swipes my sweat off) 'I am talking about you, Merlin!'

Merlin: 'What did I do? Am I not allowed to butcher meat because I am a woman?'

Me: 'Don't use that line! This young man was a teenager, probably a student. He reminds me of my son, poor thing!'

Merlin: 'I don't give a thing about how old he was, he was sniffing around me like a dog the moment I stepped out of your pickup truck, I felt vulnerable around him, and thus picked him as our today's meal. I am sorry if he reminds you something'

Me: 'He had a lot of years to live here and might have had a lot of dreams. All destroyed because of gluttony! Now I don't care about your accusation of him staring at you like a dog craving for a bone. The fact of the matter is that his behaviour was due to his teenage puberty thing, sure he would never have assaulted you in the middle of the crowd, and under no circumstances, your accusation cannot make him qualify as a meatloaf to fulfil your gut's wish'

Merlin: 'Point taken. But we need something to eat, right?'

Me: 'I have brought a whole freakin bag of potatoes!'

Merlin: 'Potatoes can irritate the digestive system, maybe we should roast some of it and make a side dish for our main course fry'

Me: 'WHAT? I am leaving this place, farewell'

Without waiting for their replies, I went outside and started the pickup truck. For the past few days, the truck has not caused any trouble in starting, luckily it started again without any gimmicks. I am not worried about the women; they can use the dead driver's vehicle to escape if they want to. The thoughts about my younger self popped in my mind and that made me determined to visit the nearby hospital, to check what is happening inside my boiling brain.

VII
Bit chalky but Flavourful

I went to the government hospital nearby, and it is in a dilapidated condition. "Ruins Ruins everywhere!" I thought. There is one big queue standing and it has taken over the parking lot also. After getting my buddy parked in a dirty spot, I joined the back of the queue. After standing there for an hour, the queue moved just an inch. Suddenly, my eyes spot a woman standing ahead of the queue wearing a fancy cartoonish outfit, she is standing in a little bent position while shaking vigorously. I broke the queue and went to meet her, she is Susan, my wife. Her face appears to be beaten with a hammer and scratched by some cat. She is not in a condition to have a good talk, but she somehow explained what caused her to stand here in such a battered position.

It turns out that the Chocolust guys have attacked my family brutally and kidnapped Susan, has taken her to multiple places. She is not sure about the places they have taken her because she was blindfolded. But she is sure that she was drugged very badly and was put into physical tortures. After suffering the madness, a group of people saved her from the place, and provided her a small house near the garbage facility. She also mentioned that the group of saviours have also brought our kids safely to the new hiding spot. She then started to curse me for not protecting them.

We then waited there for a few more hours, and finally we received the privilege to see the doctor. To my surprise, the doctor is a good man, he checked Susan with care and made me take only a single scan of my deep-fried brain. The doctor advised Susan to take an entire year of rest, and for me he has something special to offer. I am diagnosed with a condition caused by the unconventional lifestyle that I used to follow from my younger age as Susan has mentioned, but still, I am not sure if I have such a past. He named it something hard to pronounce, which I forgot the moment he said it. I have always wondered why these medical terms are hard to pronounce and write.

The doctor explained that I can live my past! Yes, the past, the one thing most human beings never ever want to live again. With my current power, I can live my past and explore all the places that my past-self visited, but I cannot explore the spots that my past-self didn't explore. Yes, the invisible wall will restrict me if I try to explore new places in my past. It is almost like some video games, you explore more places when you progress further in the game, and when you complete the whole game, you will become a mad tramp. The doctor can't say when or where will I be teleported into my past life. Susan is not shocked at all; she is still in a lot of pain, but the hospital beds are full already.

We left the hospital and went straight to Susan's new secret hiding place. The building is near a garbage ditch, covered in filth. I have to carry Susan inside the dilapidated building that is not good for any being on earth. Tears started to roll down my eyes after seeing my kid's condition. For the first time, I feel happy for my dead son who has escaped this. I became guilty making five kids, I was sure that I couldn't provide them basic living conditions. Yes, I didn't have knowledge of birth control products or the courage to abort a human life.

"Come to Bee mansion at seven o' clock" a message received on the dead taxi driver's phone, and its backside has an ID card of the driver. His name is Ted, aged forty, has a wife and two sons. Again, I feel heavy guilt, and my mind is full of thoughts about the dead man's sons but at the same time, my kids look starved like they haven't eaten anything for two weeks. Luckily, the stolen bag of potatoes is still inside my truck, and it helped to fill their small stomachs. Suddenly, I heard the tire skidding sound outside the building, four masked people, with weapons in their hands, entered our secret building.

They look less muscular and surely have no experience on how to handle a gun. "Who are you guys? take off your masks, we surrender" I said. They removed their superhero masks, they are all women, one of them started describing their masked existence. They are part of a secret organisation formed to put an end to the young women traffickers. Even though I enquired them about their findings, they didn't cooperate with me. They saved Susan from the devilish factory people. They want me to join their organisation, unfortunately they have no payment service for their employees, and that made me turn down their offer.

I need money to help rescue my family and have no issues with working for anything weird. It's time! Went out quickly, drove my way to the Bee mansion, and it is a new mansion that I haven't visited yet. I have planned to lie that I am the brother of the taxi driver, but they have no idea about the taxi driver's appearance, they mistook me for him. The workers have started to load my truck with plastic wrapped things; each has a size of two pillows. They ordered me to unload the packages into the ocean secretly, all to be done within tonight. I have signed the contract and collected the full payment of three hundred dollars, became very happy and went to the ocean quickly. When I picked one of the wrapped packages, my hands turned to red colour.

Because I know what to expect inside the package, I wonder what made me sign the contract to receive the money dipped in blood. What's more disturbing is that some of the packages have slight movements happening inside them. Without wasting any more time, unwrapped one package, it is the corpse of a young boy, and he is folded inside the package, his body is filled with red markings. Then unwrapped the package that has tiny movements, it is also a young boy who is gasping for air. "Please don't hurt me anymore, sir! Please" he begged me. He is not in a condition to make an escape move.

After placing him carefully on the ground, I have started to unwrap all of the packages. Found three women and two more men, all young. Out of the three women, two are dead. Only one of the men is dead. Dropped the dead bodies into the ocean and loaded others back inside the truck, accelerated towards the secret building. Susan and the kids are sleeping, one member of the organisation is guarding them, she helped me unload the battered bodies from the truck. They are screaming in pain, and I have noticed the small cuts made on their joints, making them unable to move freely nor stand up. I gave them baked potatoes to eat, but they are not hungry.

After a few minutes, they have started to vomit chocolate. Soon, one of the men started describing the events they all have gone through. He made it clear that he knows about the men and women lying helplessly in pain, he met them at the 'Dumhump' travel agency, and they were preparing for their respective flights, but two days before their flight, a group of muscular men kidnapped them and took them to some place, tied and... You know what happened, that. I have noticed him mentioning the travel agency, realised that the six women I met before have mentioned some travel agency thing also.

I have made up my mind to join the secret organisation, even though there is no payment for my future service. I don't know why I am so eager to join them and to take part in the investigation process, it feels like I have some instinctual inclination towards the whole detective thing. I have realised that I can't recollect my past life happened after Giggy's death, but sure I can recollect a few fragments of me getting embarrassed repeatedly, memories that everyone loves to forget forever. Anyway, because I have sworn my oath to the secret organisation, I have made my first mission myself;

to rescue the six women stranded in the middle of the forest pub.

Before getting into the dilapidated pub, the image of the coupon and my unclaimed prize sprang up in my mind. I took out the coupon and went straight to the location mentioned by the code lady. Luckily, the spot is not far away, I entered the premises by showing my coupon. "Take your tiny thing to the second floor, room 8.6" the guard said. I entered the room and a woman wearing a big robe is sitting on the bed, she looks calm, and she started a timer that shows '30:00' and it is ticking backwards. "Start when you are ready, eyes on the clock please" she said.

I have spotted the microphones and the television sized telescreen staring at my face. She has undressed herself and laid on the bed. Just like detective Susan narrated her experience, I have also tried to hug and roll her to a secluded corner, then revealed my true intentions by passing her my already written note. She made a big laugh and stuffed the note into my mouth, rolled me back to the main stage and started her role of seducing me, and I fell victim to her seduction. You know, it is hard to suppress the drives especially if it is gifted freely! After the clock ticked down to zero, the guards came inside and kicked me out of the building. I must get to the pub quickly.

I reached the pub building and there are two more cars parked outside. Merlin did a good job of luring the wealthy people! I am surprised that none of the women is coming outside to see me, am sure they must have heard my truck's screaming voice. Before getting into the pub, I have decided to take a closer look at the vehicles. None of the vehicles has any fuel left, and I found something suspicious in one of the cars, it is a stack of photos and one of it is a picture of Merlin, and she is holding an automatic rifle, her dress covered in bloodstains. All the pictures inside the stack shows some kind of brutality. Along with the pictures, documents, there are many weapons loaded in the car trunk.

On further analysing the stack, I found the faces of people that I have seen earlier. I am confused about what is happening, and a sudden feeling of fear dropped into my mind, maybe the people that I have saved, the secret freakin organisation, they all might be a large spider web of terrorist activities, and I have willingly given them my poor family. After taking the stack of pictures, I went inside the pub to find more signs of betrayal. Inside the pub is a pool made of blood, and I counted four decapitated women half drowned inside the pool. They are dressed in leaf clothes, and sure they belonged to my group. Apart from the four dead women, there are five dead bodies of men, all shot through chest and head.

"Maybe Merlin and Susan are criminals" I thought. I became angry, took a rifle from the car, accelerated to the secret hideout, fuelled with rage and blurred with guilt, stepped out of the vehicle, pointed the rifle at them. But they are not in a condition to raise their arms to announce surrender. The organisation member tried to calm me down; I threw the stack of pictures on her face. After taking a closer look, she is still standing clueless about what is the meaning behind the stack. I took the stack back from her hand and checked it whole to pick out the pictures of the refugees lying helplessly around me.

The organisation member has already found her own picture, and she does not want anyone to see it. After searching the stack, I found one of the women's pictures, and it does not look genuine. Because, in the picture, she is standing on top of a pile of dead bodies, and she has a big muscular body, thick black hair, but the same woman lying in front of me with the face of the woman on the picture, has blonde hair and very thin body. I dropped the stack and asked the organisation lady to show me the photo that she is hiding behind her back. She is nervous to show me the picture, and it is a picture of her stabbing a male soldier of some country.

She is crying hard, and I am in disbelief about what is the reality around me. She has suggested me to visit the organisation headquarters, along with the stack of photos. She gave me directions, and I quickly drove to the headquarters, but before I can get there, I have realised that I am being followed by a big car. They have overtaken me easily, and thus, I changed my route and hit the forest off-road tracks. But the spy car is equipped with mighty off-road features, again me and my poor truck failed. I have no choice other than to surrender, a pack of seven muscular men stepped out of the car, they are holding melee weapons and rifles.

Unfortunately, I have left my stolen rifle in the secret hideout. I stepped out of the truck and kneeled with both hands up in the air. They slowly walked towards me but, out of nowhere, a motorbike crashed into my truck's backside, detective Susan and Merlin, equipped with grenades and rifles. Without wasting time doing slow motion walk like the seven men, Susan and Merlin unleashed all ammunition they had into the slow-motion figures, luckily, I have rolled under the truck. Within a minute, the seven men dropped to the ground dead. Merlin took me into the truck and drove it all the way to the headquarters that I was searching.

Susan is following us on her motorbike, and she reached the destination first. Well, I am not sure Merlin has the place right, but she looks confident and swiftly drove into an abandoned farm. We went far inside the farm, and finally I can see a farmhouse standing on the other end of the farm, and surprisingly there are many makeshift buildings surrounding the most important building. The farmland looks beautiful with the vegetation cultivated by the residents there. It is like a whole new civilization living isolated from the rest of the world. Merlin parked the truck near the main farmhouse and entered the building. I followed her in and there is no security at the entrance.

Finally, I met the leader of the whole thing, she introduced herself as Zeiwo. Merlin handed her the stack of pictures, Zeiwo started analysing them one by one while comparing them with the book of register sitting on her desk. Zeiwo is shocked, a load of sweat is dripping down her face. Zeiwo took her phone and called someone, then asked me to wait, with an added please! Detective Susan has entered the room shortly, and she started discussing the matter with the leader. Meanwhile, I am observing the whole farmland through an open window. I saw a few cars parked outside the backside of the farmhouse. Detective Susan and Zeiwo called me to join their meeting.

I have narrated to them all my experience with the evil factory, and how many deliveries I have done. They started explaining to me about their findings after years of research. Before today, they made the conclusion that the factory was luring young male and female to satisfy the lust of wealthy people, and to give them away as a prize to boost the whole chocolate business like we all have been guessing so far. But now, with the stack of pictures, a new space of investigation has opened. To add more wood to burn the fire more furiously, I have revealed my findings that most of the victims were preparing to go abroad when they were kidnapped and trapped inside the plot.

Zeiwo already knows about the abroad thing, and in addition to that, she has surveyed the escaped victims' families, found that the victim's families were informed about their son/daughter died in other countries, labelled as terrorists. Zeiwo and her organisation have been rescuing the innocent human beings from the chocolate factory and other condemned places, for over five years now. They once tried to inform the authority about the matter, received no help but more issues. Zeiwo has made a new plan, to convince men and women who are planning to go abroad, about the hidden conspiracy. For executing such a plan, we are divided into teams of two, to spy on different abroad agencies out there.

Zeiwo has supplied us micro cameras for our own safety. On the first day of our "convince" mission, the agency visitors showed no interest in hearing our stories or seeing the photo evidence. They assumed that we were agents of some other agency, trying to lure people away from their agency. Zeiwo herself tried to convince some men and women, but she also received insults. Zeiwo has lost faith in the new mission. On the second day of our mission, we have decided to follow the visa seekers and sneaked into their houses to convince their parents. Again, we were slapped in the face, they scolded us for trying to ruin their son/daughter's dream life, reputed job and a luxurious life. Zeiwo has lost complete faith in the mission.

Zeiwo: 'I am tired of this crap, why don't these idiots grow up!'

Me: 'Calm down madame, we must change our strategy, I guess'

Zeiwo: 'No, nothing can change these freaks. Most of them are selfish and have no interest to get involved in the matters happening around them'

Me: 'They just want to live simple and apolitical, I believe'

Zeiwo: 'Have we asked them too much? We just want to rescue them, and they don't want to consider the facts in any manner. I mean, what's up with that?'

Me: 'Well, if you tell me to step down from an opportunity to go abroad and make a wealthy living, I would have rejected all your suggestions too. Normally, we humans are always alone and can only think about our family, and have nothing to do with the outside world, even if the authority digs a Well in the middle of a road and orders us to jump over, most of us will do the thing'

(Susan interrupts our conversation)

Susan: 'Sorry madame, the youths are not in the mood to think about the dangers they are getting into'

Me: 'I think we need to encourage local youths to motivate and help the others, may be that will help'

Susan: 'Sorry to disappoint, that won't happen! I mean, we have tried that already, but the local youths have no interest or time to participate in these external affairs. Most of the local youths are interested in higher studies, I mean very higher studies. Ironically, they are interested to sit inside a competitive exam coaching class for over a decade than to help us'

Zeiwo: 'Good heavens! I have lost faith in humanity, when did we lose our free will, courage, kindness, love!'

Me: 'We can't complain mam, it's their life, they are free to live as they wish'

Susan: 'Shut up! No one is free, and you think they are living as they wished? Think again! Distancing away from the enemy is not freedom, and there are a lot of universal enemies hovering around the world, do you think that hiding from them will give us freedom? No! I mean, even the universe has no freedom now!'

Me: (receives a text message, checks the message) 'Oh, I received a message from the Chocolust factory... Not mine, but the dead taxi driver's phone'

Susan: 'What is it? Is it a trap for you? Did they find your identity theft?'

Me: 'Nah, I don't think so. The factory has asked me to come at six o' clock sharp and should bring the anonymous S9 package from the black market. Oh, I don't know where on earth is a black market, let's ignore the text and plan our next strategy'

Susan: 'I know where the black market is! And we should use this important opportunity to our advantage'

Zeiwo: 'Yes, I think Larry should go to the factory and try to capture some video clippings of the suspicious activities conducted inside the factory. I believe we can convince some youths with the power of video evidence'

Me: 'Ok then, give me the directions to the black market'

Susan and I stepped inside the pickup truck; she has given me with the strangest directions. After passing through – a fallen bridge, mountain ruins, junkyard – we have managed to enter the black market. Susan asked me to park the truck near a pile of garbage. She then advised me to damage my shirt to expose my potbelly exclusively for them to see me clearly. I am standing bewildered listening to her mocking behaviour, but she made it clear that the market people will rip off anything attractive near them. "Point Taken" I said and walked alone, slowly into the black-market place, while randomly shaking my fat belly around to make the spectators feel my ugliness.

The scenes inside this place cannot be described with the normal English language. I can see male and female human beings tied to a pole with a silver chain, with price tags hanging around their necks, like a necklace. There are assassins sitting relaxed but eager to take their first job of the day. Fresh meats of strange shapes lined up with price tags on the thick blood stain. Advanced weapons ranging from a ten-metre sword to plasma powered guns. Suddenly, my eyes found the S9 packages resting on a massive desk, this section is bannered as 'Toxic cosmetics'. The shopkeeper happily supplied me a package after I showed him the ID pasted on the back side of the driver's phone.

I went back to my truck; Susan is hiding under the seat, sleeping. I woke her up and she is happy to see me back. "What are you doing under the seat?" I asked her. "Don't worry about that, you will understand why later" she said with a cheeky smile upon her face. Maybe she was hiding from the black-market thugs, who knows! We drove to the farmhouse headquarters. Zeiwo has been waiting for our return, she started to inspect the whole package, read out the instructions written on the side of the package outloud.

Nothing here to read you dummy!

Have pain, blow the package

Throw your mind out of the window,

Or if you're in the best mood

Throw yourself b****!

"What to expect from those pesky criminals" Susan said. Zeiwo is super excited and has decided to taste it to find out what can happen and what is inside the head of those freakish factory dawgs. Zeiwo took a handful of the powder substance from the package, stuffed it all into her mouth. "Bit chalky, but flavourful" she said. We patiently waited to see her reaction, and after half an hour, she has started to act weird, lost her stability and became unconscious but still she is murmuring something, thus, we are sure that the powder is not lethal. Show times over, I put the package inside the truck, made my way to the factory.

VIII

Missing people Paradox

I am wearing a black mask to hide my identity, and the guards have no interest to check me. After passing the package to the supply station, I went inside with a tiny camera thing attached to my shirt. Sadly, there aren't any suspicious activity happening around. This place is filled with tourists; they are thrilled to take photos and are happy to observe the factory's fantastical way of working. After waiting there for an hour, some male workers entered the main space with a wagon full of hot chocolate. The tourists have started consuming the delicious drink and still wandered around. I am observing the tourists carefully, and yes, some of them are coughing blood and have started acting weird.

Carefully, I have planted the tiny camera on one of the coughing person's shoes. Even though I am feeling guilty for not trying to save the soon be victim people, I know this is the only way to collect believable evidence. As expected, some factory workers came out of a secret door nearby, dragged the coughing people inside the secret room. Rest of the tourist crowd have started to act like nothing has happened. I took leave from the factory quickly and went to the farmhouse headquarters. Susan and Zeiwo are waiting outside, training the refugees for some future activities. Merlin is busy with her shooting practice, luckily, she has attached the silencer in.

"I have done it" me announced proudly. Zeiwo and Susan got up quickly and went inside, ordered me to follow them. Inside a room full of computers, Susan has started to play the visuals captured by the tiny camera that I have secretly pinned to the coughing man's shoe. Unfortunately, the shoe was dropped at the entrance, inside a bag of shoes. Luckily, the bag of shoes was full and the shoe with the camera is on top of the bag, it helped to capture good visuals of what is happening inside the secret spaces inside the factory. After an hour of waiting, some workers have finally brought a battered-up woman, placed her in front of a round structure made of metal. She is in no condition to fight back or talk.

Suddenly, the metal round structure started working, it is a blender thing. The workers threw the woman into it, and she is no more. After a few minutes, the workers brought a battered man and did the same thing. The blender has been attached to a large pool; after taking a closer observation, we found chocolate dripping into the pool from a metal pipe placed above it. "What in the Universal size of madness is happening here!" Zeiwo exclaimed helplessly. "I think we should not use these clips to convince anyone" Susan said. "You think?" I said and proposed the one option left for us. Zeiwo and Susan agreed to my plan, Zeiwo ordered the teams to start the mission immediately.

Merlin agreed to accompany me, we made our way to the nearest travel agency. While inside the truck, Merlin noticed a hidden drawer inside the seat cushion, but it is locked. I took a peek at the drawer, and it has a strange looking symbol on top of the tiny door. Anyway, we have arrived near a travel agency, and a group of two men and women are walking out of the office already. Merlin handed me a mask, and ordered me to wear it, she then takes out a bottle of mystery liquid and pours it into a cotton cloth. She also gave me a piece of cloth dipped in the solution and ordered me to step out of the truck.

I followed her orders, she walked up to them and sneaked behind them, pressed the cloth to their faces quickly. The two men walking ahead of Merlin have become alarmed, and now it is my turn to do the trick. I did the same thing, and they fell unconscious in a second. We then picked them up and carefully loaded them into the truck, went back to the farmhouse, and dropped them inside a makeshift prison made of wood. "My wife and kids! I am a terrible father" I thought suddenly, without telling anyone, I went to the secret building in which my wife and kids, along with the one organisation member lived secretly. The door is wide open, and there is no one inside, and there are bloodstains shattered on the ground. I fainted!

(Whining noises)

I woke up tired and naked, have no idea where I am. After observing the room closely, I am sure that I haven't been here before. There are only a desk and a bed inside this single room apartment. I searched the desk drawer and found an ID card with my face, but the card has my younger face instead, and the name 'Karl Oginfinn' written below my face. Suddenly, a tiny spark shook my brain cells, and some memories of my existence as Karl drove its way back to my mind. I remember working as an investigator, but I have no idea if I have made any significant contribution to the field. On further checking the desk, I found some pictures of me with different pet animals and their owners.

Yes, now I can remember that I was not given any human based case because of my "intelligence", but my pet finding skills were indeed great. After taking another closer look inside the drawers, I found some good pay checks for my services. I kept wondering about what caused me to plummet into a rusty pickup driver setup that will make my life miserable. I found the everyday schedule of my works and hobbies; the first thing is to exercise for thirty minutes. I am proud of my young self but have no memory of me being in good shape. Now that I checked my muscles one by one, I am feeling some electrical charge passing through my veins, and I could and did fifty push-ups in a row without getting exhausted.

I don't remember how I lost my good habits, and my great body. My thoughts engine was interrupted by a call from my 'father'. I picked his call and he is asking for the reason why am I getting late for work and home. After taking a bath, my next schedule is to visit my parents' house for something. I went inside my father's house, my mother's photo is framed on the left side wall, with a decoration light poured around her for effects. My eyes are burdened with tears, the guilt filled tears... My hard worker mother, who never had the opportunity to sit and relax for even a day. "Have a seat, son" my father greeted me inside for breakfast.

While he is making my breakfast, I went inside my old room to get some documents regarding my life and my parents. I picked up my dusty diary lying flat on the ground, covered in spider web. Walked back to the hall and sat quietly, finally father has completed his food preparation, but all he made is grilled bread with an over-fried egg dropped on top of it to make it even less appealing to eat. Luckily, for drinks he has made hot delicious chocolate. After drinking the first cup, I took another cup of drink from the flask. "Yes, I win. Give me my hundred you resolution crisis men of culture" my father said loudly.

Me: 'What bet? Am I a gambler or something!'

Father: 'What? Don't fool around, you made bet about your strict diet, and you promised to never consume any sugar in your life again. Remember Mr. Smart man?'

Me: 'Oh, sorry. I am financially burdened, will settle you next week'

Father: 'Any update on the fruit stall secret?'

Me: (after thinking for a while) 'Oh yes, I am working on it, will start the business next month!"

Father: 'What? What business are you talking about? Is it the adult toy thing again? Don't think about it again, please! You know your marriage is in next month, don't make yourself a laughingstock'

Me: (took a deep breath and a few minutes of silence) 'How is your job? Any progress?'

Father: 'Oh, they have recently bought a fully automatic chocolate mixer, it can even mix up water with oil'

Me: 'They? Who are "they"?

Father: 'My managers, why are you acting weird today? Don't you have to report for work at sharp nine?'

Me: 'Oh... Yes, I forgot, late night drinks really get me rolling nowadays. See ya'

I went out and started walking to my office nearby. Suddenly, my eyes caught the sign pasted on my father's rusty motorcycle. I am sure it is an outdated logo of the Chocolust company. "Oh, how ironical it is!" I exclaimed. My father came outside and announced that he is very close to finding the factory's secrets. For a moment I thought my father was also a detective and was on incognito mode to find out the mysteries behind that creepy factory. But to clarify my doubt, I asked him "What secrets are you talking about? The missing people paradox?". He stood bewildered and laughed hard, and replied "The secret to their unique flavour, sweet sour and delicious ingredients, mmmm". Without further talk, I continued my walk to the office mentioned on the ID.

Finally, I reached the building, and it is in dilapidated condition. The big blurry banner that has a lot of holes welcomed me into the building, surprised to see it is still holding on to the two palm trees each side. Inside, there are four desks and four chairs, nothing else. Yes, there is also a bookshelf, two more desks, two wardrobes but these are filled with hornets, ants, cockroaches and a ton of holes. There is no one inside, and I realised that my father's reference was sarcastic. Because of the building's "good" condition, I can't even take a short nap. After waiting for an hour, detective Susan has entered the building.

"Susan!" I asked. She made a small laugh then asked me "Still not over that breakup thing! Come on man, grow up". I don't understand her metaphor but agreed myself to not bother her again. She carefully sat down on one of the chairs, lit a cigarette and fell asleep. Meanwhile, I took a closer look at her ID card, and her name is written as Kaitlyn. I think I heard it before, can't recollect. Maybe we are using pseudonyms, but still I am confused. After checking my schedule, I have realised that I have no assignments today and can help complete other's cases if I wanted to. Kaitlyn asked me for help, she is investigating a missing boy's case. She is surprised to see me accept her case proposal quickly.

She promised me to share her paycheck with me if I help her, and more importantly I can get information from her about who am I and how much I have progressed from my failed teenage world. Kaitlyn and I went to the missing boy's house. During our travel, I kept asking her about what her opinion regarding my life was, and she was happy to point out my issues and fails. I found that Susan and I were lovers, but she left me when I was caught for having sex with a prostitute. I am shocked to hear my sinful action, and to further add insult to injury, Kaitlyn told me that there is a rumour spreading about me that I am an animal molester!

I received the nickname because I only have taken interest in finding missing animals, and she added that I am not a people person. Kaitlyn revealed that her original name is Anne, finally we have arrived at the missing boy's house, and she went inside the house. Again, the invisible wall blocked my entrance into the house, thus, I waited outside. After a few minutes, Kaitlyn came out of the house and questioned my strange behaviour. I remained silent. I know I can't explain her about the timeline mind-wall thing. "You child kidnapping rascal!" the missing boy's mother shouted. I can't recollect anything; she explained that I was the one who lured her and her boy into the Chocolust factory.

Kaitlyn revealed that my second job is at the factory, as a marketing man, and I have once tried to lure Kaitlyn there. I promised the mother of the boy that I will find him as soon as possible. Kaitlyn collected her payment instalment from the woman, then we went back to the office building. Kaitlyn started sleeping again, and she has no interest in finding the boy or going to the factory. Kaitlyn only wants her payment checks, and she has betrayed me there as the culprit of the case. Now it has become my responsibility to find the missing boy from the evil place, but I know he is dead already and there is nothing anyone can do. I checked my phone to see my whole dealings within my thirty's crisis.

Unfortunately, I have found some pictures of me working inside the factory, and I have a lot of friends there too! I took the keys from Kaitlyn's sleepy hand and went to the factory to find more information about the factory. Some of the workers approached me and greeted me warmly, but what caught my attention is the face of one of the child workers there. It is the missing boy, and he is doing ok with the workers. I showed him the picture of him and his mother, took him with me, handed him to his mother. The boy explained that during the tour with his mother, he sneaked inside the factory to taste the chocolate, unfortunately, he fell into an empty ditch. Next day, the workers found him and carefully managed him.

Now that I have found the missing boy, and because of the mother's reputation, the news reporters have praised me very well. Kaitlyn is furious with me for taking all of her "deserved" praises and the final payment. Kaitlyn threw two sheets of paper on my face, and it is full of dramatic conversation between her and the "missing" boy's mother. Kaitlyn was planning to play the drama thing with the mother for six more months. Kaitlyn knew about the boy working inside the factory, and she also revealed her collecting of payment from the poor factory workers to find the boy's missing mother. "The true embodiment of mischief, Kaitlyn" I said proudly.

Kaitlyn vows to take revenge on me, and her words turned into a curse. One suspicious murder case has been filed, and they have sent the details to both of us via email. Because of my newly found popularity, the police officers gave me the permission to take a closer look at the murder spot. According to the first investigation report made by the police, this incident is stated as an "accident". The dead person is a woman named Pearl, twenty-eight years old, and she was burned alive from the accidental blast caused by the firecrackers she had kept inside her car. But this incident doesn't look accidental to me, for one reason - the car is in a parked position, and there are clear signs of her trying to open the door.

Most importantly, her friends mentioned that she was a non-smoker, and one suspicious blown out lighter is resting on the seat. Kaitlyn also sneaked her way inside the crime spot, started to observe the picture more closely. Her face shows bold confidence, and she challenged me for a bet. If she wins the case, I must give her a thousand dollars and she will change her name to Susan, my love's name! I am not enjoying her madness, but I must play with her because the timeline demands it! And I am very confident about the progress that I am having now. I have also made my demands that if I win, she must give me a thousand dollars and must change her name to 'Stupid', she agreed confidently. Kaitlyn even wrote a "legal" document for our bet contract.

Even though I tried to recollect what kind of mistakes I will be making in this case investigation, not a single piece of memory can be recollected, except for the memories of my hopeless expressions and screaming face. Kaitlyn has already made a big report on the whole case and casually put it on her desk; I tried to look at that meaty file while she went outside to take a call. "You will lose, loser, pathetic animal molester, pervert petter" written on the first page. Kaitlyn has set me up, and I fell into her trap, she returned and laughed hard at me. I went outside and have decided to visit Pearl's house, rented a car and reached there. Pearl was living alone in a middle-class house.

The gate is not locked, and there are signs of vehicles hovering around the compound lately. Her house is also not locked and is in a ransacked condition. After searching the house for an hour, I couldn't find any valuable evidence to progress the case. Suddenly, my eyes caught a small hole on the wall, it is not that visible, but one can spot the colour difference between the wall paint and the plastic cap used to cover the hole. I am sure I have made one of these hidden holes in my house also, people usually store their valuable documents inside these tiny holes. I have opened the plastic cap door of the tiny hole, and there is one thick sheet of paper resting inside the hole.

I carefully took out the prize and started the engine to go home, made sure no one is following me. Unfortunately, a white car is following me. An instinctual reflex jerked in my mind, and I took the rough forest path. The paths brought the nostalgic feelings back, and I just remembered that Zeiwo's farmhouse is near this forest. Yes, I have found the future headquarters of our secret organisation. I drove deep into the farm and finally reached the single building standing proudly at the end of the farm. Sadly, the farm is in an abandoned condition.

My bad, Zeiwo is not inside the farmhouse, and I quickly looked around the whole farmhouse. Luckily, my enemy followers have lost track of me. I sneaked my way into the farmhouse and started reading Pearl's documents. I have realised that the rolled-up paper folder contains at least one hundred pages, and it is just a copy of its original, and there is one USB drive attached to the document also. From the short preface, I have found that Pearl was working as the leader of foreign affairs ministry, and she has taken a lot of pictures of the Chocolust factory, she was doing research alone. Pearl was sure about the corporate world's secret partnership contract made with the factory, and she had a lot of interest in the man missing incidents happened at that time.

She has taken pictures of government embassies as well. She has provided a short narration in the most realistic way, like she is going through the events right now, and she intends her document to be read by everyone in the world, but she also mentions the impossibility of her wish (Narration starts) — 'The narration starts with her declaration that she has found evidence of trillions of dollars transactions done across the world by the top ruling corporates. They have taken control of the governments also, and they are trying to establish the almighty authority over the entire world. To achieve their mission, all the corporate companies formed an alliance with the biggest corporate, the Chocolust factory that sells both chocolate and people! She mentioned her helpless state because she was the only one who was interested in fighting against this madness. The factory has given a hefty amount of money to her office, and it was enough to make other workers sit quiet like a puppet.

Pearl was threatened by her lower grade employees also; she realised that her high reputed job was not giving her any power because of the real power's arrival. "Everyone keeps blabbering about their power until the real power walks in" she quoted. Sorry readers, I guess I should read exactly what she has written.

"Because of my attitude, they fired me from the office without any legal letter or a word of reason. I have become devastated, the job that I once achieved with mighty hard work and dedication, even sacrificed my own happiness and my time with my loved ones. From then, I was after the factory and its leaders.

I took a job at the factory, disguised as a man. After working there for three months, took secret photos of the factory facilities and its managers, but they always wore masks to conceal their identity from everyone. By looking at the size of them, I was sure that women were in the group, found an ally shortly, it was a he and he was a disguised police officer named Gin, and he assured me that they were not alone in the battle against the devils. He revealed that there exists a secret group named 'Alliance'. While working together, they found and recorded events of brutality and absurdness. With Gin's friends, I managed to sabotage the surveillance system inside the factory.

The factory people were not concerned about the camera eyes, because they had hundreds of super soldiers lined up around the factory, carrying some of the heaviest weapons. I managed to enter the restricted area sneakily with the help of the 'Alliance'. The room was dark but the rays from one shiny metal kept the whole room illuminated in blue light. There were many white square barrels lined up, touching them felt chills in my hand. The most horrible thing I have ever seen was inside these barrels, I don't want to say it in full picture. But for the sake of curiosity, the barrels contained human organs sorted out separately into each. "Are they organ harvesters!" I thought.

If you have been reading this till now, I have a reminder for you; the stuff that I have narrated so far is nothing compared to what I am about to narrate! (continue) Then I went inside a cubicle, and found some documents stacked inside the drawer, they were contracts made by the Toy factory. Surprisingly, all the transactions were above fifteen-digit numbers! After searching the whole documents, I could only find one name or maybe it was a pseudonym, I didn't know. It read "Maggy GTM 23" what is this GTM thing means?

I went outside the cubicle and walked straight to find more mysteries, came near a big hall. In front of my view, there was one green door with a password lock. Surprisingly, there were no instructions written on anywhere near the door, and this absence of warnings and my own curiosity made me put the password on screen. I was expecting some error messages to pop up on the screen any second, but another fear of the thing triggering an alarm scared me more. It quickly analysed my code and opened the door slightly, bright yellow light blasted out of the small opening, and I walked into the light.

IX

Member of the GTM

My eyes felt immense pleasure looking at the most vibrant world that was in front of me. Suddenly, the door behind me closed with a thud sound. Luckily, there was one more password screen placed on the wall for me to exit the place. I walked forward into the land full of identical trees but didn't know what they were. After getting more close to the trees, found cocoa beans shaking joyfully on the tree branches. The fresh air cuddling me and the trees, felt nothing like the natural wind, and there was no one to speak to. I moved slowly and stealthily through the cocoa forest, an amazing fact about the place was that there was no other form of vegetation, not even grass. Cocoa trees everywhere.

After walking for a few miles, I lost all my energy and almost slipped into the unconscious realm, found a small colony built with bricks, before losing all my conscious mind, saw some young white men approaching me. I woke up inside one of the small brick buildings, and it was nicely set up inside. There were no electric appliances inside, only wooden furniture. One cup of milk placed on the bedside for me probably, drank it happily, it tasted chocolaty. I went out, and observed the scene more closely, could only see young people, mostly men. Even though they looked like human, there was something suspicious about their body shape.

They lacked beard, moustache, hair. Sure, they didn't spend valuable time everyday shaving themselves. They were all dressed up in green colour robes. For another surprise, every single one of them was skinny and shorter. It was hard to identify male and female, but males were a little bigger in size. They were riding a cart like thing that had a pedal system. It was strange that they were living in an ancient mode of living. Suddenly, an alarm went off, all of them started running to the corner of the forest, they were fast and hard workers. Luckily, one of the men gave me a lift in his cart vehicle. Finally, we reached the corner and there are three big square pipes ending with a square container placed on the ground.

Some of them picked something from the big open containers and put it into their small sacks. After a few minutes, the crowd became shorter. I took one closer look inside the containers, and there were buns, tomato slices covered in lettuce, and patties of meat found in each of the three containers. I made one and tried it myself, it tasted too spicy for me. The man who gave me a ride waited for me to enter the thing again, and he kind-fully took me back to the centre of the colony. They ate the burger thing quickly and went back to the cocoa forest, started collecting ripened cocoa beans, added minerals and powders to the trees.

They collected at least three good cocoa beans from each tree, and there were an uncountable number of trees surrounding the small colony of buildings. I became sleepy and tired watching their work, and sure that the time should have become night. Yes, there was no sun inside that artificial civilization setup, could see a lot of greenish lights that scattered out packs of light all over the place. But how could they sleep with the lights on? "Will the factory people don't switch off the light" I asked one of the women, but she had no answer for me. After questioning some of them, realised that they didn't talk language. They worked, ate and slept for a few mandatory hours, and repeat! Robots without intelligence.

Now that I saw most of the five hundred plus residents living inside the small colony, surprisingly, I didn't see an older person or a middle-aged person. There was no form of love, anger, happiness, festivals, ceremonies happening there, even though I saw children there with them. They worked repeatedly and had no problem with that. They worked like us but instead of money, they received food. My mind was full of research about why was there not one older person, was it because their lifestyle prevented them from aging? Or was there a strong reason behind them that I didn't know.

Next day, the alarm went off. All the residents lined up like students did in a school assembly ground. A few factory workers entered the place; I hid behind a big cocoa tree. The workers performed a closer analysis of the residents, picked three men and two women, escorted them out of the cocoa world. All of my questions have answered. I knew they were not coming back, and surprisingly the crowd had no problem with their recent loss of teammates. They worked as usual and collected all the good cocoa beans, this time I decided to follow them all around, found out that the cocoa forest was divided into four sections, and the residents were equally divided for each section.

After following one of the team, I observed their whole process of work. They didn't climb the trees but used one large metal sickle to cut the beans from the branch. They spent at least five minutes on each tree, from checking the tree's condition, pouring minerals and water, to finding the perfect cocoa beans. They did take care of hundred trees before getting back to the colony, I surrendered my mission before they covered about sixty-five trees. Luckily, the cart driver gave me a ride back to a nearby outpost like building, he even placed me inside a small bed there. As I laid there, thoughts about my life sprouted back to my head.

First, I entered the secret place to find the mysterious crimes associated with the chocolate factory. Now that I was inside the biggest fantasy world, I was hypnotized with its magic. I pledged myself to leave the place within two more days of observation. After taking a short nap, I woke up with a whole load of sweat all over my body and stepped out of the building. My eyes could only see the cocoa bean piles surrounding the four sides of the small building that I was taken into, only a narrow space left for entrance and exit.

Surprisingly, the outpost area was so much hotter than the main colony. I walked out of the pile of cocoas, and went to the main colony, which was two miles away from the outpost.

Finally, I saw them taking rest by doing nothing, but some of them were nurturing human babies. I was confused, not about their ability to perceive a child, but the lack of any hospital and elder people in that place. After two more days living there, I decided to stay there for another week to find out the mysteries. Next day, an alarm went off, it was the recorded sound of a human baby, the cocoa people ran to the food container area. Again, the cart man helped me with the ride, there was one big platter placed on a pedestal near the food drop-box. On top of the platter laid seventy plus human babies, definitely less than two years of age. The cocoa people picked the babies and retreated to their colony.

The whole incident appeared less surprising to me, because of the number fact about how many human babies are abandoned each year. The cocoa colony people were happy to raise them, happy to be engaged in some kind of activities while they were resting and waiting for the new harvest season. I didn't know the process behind making chocolate, had no idea what they were going to do with the pile, collected over all those days. I was surprised to know how much cunning those factory giants were. They gave human babies to those people only to continue running their secret cocoa farm. The cocoa workers started grinding the cocoa beans with a traditional wooden grinder, and after that they packed the crushed cocoa into bags and then disposed it into a big ditch in the corner of the place.

I finally decided to get out of the cocoa setup next day. In the evening, again the alarm went off. Cocoa workers were all lined up perfectly. Some of the factory workers entered the place, took three women with them. Unfortunately, they found me hiding behind a thin cocoa tree and took me outside. The people who were taken out of the cocoa place were pushed into a metal box container and then filled the whole box with chocolate. I was expecting the same fate, but the manager of the factory, wearing a mask, sold me to the black market. And then..." — (door opening sound) "Thief! Put your hands up!" Zeiwo commanded me while pointing her gun at me.

Me: 'Please don't shoot! We know each other, in the future'

Zeiwo: 'I said put your hands up in the air'

Me: 'As you wish' (raised my hands up)

Zeiwo: 'Surrender all of the things you have stolen from here'

Me: (laughs) 'Even this whole house is worth nothing'

Zeiwo: 'Good point. Then what are you doing here, boy! Turn around and reveal yourself'

Me: (turns around) 'Ta Da!'

Zeiwo: 'Mr Oginfinn? What are you doing in my house?'

Me: 'You know me? Good. I have turned myself into one traveller who switches between timelines inside his own head. Now, let's not waste our valuable time and make our plans'

Zeiwo: 'What happened to you, boy? Are you drunk? I was your egg supplier once, and that was all the relation we had. Now please leave'

Me: 'Like I said, I am a mind traveller, and in my middle-aged time, we will become friends and strengthen our alliance together'

Zeiwo: 'Alliance? For what? What is the need of an alliance in this beautiful world'

Me: 'Sarcasm! Great one' (points my finger at the girl standing beside Zeiwo) 'Who are you dear? I have seen you somewhere!'

Zeiwo: 'Stop staring at my daughter, you creep! And get out of here!'

Me: 'This is not the right time to argue; we have to stop that devilish factory people or else they will destroy the already chaotic world'

Zeiwo: 'Get out of here or I will call the police. My daughter has to prepare for her flight next week, please leave Mr Finn!'

Me: 'Your daughter's what! Have you lost your mind you sicko! We are on a mission to convince youngsters out of the abroad trap, and you say this...'

Zeiwo: 'Come Mr OFinn, let me take you to the hospital nearby, you will get better'

Me: 'Take yourself there, stop playing around you fool! We must plan now, I don't know if it would renew the timeline or our future, but we have to make this opportunity count'

Zeiwo: (Scratches her head) 'Ok. Tell me what your plan is'

Me: 'I have found the secret notes of Pearl, who is one of the fighters against the devils. She found major evidence against the chocolate factory; we must somehow make the people enlighten about this new information. Must stop every flight taker'

Zeiwo: 'Why are you keep blaming the factory? And what is your problem with the people going abroad?'

Me: 'They will kidnap and enslave the flight takers, and do weird things with their pictures, I don't know the full details'

Zeiwo: 'If that is what concerns you, confess this to the police, police officers are recruited for dealing with such stuff!'

Me: 'This is beyond their reach, hurry up! We must get our planning going'

Zeiwo: 'Please don't make it a lot harder. Please get out of here and never return'

I see no other reason to further explain to her, went to the detective office. Kaitlyn is flirting with some random guy she has met in the street. I have decided to hide the documents collected from Pearl's house, because I thought there was no need to read her sufferings anymore. After hiding the documents inside a secret hole in the wall, I searched Kaitlyn's desk to find any evidence she has collected. Shockingly, I have found a solid report she made on Pearl's murder case, and she has concluded her report by stating that Pearl committed suicide by lighting the firecrackers she brought inside her car. "Oh, Kaitlyn, What a loser!" I thought but then noticed a strange document rolled into her waste bin. It says,

Name: Jessica

Age: Unknown

Member of the GTM

Residential address: near the Henway mountain

The surveillance camera of Barbeque shop near the old bridge has recorded her last seen with Pearl on the date of her death. It is clear that Jessica has brought the fireworks into Pearl's car.

Case concluded.

Kaitlyn has also pasted a photo of Jessica, but she is wearing a golden mask with diamonds placed into her eye sockets. Kaitlyn seems lazy to follow this Jessica person, and I will not be like lazy Kaitlyn. I promised myself that I will find this Jessica person and put her inside the jail for the soul of Pearl. Kaitlyn is still flirting with a man, and I went to the location mentioned in Jessica's bio. While driving, I thought maybe Kaitlyn had set me up again, if not, why did she put her reports and findings openly on her desk, and flirt with some random man for an hour? Anyway, I have decided to get to the location to see if there is indeed a house near the wide-open mountain terrains.

But first I went to the Barbeque shop near the old bridge, mentioned by Kaitlyn in her conclusion report. Unfortunately, there is no building standing in the spot, but there is one recently burned down building resting in peace inside the still smoky ash. I have enquired one middle aged man about the incident, and he replied that the building was indeed the Barbeque shop, but it was burned down two days ago. "Who did this? Any information?" I asked him. "No idea about the culprits but who cares, was cool to watch all those flames and smoke, circling around like one big old hurricane. I mean, they have money, they will build a new one in a month" he said.

My mind is still equipped with Kaitlyn and her cowardly attitude; I have a feeling about the possibility of the whole Kaitlyn report thing being true. Finally, I went to the place where Jessica resides, as mentioned in the note. Surprisingly, there is indeed one giant mansion proudly standing alone in a thousand plus acres of land. The true definition of 'Rich' is evident here. For sure I know there is no way I can get my poor foot inside the compound. Strangely, there isn't any security or a gate, and no signs of high weaponry anywhere. It is just one luxurious mansion painted with the finest gold paint or pure gold. There are a lot of flowering plants covering the entire compound, and it is very peaceful to see such a scene in the middle of the deserted mountain terrains.

I am not alone, there are a lot of human workers, male and female, doing different works. Looks like they don't care about my presence. I have walked at least a mile and still not reached the mansion building, and I am getting very thirsty. Finally, I have reached the mansion building and went inside. It is just a big hall with the four walls decorated with every possible luxurious item anyone can think of. I am confused why Kaitlyn mentioned this place, and where is Jessica? After walking a mile or two inside the building, finally reached near an arena, more like a wrestling ring, with two men fighting, but there is no referee, no pinfalls, no submission, it looks like they are fighting for their lives. Both are covered in blood and are still exchanging blows.

There is one masked man or woman sitting behind the arena ring, on a fluffy royal chair. This person appears to be very muscular and tall, but has long hair and nails polished with shiny liquefied gold. Speaking about gold, this person is wearing gold plated armour around their chest and stomach, also wearing gold plated stockings and brief as well. This person has tanned skin with no body hair, hips are huge and muscular, heavy arms and fifteen pack stomach. Still, I can't distinguish this person's gender, but I think this person will be a 'He'. He is clearly enjoying the fight, throwing food at the fighters like he is feeding some zoo animals. The fighters are eating some of that food, also using it to beat each other. He is laughing loudly. Meanwhile, the two men have started biting each other, ripping off a good amount of flesh with each bite.

The whole brutality came to an end with one of them choking the other one with his raged-up biceps. The victorious man somehow managed to get back to his feet, and then suddenly, the person enjoying the whole show jumped into the arena ring and swung his mighty hand, hit the man hard and he was blown into pieces. The big bicep of the masked person is still standing tall, and then he turned his attention to me. Without having a word, he grabbed my throat. "I came... Question... Pearl... Murder" I said while gasping for breath. Luckily, he threw me to the ground and unmasked himself.

His slowest unmasking surprised me with every second, the red lips, diamond pierced nose and ears, blue eyes, black eyebrows, smooth forehead, black hair. He is she, and she offered a cheeky smile for me. She is very beautiful and has flawless skin, with strong perfumes covering her whole body. She then poured a big glass of something and offered me, she is getting angry while I am standing stymied with fear, I finally took the glass from her and drank it all in one sip. "Jessica?" I asked her in a low register. Without giving me an answer, she walked to her seat and ordered me to enter the lonely arena ring. She took one big sword out of the secret compartment inside her chair handle.

She: 'Undress yourself and dance now!'

Me: 'No! You are under arrest lady, surrender now or...'

She: 'I assume you are not blind, this sword I am holding proudly, can wound you just with its air'

(She swings the sword slightly, and a small cut appears across my chest area, followed by irritating pain)

Me: 'Ok. chill lady!' (starts dancing)

She: 'That's my boy. Now, tell me the matter, but don't stop the dance'

Me: 'Are you... Jessica?'

She: 'Yes. Anything else'

Me: 'You know... Pearl, recently... murdered!'

Jessica: 'Don't lie, boy, I killed her by blowing her up into pieces'

Me: (Stops dancing) 'What! Why did you kill her for? You think you're some kind of almighty thing! After all, you are just a hidden dot inside one evil factory thing'

(She swings the sword again, another slight cut appears on my stomach, resumes my dance)

Jessica: 'She killed my friend! Keep dancing you fool!'

Me: 'I have... Collected solid... Evidence about you! Keep... In mind'

Jessica: 'Dance Dance Dance!'

Me: (stops dancing) 'I am done you sicko! Kill me or do whatever you want'

Jessica: 'Wow. The breaking point! Good. Don't worry, you can go now, please report me to the authority. In the meantime, I will pack up my things. Farewell!'

Jessica has started to take out different kind of weapons from the inside of her royal spacious chair, I know she is playing with me, but I have no other option left than to obey her "advise". I took leave from the mansion and entered my car. Before getting to the detective office, a pack of police men stopped my ride, ordered me to get out of the car, they covered my face with a bag and forcedly took me into their spacious vehicle. I don't know where they are taking me to or are they real police officers? I kept wondering what happened to my reflexes, my questioning ability. I am a middle-aged man inside! Finally, they unmasked me and as expected; I am inside jail.

X

Coupon redeem Place

Strangely, no one cared to offer some of their few minutes to enlighten me about my crime. "HEY…" I screamed loudly, but again no one cared. "Mr Oginfinn" a familiar voice came from the dark backside of the prison cell. The person slowly walked to my side. It is Zeiwo, and she was brought here yesterday. First, she kneeled and made her apology speech, and then explained what happened to her daughter. Just before two days for her flight, while preparing for her life changing journey, some huge men charged inside the farmhouse and kidnapped her. Zeiwo then went to the local police station for help, but they arrested Zeiwo instead and honoured her with false crimes including mass murdering.

The small talk between me and Zeiwo is interrupted by another call of my name "Mr Oginfinn!", in a mocking voice. It is Kaitlyn, she gave me a strange bow of honour and shown me a payment cheque she received for successfully completing the Pearl murder case. She has submitted her report stating that Pearl has committed suicide, and the authority has accepted her final report without any evidence. "I know you know that Pearl was murdered by the person you first made a detailed report on, starting with the letter J. You coward! How much she paid you!" I asked her angrily.

She made one strange laugh and nodded her head repeatedly, at the same time grabbed the metal rods of the prison cell tightly.

Her eyes indicated her unquenched anger and helplessness at the same time. "I don't know what you just said! Pearl was suffering from loneliness and that made her buy some explosive stuff and explode herself with it. Now, remember our bet, forget Kaitlyn! I am now Susan!" She said mockingly. "Take whatever lady, you sold your spine to that J person, remember it all the time!" I replied. Once again, her facial expressions changed from mocking happiness to helpless anger plus fear.

She replied "Stop speaking like movie heroes, you prison boy! I know you went to J's mansion and ran away while peeing your pants! Nonetheless, we all sold our souls to them, I wish you would find that sooner than later. Bye my friend". Before Kaitlyn walked away, I have explained to her about the whole Chocolust chaos. Again, she made one hysterical laugh and galloped away while loudly saying "I am Susan, I won Susan, I am the great Susan". Zeiwo stands bewildered, she heard our madness talk.

Zeiwo asked for an explanation about the whole crime-full atmosphere that is ruling the world. I have narrated to her all my findings regarding the crazy factory setup and the details about the corporate companies joining hands to destroy humanity. As expected, Zeiwo then put forward the notion of forming a community with the already victims and the would-be victims. But first, we have to escape this disgusting prison, luckily, Zeiwo's sister-in-law Margaret is working inside the prison structure, and will help us get out of here. "Don't worry, she will" Zeiwo said confidently, and Margaret did it shortly.

After the sneaky escape through the hidden door inside a specific wall, we kept moving to the middle of nowhere. Margaret has also joined our small team; she guided us into a forest nearby. Surprisingly, Margaret has arranged a minivan for our travel to somewhere. We entered the vehicle, and a masked driver took us straight to one luxurious pub. Yes, I know this pub will soon earn the badge of dilapidated. There are a few good-looking cars parked outside, and it looked like an ordinary pub with alcohol and strippers everywhere. But Zeiwo and Margaret led me into a big room that has a huge bed.

Soon, I have realised that the whole pub serves as a hideout for a secret organisation, established exclusively for saving the flight trap victims. Pure coincidence! But Zeiwo is not the leader of the whole thing, and the actual leader, Jill, is delivering one ear catching speech on the subject. I keep wondering why the invisible wall didn't block my entrance into the pub and the jail. It means that I have visited these places in my actual timeline. From Jill's speech, I am sure that they have detailed information about the entire illegal activities happening around the world. Jill has mentioned about the Chocolust, toy factory, and some of the leading freaking corporate companies around the world, and their cruel plans.

Even though Jill has information about the plans, she doesn't know the exact plot. She received evidence of fund transactions up to fifteen-digit numbers between these companies. By the time Jill ended her speech, the workers have started supplying bread and drinks to everyone. While eating the bread slowly, I kept thinking about the possibility of this kind of an organisation that might have existed in my adult years, failed to sabotage the brutal plans made by the companies. I believe that if I can change the small mistakes that might happen with Jill's plan, I would be able to change the future.

I had a small conversation with Jill, and her plan seems solid. She explained that her team has received information about a group of leaders, of the biggest corporate company 'Fictional Qwerck', will visit the Chocolust factory tomorrow. Jill's team has planned to kidnap them and to squeeze them hard to get vital information. I don't know what to do instead, thus followed her plan. Jill then escorted me to the outside of the pub, swiped off the sand to reveal a hidden door on the ground. She then opened it and invited me to join her, we climbed down at least twenty steps, there is darkness everywhere. Jill turned on the light, illuminating the massive weaponry.

There are at least thirty varieties of weapons here, including big explosives stacked up to the ceiling. The strong smell of gunpowder filled up my nostrils, one little spark can blast the whole area now. Jill revealed that she has sold all her wealth, spent it all to buy this massive collection of weaponry, enough to blow the Chocolust and the Toy factory completely into ashes. We went back to the pub and started preparations. The pub functions like a real one, and people outside the organisation also visit here regularly. Jill has requested us to do pub stuff to keep it going without giving any doubt. Jill owns the pub, she turned the whole thing into a hideout after losing her precious daughter, obviously to the factory devil's.

All of us are in preparation for the kidnap planned tomorrow, can see the spirit of rage in each of the member's eyes. Me and Margaret are performing as strippers for the crowd, she is dancing and singing vigorously. Finally, the day of kidnap has arrived; Jill has made a good plan on how to attack the invincible car they are travelling. She brought several explosives from the basement, has planted every single one of them on the road, luckily, the road is full of potholes. We waited eagerly for their arrival, and after waiting almost four nail biting hours, one big car appeared out of nowhere and drove straight into our trap. The powerful blast caused the car to fly up and land upside down, without wasting a minute, our infantry team moved forward with rifles.

As expected, none of the passengers are injured, thanks to the billion-dollar car, and we have taken all five of them hostage. Jill and we are happy with our victory. Luxurious feast with different varieties of food I haven't seen before, welcomed all of us. After the feast, Jill has also called me to attend the questionnaire between the five captives. They are seated in a circle and are given food. "Listen guys, we don't want to hurt you, we just want to know about all the evil contracts that you people made with the devilish chocolate factory and all other people around the world. We just want to save humanity!" Jill said calmly.

Person One: 'You fools! Go get an appointment in the mental asylum'

Me: 'How dare you mock us, you greedy little piece of money'

Jill: 'Stay calm Ogin, they will tell us, be patient'

Person Two: 'Release us NOW!'

Me: 'Or else what? Remember that you guys have a lot to lose, think about all those hefty digits of unused money, those skyscrapers built in every country for just vacation life, those followers. If you guys answer all our queries, we will release you soon. Deal?'

Person Three: 'Ok. Fine. Ask your stupid questions'

Jill: 'What is that contract you people made with the Chocolust factory'

Person Four: 'We just wanted to eliminate our enemies, most of our targets were resigned employees from our global company, and they searched for "better" lifestyle abroad! I don't know about what other companies want to do with making a contract with the factory'

Me: 'Tell us more about the Chocolust factory, how did you people find them and their brutal power?'

Person One: 'We received information that one of the twenty-five lords of the GTM owns the factory, that was all the information we needed to know as far as power is concerned'

Jill: 'What is GTM?'

Person Two: 'We don't know the full form, there is no way to find more about them, and they are untouchable by any law'

Me: 'Why do they make people into sex slaves? Is that what you guys made contract with?'

Person One: 'There is no way to tell them what to do, all they want is to abuse their invincible power! They can even steal our entire company If they want'

Person Three: 'If you people want to save humanity, do something against GTM, not us. We are just people who became successful with hard work and dedication, and there is no power in our hands! Let us go, freaks!'

Jill ordered us to kill them; she explained that it is not safe for us to let them go. In a minute, all of them are gunned down, and our meeting has dispersed. Jill has no idea about what to do next, she appears helpless. I kept observing her face, in a few minutes, she has broken down in tears. "We failed! There is no way to bring the truth, we can't save humanity!" she said while weeping. My mind is equipped with Jessica, who according to Kaitlyn, is a member of the GTM. I have put my findings in front of Jill and her sad face transformed back to happiness. "Please, Ogin, go now" she requested me. Zeiwo joined me, and we went to the detective office to question Kaitlyn and to retrieve Pearl's documents.

Before we can reach our destination, we are chased by the police. I have realised that we are escapees and should not have undertaken this mission by ourselves. Luckily, we are not inside my rusty old pickup truck but one powerful car, and it helped us to get away from the chase very quickly. But there is no way we can get back to the detective office anytime soon. I have made a quick plan to reassign my mission to another member, but when we returned to the pub hideout, we can only see death and destruction. Zeiwo and me quickly rolled underneath the car to avoid getting detected by the giant human beings hovering around the pub, they are carrying swords and rifles.

After making sure that no one is alive and the pub will never be the same again, they left peacefully in a big truck. Zeiwo and me rolled out of the spot, entered the pub to see if there is anyone left alive. No, there is no one left, the giant mercenaries have made sure to spare no one, and the pub is burning down slowly. Zeiwo and me are the only survivors of the secret organisation. Zeiwo has sworn an oath to always fight for our cause, and to rebuild this burned down organisation again by herself. "Yes, you will surely do" I said. Zeiwo asked me to join her new team, and I have agreed to her proposal, we went to her farmhouse. Suddenly, my head turned heavy and dizzy, I fainted. (Whining noises)

My mind has restarted again and first came the sense of pain. The pain is escalating slowly, but I can't see what is happening around me. In a few minutes, I have my vision back and there is one cat sitting on my chest, casually biting my nose like it was some kind of canned fish. I shook him off my body, dressed my bleeding nose with my own dress. My eyes found one suspicious looking paper pasted on the wall there, I am relieved after reading the content written on it. It is Susan's note explaining that she and the kids are safe, they are relocated to a spot near the JPK Mall complex. Immediately, I jumped into the pickup truck, drove quickly to the location mentioned by Susan.

Unfortunately, they are living in a single room house, walled with old clothes and a plastic sheet ceiling. My heart crushed with guilt and helplessness. It is evident that Susan and the kids have not eaten anything for two days but water. "I am one big sinner, already killed one child and progressing my way to kill the other four by starving them. I shouldn't have married and shouldn't have had kids without earning proper wealth and stability" I thought. Susan welcomed me with a smile face, and there is no way her smile is real. "Why did you marry one poor ugly beggar like me?" I asked her seriously.

She stands there still without giving me an answer, started to cry like one big waterfall. I thought she was cursing her poor decision taken at the marriage time, but she started cursing herself for my poor state of wealth. She kept blabbering about the sacrifices I have done for her all these years. For some weird reason, I can't remember anything happened more than a year ago. I am getting angry and frustrated with my condition, it is like when you wake up one day questioning who you are! I have realised that there is only one way to cure my dilemma; to seek help from Susan herself. Without wasting anymore time, I have narrated to her every problem that I am having including the mind travelling thing!

Susan calmly listened to my problems, carefully filled my memory gaps. After completing her pre-graduation studies, she joined law school and became a lawyer, and she then met me during my time as detective Karl Oginfinn, after I was jailed again, she was the one who bailed me out. Yes, I know what you guys are thinking, even I am also standing bewildered listening to her different narration of my own life. After bailing me out, we were married, and we were very wealthy and stable until Susan was trapped in a controversial murder case. Susan received death threats, but she bravely fought to bring forth the truth against a rich man. But all of her attempts backfired, and she was fined a huge amount of money.

We had to sell our home, furniture and appliances. I was fired from the detective office. Since then, I was working different jobs, but the shocking thing she said was that I used to work for the Chocolust factory long before I bought the junky pickup truck, and for another surprise I worked there as a worker for three whole months, without visiting Susan and kids. Yes, I got what I wanted to know, I am sure that the factory people have done something crazier to me back then and now, and forever I believe. After taking Susan and kids to Zeiwo's farmhouse hideout, I went to the detective office to retrieve Pearl's documents.

When I reached the office, I have found that the whole building has changed into one coupon redeem place by the Chocolust freaks! I kept wondering what to do next, and my eyes caught the secret door on the seat, and it is locked! But I have realised that the ignition key can be used to unlock this secret door thing. My detective mind is thrilled to see this mystery hiding behind the door. I found five vials of different coloured liquids: green, golden, black, blood red, sky blue. I am eager to have a taste of one of them. It is a universal thing that if all our chances are blocked, some kind of deux-machina will help us, and having faith in this theory, took the green vial.

It has produced a heavy fragrance like that of gasoline, without wasting no time, drank the whole vial in one shot. As expected, I have experienced a burning sensation throughout my body, followed by the feeling that we all sometimes experience during our sleep, the feeling of our soul getting lifted from our body slightly and then getting dropped down with a big jerk. I have become invisible! This rusty pickup truck thing might have been owned by some magician probably. Anyway, I am happy to be invisible now because, I can easily enter the coupon redeem building and take the documents with ease, and if I am in the mood, no! not what you guys think! I mean, if I am in the mood, maybe I can scare the brutish guards inside. Am I in the mood? Yes!

XI

Cocoa Civilization

I slowly made my way into the compound, and successfully went past the two guards, but the automatic gun is not something I can cheat, luckily, I heard the gun's squeaky sound when it moved up to aim me, but it didn't shoot. I might have made some big footsteps, thus slowed down more, and now I am moving like a snail. My cabin was upstairs, I started climbing slowly, but one stupid old step decided to make a crunch sound that alerted the guards and the gun. Quickly, I jumped through the window in front of me, took a brutal landing, somehow entered the truck and stomped down the speed pedal. The guards would have killed me if my good old friend didn't start.

I am surprised about how I manipulated the camera and the automatic gun with my invisibility power! Then I went to the Chocolust factory to try my new invisibility power there. Luckily, I will not be caught for my noisy footsteps, because of the crowd-ful noise there, but I am not sure if the cameras can spot me or not. Anyway, I have decided to get in with my power. There are many tourists wandering around, and I am shocked that why everyone still behaves like there is nothing suspicious going on with the factory and the missing people record it has. I have successfully entered the restricted area with ease, and the whole setup looks exactly like what Pearl mentioned in her dystopian documents.

Again, my detective mind made me look out for the secret place where the secret civilization of cocoa people lives. Yes, found it! The door is locked with a captcha code shown above, only need to type the six alphabets into the screen. The door is opened, I slowly walked inside cocoa world, my eyes are mesmerised by the beauty of the whole setup. After walking for some time, I have landed on the main colony. The cocoa people can't see me, I have started to explore each building there. They are made of claylike substance, and it is very cool inside the building. There are no appliances in any of the building, but surprisingly, I found a textbook lying under an unpolished wooden table.

I kept wondering that if they know how to read and understand texts, they would have escaped from here long ago. Luckily, I found the name Pearl on the first page of the textbook, clearing all of my doubts. The text is not a document or her findings about the place, instead it is one short story written by herself, probably written during her stay here. I am very excited to read this thing because I know it is for sure not just a story of fantasy, should have hidden politics to decipher. The story starts with a nameless King, and he was ruling one big kingdom that never tasted the brutality of war yet, and he didn't want anyone to think about overpowering him and taking the throne away from him.

For this, the King conducted fake battles between him and his own soldiers dressed up like pirates, ending with the King defeating all of them, and by smearing bull's blood over his body and the fake dead soldiers laid around him to make an authentic view of battle. The spectators offered praises for the King's bravery and fearless behaviour, and he started to take pride in his dramatic battles. The King started to elevate his style during the dramatic displays, often by making real cuts on the soldier's body. After many fake battles, the battles turned more violent because, the King started to end each of his fake battles by beheading one random soldier and raising the head like a trophy.

After a few more of these violent endings, the soldiers became enraged and decided to take revenge against the cowardly King.

In the next battle, the well-prepared soldiers started defending themselves from the King's sword swings. They surrounded the King without letting him escape from the mighty circle of defence formed by the soldiers. Finally, they started to attack the King mercilessly, but shockingly the King showed his true power, and easily eliminated all the soldiers dressed up as pirates. The crowd cheered and threw flowers over him, meanwhile, the King chose his new soldiers from the crowd who joined him without any questions regarding the previous recruits.

The King then started his routine of fake battles with his newly recruited batch of soldiers. One day, the King decided to explore the outskirts of his kingdom all by himself, and he was surprised to see that even the tribal groups had respect towards him. After exploring most of the land, he entered the forest setting and started to hunt every animal he saw. After killing numerous animals, he met a small fairy hovering around one mango tree. The fairy offered a special cup of juice to the tired King, and it replenished all his lost energy and power. "Thank you, dear fairy! Ask me anything you want in return" King asked fairy. The fairy made a smirk on its face and flew away.

The King became furious, took out his blood covered sword, threatened to kill the fairy and its whole ancestors. The fairy calmly explained that the King did not possess the thing that the fairy always wanted. The King angrily ordered to spell out what was he missing out! Finally, the fairy said "Peace..." The king stood without any response, and the fairy explained it's answer to the king. "You have won everything, but did you ever experience the feeling of having a peaceful mind, empty of thoughts!" Fairy asked the King; he thought about it seriously and agreed to the fairy's conclusion. The King then demanded the fairy to give him some taste of delicious Peace!

Without further questions and answers, the fairy granted the mighty King's wish. The King fell to the ground dead! — end of Pearl's story. My little brain is unable to decipher the hidden politics presented by Pearl, and the cocoa people have started to settle in their respective houses. One of them entered the house that I am staying now, and she screamed seeing the textbook levitating in mid-air. She ran outside and made loud screams, gathered backup men and women to fight their invisible intruder. I have decided to play along with their feeling of fear! Gave them a few gentle taps and threw cocoa beans at them. I was wrong, they don't possess any feelings related to fictional ghost figures.

What they do believe in is that there is one invisible intruder around them. They have gathered, holding sickle and knives, stabbing the poor air violently. I hid behind one cocoa tree and enjoyed the scene. It is true that with great power comes great entertainment! While examining their outfits and odd human form, I have noticed that they are very pretty, have smooth skin and wore the shortest outfits possible supplied by the creepy factory people! Suddenly, the alarm went off and the whole crazy crowd lined up. The main door has opened, some masked men entered the cocoa world, they have started to examine the cocoa people standing in a very disciplined way.

After one hour of examining the whole cocoa crowd, they picked two men and three women from the crowd, took them to the entrance door. I have secretly followed the gang, observed the disturbing things that I have expected to see. The masked men forcedly undressed the five Cocoa people, tied a collar to each of their necks. Out of nowhere, a forklift came and dropped one metal box into a good-looking pickup truck. The workers placed the five people inside the metal box! this scene caused me to lose my inactive status. I made one furious jump and pushed the masked men to the ground, then took control of the pickup truck that has the metal box.

I drove the truck straight to Zeiwo's farmhouse hideout, made sure no one followed me. This new truck is very fast and powerful, and I have decided to make it my own. I have somehow managed to convince Zeiwo about my newly found powers. Zeiwo and her team carefully opened the metal box and carried the five Cocoa people into our farmhouse hideout, offered them clothes. We have observed them for some time, but they are not responding to any of our questions. The collar tied to their necks has a symbol of a dinosaur, not even detective Susan knows the meaning behind this symbol. What is more surprising is that they haven't expressed fear, they have absolutely no idea about their own lives.

After an hour, my invisibility power has worn off. I must retrieve the four vials of magic liquid, so that I can enter the coupon redeem building again to take Pearl's documents. But the dangerous thing is that I parked my rusty pickup truck, which contains the vials, beside the chocolate factory. Detective Susan accompanied me to the factory, and I can't find my truck near the spot I believe I parked it. After searching the place for a while, Susan has found the truck parked inside the factory premises! We both know it is a trap but there is no other way to retrieve Pearl's documents without the help of the mysterious vials.

Without wasting any time, I went inside the factory compound carefully and the gates are shut down immediately, trapping me inside the factory surroundings. The walls are decorated with electric coils; I have only one option left to do! Quickly entered the truck, thanks to its window-less door, and took the yellow vial from the secret cabin. The factory maniacs are coming to take my soul away; I quickly drank the whole vial in one sip. I stepped out of the vehicle and waited for the invisibility power to kick in, but nothing is happening inside me, and I can still see my hands. The factory people are waiting for my move, while tightly squeezing their tools in hand.

I have decided to accept my fate, kneeled and ordered them to take me to hell. Suddenly, my vision blurred and I fell to the ground unconscious... When I woke up, I am inside a big luxurious hall of some mansion, probably Jessica's. No, this is not Jessica's power-dome, this building is adorned with all types of surrealist items. I can see a pool filled with money, a tree that grows diamonds, a cartoonish drawing of me that keeps performing absurd moves, floating furniture hovering around the place. All of this look weird to me. Suddenly, some kind of cartoonish thing appeared in front of me and started giving a one-sided speech about the situation that I am in.

"Greetings Larry, this is your second time here! I am surprised to see you back. I believe you lost the previous time, so I must explain to you about the whole game thing again. The whole objective of this game is that you need to keep the percentage counter planted on your wrist to zero, for a minimum of thirty minutes. If you fail to pass the test within twelve hours, all your memories will be erased from your small brain. Wishing you all the best, Larry. The game starts now!" The cartoonish thing disappeared. Just like it mentioned, there is one wristwatch on my left hand, and it is currently showing Zero percentage. I don't know what to do.

I have noticed a timer inside the wristwatch, and it is ticking backwards, currently at "18:34" and I think I have to wait for only eighteen more minutes to free myself, hopefully! The percentage timer is showing thirty five percent currently. Even though my mind asked me to explore the place, I have decided to remain seated on a comfy chair for the next eighteen minutes, but suddenly the timer has restarted to "30:00" along with the percentage getting back to Zero! I am shocked and confused about what am I supposed to do. I want the cartoonish thing to appear again to advise me. I have started to take a walk around the luxurious setup. I am mesmerized by the beauty of every single element presented inside the hall.

My eyes caught a huge diamond placed on a metal pedestal. I went near it and admired the thing; thought about the wealth I can gain from this single piece of diamond. Unfortunately, the timer and the percent thing have restarted again. I am getting ferocious with the whole setup, threw a whole load of valuable items around the place. I went outside and walked through the garden, received a slight amount peace. The percent has reached forty-five, suddenly, a woodpecker appeared out of nowhere and started to irritate my peace by pecking on a nearby orange tree. I became very frustrated, threw a huge rock at it. The woodpecker has disappeared, and at the same time, the timer and percent restarted again!

I think I have an idea about what I have to do to escape this place, but still not sure why do I want to escape this place. It is very beautiful and appealing for any human being, and for sure people like me can never live in a place like this. Yes, I know what you guys are thinking, where am I right now? Am I inside a real place or not? I believe this is also a creepy place built by the factory people, just like the whole cocoa civilization they built inside the factory. I mean, what on earth was that! Cocoa people! Who thought about such an idea, like "Hey, let's build a new place and plant some cocoa trees there, and then create a civilization of workers in there"

But still, I prefer the cocoa civilization to the modern world! I mean, come on guys, who will reject such an offer? Human beings have to endure the lifetime process of studying and working for some weirdos, but when it comes to the Cocoa place, there is only one freakish thing to do for your entire life, to harvest cocoa beans. Wow! The timer ticked down to "09:23", only nine more minutes to go! I am happy that my philosophical blabbering's had some kind of use finally. I continued to wander around and reached near a wooden shelter, walked inside it and found a platter of mouth-watering food staring at me. There is ice cream, roasted meat, fruit salad, noodles etc. Even though I feel no hunger, I have decided to taste some of the food.

I took one big scoop of chocolate ice cream and stuffed it inside my mouth, ouch! The brain freeze thing! Unfortunately, the watch thing has restarted again, I am sure I saw it getting down to "05:52". Yes, I finally have the whole idea behind the game. I must try to clear my mind from all the cravings of human mind! Suddenly, an idea popped inside my mind, I can close my eyes shut and wait thirty minutes to pass the test. But no, I can't close my eyes for even a second. "This is impossible to pass" I thought. The timer ticked down to "20:34" and I must somehow manage to achieve the goal this time. The scorching sun's heavy punches made me retreat to the mansion.

The comfy chairs and beds scattered around the hall provoked me to take some rest on them, but I know laziness is considered a sin for human beings. What! I mean, how is laziness a sin! Even though we are living inside the most advanced age, human beings are still not allowed to take some rest! (gasps) Anyway, I have decided not to take the catch, started marching around the hall, slowly. Again, the timer ticked down to "10:28" Suddenly, a secret door is opened and came three women, dressed in princessy attire. They look very beautiful and charming; they approached me and asked me for help.

They want me to protect them from some evil creature hiding behind the secret door, which is still open. Strangely, I am unable to locate any wild creature standing behind the door. The three women are holding on to my body, they look frightened, but I started to experience a spike of energy from their touch. Suddenly, they have disappeared, and my timer is restarted for the fifth time I believe. I have lost faith in completing this challenge thing, but I can't imagine losing all my memory that I have regained recently from my mind travels. I must win the challenge somehow, or else there will be no hope for the world becoming free from the evil hands of the Chocolust creeps!

Yes, I know what you guys are thinking. Am I being too much prideful? No, I must lead Zeiwo and her team of victims, because they won't get help from others. First, I must retrieve Pearl's documents, then plan a full-scale attack against the Chocolust factory with the weapons hidden inside the secret basement of the dilapidated pub, there should be enough ammo to destroy the entire factory thing. Back to my mission, I have noticed the timer ticked down to "20:35" and should complete the task this time. Again, I wandered around slowly through the garden.

I have found a swimming pool in the middle of this garden, and there is one massage chair placed beside the pool. Even though I know the scene is a trap, took a quick peek to see who is lying on the chair. It is one big man with a bucket-belly, and he is enjoying a massage by some women. He is adorned with golden chains and bracelets, and the women are feeding him exotic fruits and other delicious smelling dishes. Unfortunately, a small sense of envy rolled into my brain and that caused the timer to restart again. The pool side scene disappeared, and I have started cursing my eyes. I am unable to close my eyes, and they are not blinking either.

I pledged myself to not look at such tempting scenes again. I can't take some rest, must continue walking around for thirty minutes. I have decided to walk with eyes focused on the ground. Again, I have managed to get the time down to "15:24". Out of nowhere, a security guard came near my side and questioned my presence there. Even though I am staring at the ground, he forcefully made me look at his angry face. "Who are you? Where did you come from?" he asked. I explained to him my whereabouts, and my thirty minutes challenge. He started laughing and called me a madman, and he announced that I am one poor uneducated local born man.

My mind has become stymied to provide one good reply. I felt ashamed to admit his accusation of me as a local born beggar! Thus, my proud mind made me lie to him with a fake royal ancestry story. The guard started laughing in an evil way and disappeared. As expected, the timer has again restarted! I became hopeless with the challenge thing. Luckily, I saw one luxury car resting next to the mansion entrance. Most importantly, the entrance shocked me. It is just two concrete poles each side with no gate, only a blank space staring at me. I went closer to the gate space and there is nothing to look at, except for the invisible wall blocking me from walking forward.

Anyway, I entered the sports car, sadly its interior looks like the rusty old pickup truck of mine. The engine took time to get back to life, and I slowly drove it around the place, luckily, the timer hasn't restarted! Then I saw a special crowd near a carnival like setting. All the people are dressed in animal costumes, and again I am tempted with the scene. But I am sure that nothing can tempt me enough to restart the timer thing.

XII

Temptation control Method

This carnival is very exciting to watch; I have received a ware wolf costume. There are cats, dogs, toads, bulls, crocodiles, snakes etc. It is always fun to watch snakes standing up! There is also a vivid display of different foods surrounding me, and I am so careful to not taste them. The costume people are happily eating the feast, and I noticed that they are acting like real animals. There is no carnival without games, and I have participated in some of them, but made sure not to get competitive with any of them. I am so happy to see the timer getting down to "15:23". Then I saw another big crowd standing near a stage that is decorated with flowers and electric speakers. An announcement has been made about the upcoming play by team 'Gold'. After some time, two cats and a bull appeared on the stage, they introduced themselves and officially started the play.

Cat B: 'Good morning, A, why are you crying?'

Bull A: 'I have received news about my death bell! They say my prime days are over, and should be killed for meat'

Cat C: 'Don't worry A, you are stronger than your cruel human owner, you can beat him with one strike, remember!'

Bull A: 'I can't do anything, I have secretly tried to kill him multiple times, but he has incredible reflexes! I must accept my fate now'

Cat B: 'Don't worry A, we should discuss the matter with councillor D'

(The two cats and the Bull walked to the backstage, a wild Boar enters the stage, it starts sleeping on the ground. The cats and the Bull walked back to the stage)

Boar D: 'Good morning, guys, what's the issue?'

Cat B: 'A's owner is planning to put him down'

Boar D: 'Well, isn't it a natural thing? The owner has the right to do stuff to his stuff'

Bull A: 'I am not his stuff, he stole me from the wild forest, and I have no attachment with him. He is only alive because of my old age'

Boar D: 'Does he have any weapon?'

Bull A: 'Yes, he has many rifles inside his shelf'

Boar D: 'Ok then. We must recruit an army of protesters to have a fighting chance. Hurry up!'

Cat C: 'Are we going to war? Is there any other option left?'

Boar D: 'There is no easy way to deal with the human power, we must war'

The Boar then returned to sleep, meanwhile, the trio has started their search to raise an army of protesters. They have met chickens, lambs, goats, horses, elephants, crocodiles, snakes, etc. Most of them showed negative response to the trio's suggestions, and they have no problem with the bull's problem. According to many animals the trio has visited, they have no problems with their owners till now since they are given good food and shelter. But still, the trio has managed to form a fifteen-member army with five roosters, four goats, three pigs and the trio themselves. The wild Boar D has appeared again and congratulated them.

Boar D ordered them to strike tonight, offered it's wishes to the army. The army waited till midnight, the stage turned dark and changed to Bull A's owner's house. They sneakily entered the house and searched all corners of the stage, found no one. My wrist timer ticked down to "02:12", meanwhile, they are standing helplessly in the middle of the stage, lights turned on! From the middle of the crowd, the wild Boar D and the Bull's owner walked into the stage, both are holding automatic rifles in hand. "You should never think about turning against your owner, folks! If you ever do, the following shall be your fate!" Boar D addressed the crowd. They mercilessly gunned down the army into just meat!

With less than a minute left to complete my challenge, I became extremely angry. Again, the timer has restarted and the whole carnival disappeared. I am tired from the whole loop situation and fell to the ground. After half an hour of taking rest, got back to my feet and observed the place. Again, I found a strange crowd standing in distance. I took one shovel from the garden box and started digging the ground continuously. The timer ticked down to "15:56", I can no longer see the outside temptations because of the depth that I have dug into. Without sparing a single second, I continued digging hard.

When the timer has reached "09:34", my shovel has detected something hard in the ground. Soon realised that it is a big piece of golden brick, shiny and pretty. But no, I continued my digging journey and spared no time to take a closer look at the thing. After digging for some time, I noticed the timer ticked down to "02:45", again, something blocked my smooth digging. It is one big red diamond attached to a platinum brick but continued digging again. Finally, the timer ticked down to the last five seconds. I became unconscious and fell to the ground.

(Whining noises)

Boom! I woke up inside a laboratory like setting. I am tightened to a chair, and I have a feeling that my face received a cut.

Someone: 'Greetings Larry, Oginfinn, Billy, my name is Fobbi'

Me: 'Good to see you sir, release me?'

Fobbi: 'Not so fast, my boy. Please wait twelve hours for your face to stick perfectly'

Me: 'What happened to my face? I am feeling a weird sensation! How did I end up here? I have completed the challenge'

(Fobbi ignored my questions, he brings a mirror and shows it straight to my face, my face has changed! I am somebody much younger and handsome, to be honest)

Fobbi: 'We have made you more pretty, happy?'

Me: 'You sick freaks! I know all your tricks, and I have solid evidence to lock you all in prison'

Fobbi: (laughs) 'I am scared, I am a little girl, hiding in the closet!' (laughs hard) 'Please take all of your solid metal evidence and roll it all into a ball, then push it straight into your throat!'

Me: 'Don't let power take control of you! You people can't defeat the world, remember. The power of solidarity is beyond everything'

Fobbi: 'Good hope. Keep it up, but things are much difficult than you can ever think of, my boy! Power can corrupt anything, animals, insects, even plants!'

Me: 'Enough of your boring philosophy! Why did you give me this made-up face?'

Fobbi: 'You have misunderstood us. Your new face is not made but was cut out from a pretty young man! Low budget issues'

Me: 'What! Devils! Stop this madness, I beg you Sir!'

Fobbi: 'Now, that's what power can do! It can make you "Sir", even though you never stepped into any academic institution in your life. And with power, these room temperature IQ people can trap your whole life inside one academic jar of nothingness, for your entire lifetime!'

Me: 'Point taken! Now release me Sir, I must complete my mission'

Fobbi: 'I wish I were that powerful enough to let you go now. Sadly, there exists one supreme power! Sorry my boy, make yourself comfortable'

Me: 'Tell your supreme dawgs that me and my team will soon destroy these pesky buildings along with you people into ashes'

Fobbi: (laughs hard) 'Enough of your trash talks! No more healing time for you, just suffer the pain!' (takes a map from his desk and sticks it straight to my face) 'Look boy, you will be dropped in here, and you should obey the commands, nothing else'

Fobbi then rolls the map and stabs it inside a backpack, then calls the workers. They have started planting the backpack and guns to my body, and attached a metal collar around my neck, finally took me into a helicopter resting casually on the helipad. I am tied inside the helicopter, and I am alone except the driver who doesn't care to answer any of my queries, not even his name! After three or more hours, the helicopter has stymied in middle of the freaking sky, and the driver pressed a button that unlocked me, then he titled the copter to the left side, slowly I slid my way into the air! Free falling straight into some wasteland looking canvas. Luckily, the parachute opened automatically and safely made me land on a pile of concrete waste.

I have started wandering the place, the scorching sun is heating me up crazily. I have no idea where to go, took out the map, I am shocked! This map is completely different from the maps I have seen before. My first thought was that the map might be a map of some fictional place like the previous one I have gone through or maybe even some video game space. Surprisingly, the map has some familiar country names marked, but they look not the same as in the popular maps. After walking a mile through the ruined place, I noticed a pile of fired bullets shattered across the canvas. Suddenly, a beep sound is heard, the metal collar attached around my neck started to glow. At first, I thought the collar thing was a gimmick or an adornment, but my thoughts dropped to waste when the thing produced one painful electric current into my brain.

Yes, I know you have heard of these kinds of collars in some recent fictional works, but you must know that these things are no joke! It is painful enough to make you do the things that you have sworn oath to not do in your whole life. I have continued wandering the place. After walking for almost an hour or so, a voice trembled out of some hidden speaker source planted on my bodysuit. "Your mission is detailed in the notebook placed inside your backpack, finish them in the mentioned order. Let the showdown begin woo hoo!" the anonymous caller announced. Yes, there is one hard bind notebook inside the leather backpack, and each of its pages has a detailed description of the mission along with a short narration on how to do it successfully, ending with a 'best wishes' comment!

Mission one - The Grenade Throw

Slowly take one red grenade from your grenade box placed inside your backpack, gently adjust the timer using the touchpad on it, after that, slightly press the button placed on the bottom of the grenade. Now, erase all the careful instructions provided to you till now, and throw the grenade straight into the red building standing between the two oak trees, better aim for the 'X' mark drawn on the building window.

Best Wishes!

I checked the backpack and found a box of red and blue colour grenades. The blue colour one is a traditional grenade with no display screen. I took the red one and analysed it closely, the timer can be adjusted to a maximum of forty seconds, and a minimum of fifteen seconds. Again, I took a long walk through the dusty road, finally reached near the exact location mentioned in the notebook. I have noticed that a blue drone is spying me from a distance. The red building looks dilapidated and abandoned, but I have decided not to throw the grenade into it just because someone ordered me to, dropped the grenade to the ground without adjusting. For the second time, the painful current splashed through my nervous system, and it made me pick up the grenade, set timer, click the button and throw it straight into the window!

I fell to the ground due to the excruciating pain. The grenade exploded with a loud sound, and my eyes are shocked to see numerous children running bewildered while screaming their souls out of their small body. The children are covered with ash and fear! I have realised that it is a school, and I just bombed a school, and probably caused at least fifty causalities. "Congratulations, you have completed your first mission. Move to the next one" the anonymous voice announced. I became furious and poured curse words out loud; sure, the anonymous man heard me because he gifted me the third electric treatment! I took out the notebook again, read the second page;

Mission Two - The Rifle refiller

Take the rifle attached to the side of your backpack, take out the 7.66 mm magazine from the backpack, gently push it into rifle's cavity, adjust the shooting speed and power, adjust the scope, go to the old park that is six miles away from your current location. Finally, shoot a minimum of five magazines there.

Best Wishes!

In fear of the fourth electric strike, and because it is just one rusty old park, I went to the location mentioned in the notebook. It is beautiful to think about the things fear can do to us; it can make us live the most pathetic life, turn us into a slave to those who are fearless! Anyway, I reached the destination, but the park is not old, it is well maintained and beautiful, and it is occupied by many children and their mothers. The kids are learning how to cycle and climb, they are enjoying their newly formed friendships. "Why... Why you frea... What wro...' I lost words! I have pledged myself not to touch my weapon, and I don't care if they electrocute me for a hundred times more! I have slowly started walking back to the deserted place.

The metal collar started to inflict pain upon my whole body. I tried my best to resist it for some time, but eventually the pain made me do the unthinkable! I took the rifle, loaded it with the required magazine, and aimed at the slightly crowded park. Even though my body is filled with pain, my mind made me lift the rifle and shoot the sky instead. Unfortunately, this rifle is not an ordinary gun, it is also a grenade launcher thing! By tilting the gun up, the launcher was activated and it shot three volleys of exploding shells. The park burned down within a second, chunks of burnt flesh are scattered across the surroundings. This incident has caused me to stand there without any movement. After a few minutes, a group of people came up to me and ferociously beat the life out of me! They kept kicking me till I became unconscious.

XIII

Giga grudgers Unleashed!

When I regained my consciousness, am inside a big room that has a prison like door, and a metal table in front of me. Luckily, someone has dressed my wounds, and the metal collar has damaged from the brutal kicks offered by the people. I am handcuffed to the metal table, and there is a button next to my left hand. I gently pressed the button, and it caused the speakers surrounding the room to produce one squeaky sound. One police officer charged into the room and points his gun at me.

"Reveal all the information about your gang, you scoundrel!" he shouted. I have narrated the events in great clarity, and surprisingly, he is not a corrupted officer. He is one helpless man who is unable to bring peace to the place because of the violence spread out by collar wearers like me. He knows about the secret mission the evils of the whole world have jointly executing so far. He then handed me a short notebook, which is the diary of a man he met inside the prison who was also from my country, a year ago. The police man then released me and revealed a secret path to escape safely from the compound unnoticed. He made it clear that he was ordered by his superiors to kill me mercilessly and then load me into a waste container.

"I know I am a useless piece of flesh, even though I have gained a lot of knowledge and won many exams, still lacks the courage and determination to challenge the unjust authorities. we need more brave people like you, I hope you bring light to this world" he said. I bid him farewell and sneakily went out into the forest surrounding the station building. It is almost night; after walking through the dark forest for some time, something jumped on top of me, the impact caused me to lose my balance and fell. It is one teenage girl, and she was hiding on top of a tree, lost balance and fell on top of me. "Forgive me Sir, please don't hurt me" she begged me.

"Relax child, I am okay, hiding from what you say?" I asked her. She explained that she doesn't know what exactly is happening around, all she knows is that it is not safe to wander anymore, especially for a girl! She then revealed that she is not alone in her hide game; I can see many young women holding on to the tree branches tightly. Since night is falling, I must keep moving fast to reach the 'people area' of the random place that I am in. The girl climbed back to the tree, I noticed deep fingernail markings on the tree, indicating how much fear they are holding in themselves. "Please don't reveal our location" she shouted from above.

After walking for over an hour, finally reached the people living area of the place. I checked my pockets to find something, I still have the map and the notebook of the helpless man, but have no money left sadly. There are only a few houses here and there, still not found a single person. I made knocks on some doors, but no responses received. "Maybe there is some festival happening around" I thought. Luckily, I found a mini van parked outside one big house, so there must be someone inside. I went inside the house compound, still no sign of anyone, and there is no light shining anywhere except from the backside of the house that I am in now. Slowly made my way to the backside, the back door was open and there are signs of violence spread across.

My detective mind forced me to inspect the situation further! Entered the room and found a beheaded corpse inside a pool of blood. Out of nowhere, a man leaped onto me, holding a big meat machete. My quick reflexes were enough to save me, he fell to the ground and growled in pain, still holding the machete tightly. I went outside, ran for my life, went inside the forest again. Night has fallen in; darkness came to my advantage. He failed to locate me, went further inside the deep forest. Meanwhile, I returned to the man's house and broke into the mini van parked outside.

Luckily, the keys are still inside the vehicle, drove it through the empty street, I can see a crowd standing in distant. When I reached closer to them, realised my mistake, they are holding thick wooden sticks and machete's. Suddenly, one middle sized stone shattered my mini van's glass, and it hit my chest with sheer power, lost my breath for a minute. The crowd pulled me out of the van, and started kicking me for some reason, destroyed the van completely. Luckily, they left me and entered a random building. Surprisingly, one man lifted me up and took me to a hiding spot, offered me water and food, dressed up my wounds. He introduced himself as Ivan, and we both exchanged stories of our lives.

Ivan is one good listener, also a good narrator. He explained that the place is undergoing a violent situation. People turned violent after the random terrorist attacks happened inside the country. People have overthrown the government and started destroying the whole infrastructure. According to Ivan, the beating I received earlier was not because of any personal grudge or dislike, but for the sake of violence alone. This whole country is undergoing one merciless Anarchy! Rules and regulations don't matter anymore. The strongest men strive and conquer everything in their path. Every suppressed desire will be explored with bestiality!

Ivan advised me to join a group, because the crowd will target solo people first, and satisfy their desires on them. Ivan escorted me into a group of young people; they are planning to eradicate all middle aged and older people out of the place and then to take over the whole place. My younger face helped me to manipulate the poor youngsters. After a few hours, the youngster group became enlarged with teenagers and adults. Surprisingly, there is no woman inside this strange group. Our group first entered a bank, and there is another youngster gang inside already. Both groups started the battle for power, there is no voting or succession, strength is all that matters.

The second gang is defeated quickly by our big gang; our gang then ransacked all the money locked up inside the bank lockers. They celebrated their victory of becoming rich by throwing money around. Some of our members have started to sexually assault the female members of the defeated team, loud screams are heard from everywhere. The leader of our group ordered us to sit down on the ground, and he delivered a thunderous youngster worthy speech! "Hear me, fellow youth, from now on, our gang will be known as 'Giga Grudgers', and I must remember you that there is no need to loot money or any other precious item. This whole country is ours to feast. We should focus our attention to establishing dominance over this country, we must form our own government here!"

The young members started to cheer, and then the Giga Grudgers again wandered through the streets, while randomly beating old men gangs, recruited new youngsters as well. Grudgers then entered a nearby grocery store and ransacked it completely. Then we marched to a medium sized mansion, pulled out the gates with all youth power, and easily killed the two big guardian dogs. The mansion compound is filled with our members, sure that our gang has exceeded five hundred plus members. Gang members started to pour chaos around the mansion. Destroyed the luxury cars, burned down the gardens and statues, killed every pet, throwing rocks constantly at the mansion.

With sheer manpower, they have managed to crash the expensive front door, rampaged into the hall. They started searching the whole place to find the owners, or something else maybe. I keep wondering what if these gangs used their youthful energy to disintegrate the worldly evils like the Chocolust freaks and every other illegal power holder! I am thinking about making a speech to the Giga Grudgers about my findings, but they are busy assaulting the male and female members of the mansion, some teenage members are sexually abusing the female maids, they are screaming for help, but sadly there won't be any help.

I went upstairs and observed the scenes happening outside the mansion, through a large broken window. The entire town is getting eaten by fire, gunshots left and right, dark smoke suffocated the moonlit sky, even the sun won't be able to offer day here anymore. I have decided to steal a random vehicle and get to my native country somehow. Meanwhile, most of our gang members have become intoxicated with the precious wine and liquor collection sealed inside this mansion. I also have the opportunity to drink plenty, but my responsibility mind stopped me. I took one big machete from an unconscious gang member and slowly sneaked way out.

While making my way out of the big mansion, I heard the scream of a little child, coming from a nearby room. The door is locked from inside, and the screams are getting louder and louder. Luckily, my eyes detected a metal statue of some cartoon character, broke the door with the statue and finally entered the room. What awaited me inside is the most disturbing scene ever, unbearable to watch, especially as a father of three girls. It is a boy, less than fifteen years of age, standing alone in the room, and he is sexually abusing a girl of less than twelve years of age! "This is mine, get out of here man!" he yelled at me.

I stood there like a statue, while my eyes kept analysing the boy's face and body. Short hair, no sign of beard or moustache, a little obese, almost five-foot height, no upper body clothes. "What is your problem! Enjoying the scene? Get out you creepy adult fellow" he said mockingly. I am getting more angry and violent every second with the girl's helpless cries ringing inside my brain like one electric shock. The moment of unleash has finally came, tightly clutched the machete and swung it hard on him. The entire room is splashed with the quick burst of blood! His headless body fell flat to the ground.

After a few minutes of silence, a sense of relief blossomed on her face. She asked me for help, introduced herself as Opaoul. Like I guessed, she is only twelve years old and today is her twelfth birthday, and she is a member of this mansion. She explained that while she was eating birthday dinner with her family, a group of men charged through the door and chased them. She made it clear that this mansion has noise cancelling properties, and her family has spent the whole day with her inside this mansion. We then managed to exit the mansion, luckily, most of our gang members are drunk unconscious.

While running through the streets, looking for a vehicle, both young and old men tried to assault us and tried to take Opaoul with them. I had to use the machete again to protect her, and since there is no law withdrawing me from anything, being aggressive is the most important objective. Unfortunately, we can't find any vehicle with healthy wheels, because the riot people have intentionally busted open every wheel. The people are competitively throwing rocks and spreading fire to every single building. Loud screams are heard from school buildings, but I have decided not to investigate big buildings anymore.

Me and Opaoul are getting heavy thirsty, we entered one already destroyed house sneakily. The disturbing image inside the well startled me, it is piled up with corpses! We are left with no other option than to run, because people have started to throw rocks at us, and started chasing us. Sounds of glass shattering, gunshots, vehicle smashing and crashing, thunderous sounds of trees and posts getting ripped off from their roots, sounds of rapidly burning fire etc. filled my ears. Finally, we have arrived at the railway station, thanks to Opaoul for giving accurate directions. She possesses a lot more knowledge than other twelve-year-olds.

The railway station is also empty, and there are signs of violence hanging around the premises. We found a hidden spot, hard to notice straight away, I handed her the map and waited for her answer about the thing. While she is studying the map, I am watching a TV screen pasted on top of the station pillar. It is currently showing the major news regarding the recent traumatic events. Headlines such as,

—"People say they don't want useless leaders anymore; they will make crucial decisions themselves from now on"

—"Half of the country is devoured by violence"

—"Police have not yet identified the real culprit; clues hint that he may be one of the leaders of the terrorist group, Nameless"

—"All train services have stopped"

—"Hints of a third world war"

—"Try to reach the border somehow for help"

—"Women must find a hiding spot as soon as possible, must evacuate their households"

The news channel is also showing live drone footages of the horrific events; the scenes indeed resemble a world war battleground. People now focus on destroying buildings with the help of bulldozers and big trucks. The drone shots are getting zoomed in and it clearly shows what the violent mass is doing. They are tying thick ropes around the pillars of different buildings, pulling them off with the help of big trucks. I am stunned seeing the absurd acts of the crazy people out there. The drone then decided to show one larger gathering in the middle of the highway road, surrounded by meat wastes and empty bottles, they are preparing barbeque and consuming alcohol in excess amount possible.

I guess they know their freedom will end after the establishment of a new and powerful government. Human beings are always frustrated about the ways they are shackled to the laws of governments, and I was one of them. But the horrible scenes playing around me changed my mind. I have never imagined how much dangerous common people can be, even though most human beings tend to lead a disciplined life, the remaining amount is more than enough to cause irreversible damage to the entire planet! The world has forgot the fact that a human being is also an animal! And if they are given excess freedom, things like these will occur. Opaoul broke me from my deep philosophical thinking, and we continued waiting for a train to appear even though I heard the negative news.

Opaoul has finally reached a conclusion that the map is a genuine one, but has many differences compared to the popular one everyone knows. This map contains more countries and islands, and in this map, most of the countries are shaped different than the popular map. While discussing more about the map issue, I have realised that the popular map she has been referring to, is not the one I call the popular one. According to her, there are only ten countries inside their own map. She has found my native country in the map, and luckily, it is only three countries away. Suddenly, a train whistle sound cheered inside my ear.

Yes, it is a train, and it is heading our way. We are excited and entered the train as soon as it slowed a little. The train is full of middle-aged men, children, and mostly women. Most of the women look like they have escaped from prison — clothes tore off, blood marks here and there, nail scratches, missing footwear — and they are not enjoying my presence there with my young-looking face. Me and Opaoul went to the front compartment and took the opportunity to make a small discussion with the crew there. The engine crew consists of young men and women, and not surprisingly they are holding knives and guns for you know why. Even though they mistook me for kidnapping a girl, Opaoul bravely defended me and helped me.

They explained that they are martial artists and have come to this country for some competition, without having any idea about the country. They also revealed that they have stolen this train. I showed them the unusual map, they became bewildered, except one guy, he is sure that he has seen this map elsewhere. He can't recollect where, but he is sure that this map is indeed the most genuine piece of land information available. I made him recollect the crucial point that whether he has visited my country or not? He replied negative. Anyway, I just want to return to my native place, to continue my Chocolust eradication mission and to visit my family.

Somehow, I have damaged to understand the map and where is the train currently at, thanks to Opaoul's intellect. I must wait for twelve hours for the train to reach the wintery forest entrance, then cross the wintery forest to reach the next destination, which is a desert! I am losing my hope of getting back to my homeland,

and I am also worried about how to convince Susan about my face transplant or stolen incident. Opaoul has started to sleep peacefully on my lap, thus restricting me from further observing the train and its members. While sitting idly for some time, a big connection between the map and the wintery forest started to sprout inside my head, it is about the dangerous routes that connect these hidden countries to the main countries that are marked inside the popular map. Because of my terrorist activities, I should find a sneaky way to escape this place.

After taking a closer look at the map for a shortcut, I have realised that to reach my homeland, I must cross a volcanic ground, a dense forest that is not explored yet I guess, along with the two other places mentioned earlier. The chances of my survival have become very little, and I have decided to leave Opaoul inside the train. To kill more time, I have started to further analyse the map and found many dinosaur signs placed on random countries. My home country has two of those markings. Rolled the map back into my pocket, and took the notebook gifted by the good police officer, who helped me escape earlier. The notebook looks very fresh, must have written this year or the previous.

The diary of a man of nothingness

Hello everyone, this is not a diary recording my every day or monthly events, but this is a record of my life. I am not writing this to inform you about my mistakes and milestones, but to warn you about the dangers I have experienced in the last one year of pain. All other medias are under their control except writing, at least I believe so. If you find this book, please read this fully and educate others. My name is Harry, and I was working in the Toy factory. I received very good payment and only had to work ten hours a day. My work there was to make fancy costumes for dolls and statues, but I always wondered why they made me tailor each outfit in specific sizes. I decided not to investigate on that subject any further since it was none of my business. And it was my first mistake! If you ever find anything suspicious, take your time to investigate the matter further, at least inform your close friends!

Before revealing my next mistake, I must introduce my small family, my wife, my teenage daughter, who was studying graduation course in journalism. My daughter was very curious about the toy factory for some reason, and she always pecked me for helping her get some work materials from the factory. The factory had strict policies against theft of even one single line of thread! But still, my adventurous mind made me do the unthinkable for my daughter. She explained to me that it was for her final year dissertation. It was my second mistake.

Even though the factory people didn't say a word about my several cunning thefts, they were just toying with me. Back to my factory worker life, one day, while unloading boxes of raw materials from the truck, from one of the boxes, I heard someone screaming my name, the voice was similar to my daughter's...

XIV
Caves and more Caves

(Train whistles loudly) I woke up, realised that I fell asleep while reading the diary notebook thing. My drop point has arrived, and luckily Opaoul is still sleeping, and she is not sleeping on my lap. Without wasting any more time, I bid farewell to the main crew and jumped out. A big white frozen canvas is staring at me. The train has disappeared in the fog, and I started my journey through the snow. Even though this spot is marked as the entrance, there is no sign of a border or a gate. I slowly moved forward, carefully slamming down the thick snow. The whole scenery looks awkward to me; the deep snow-covered ground has no sign of a sturdy sandy ground below. Also, the trees look branchless and are very tall, and the sky looks like a group of thick curdy-clouds hanging.

(Splash!) Someone threw a snowball at my back! But I can't find who it is. By following the deep snow tracks shattered behind me, found the snowball thrower, it was Opaoul and she greeted me with a cheeky smile. "Oh, what have you done dear!" I asked. She has started to make another snowball and hit me again, again threw one but hit one of the trees. She is laughing at me, suddenly, a piece of white snow fell on top of her, and she fell. I picked the snow piece; it is very heavy and full of white milky liquid. Opaoul's forehead received a small cut from that, and she is crying out loud. The wound froze quickly and it offered her some relief.

Luckily, she is done with her snowball game. We slowly made our way through the snow, and a big piece of milky snow fell on my head, almost lost my consciousness. Many more of the puffy snow started to rain down from the ceiling, and luckily, we found a snowy cave. I made a fire inside the cave with a few papers from the notebook of the factory worker, and by slapping two sharp rocks. I am sure that this cave has warmed up plenty of travellers. I have found plastic covers, half burned twigs, neck tags, empty rum bottles. Unfortunately, the fire is not sufficient to help my eyes read the factory worker's notebook.

Surprisingly, I found a revolver hidden underneath a stone, and it still has four shots left. We can't rest any longer because of the freezing temperature, left the cave and resumed our journey. The surroundings look very strange, with all the trees looking identical; brown colour and tall, filtering the fresh yellow blessings from the sun through the milky snow biting on to the treetops. The snowy ground looks deep enough to fit one skyscraper; the whole place has only brown and white colours. An obstacle appeared in front of us —it is not making any sound, has thin hands like a twig, round big belly full of probably all of the animals ever lived here, sharp and lengthy nose, dead eyes staring mercilessly, round ears, big hips but legs are hidden under the snowy ground— it is a Snowman!

Yes, I know I have exaggerated that hard, but you must understand the situation that I am in. Alone in a freezing forest, face to face with death any moment, and out of nowhere; a Snowman! Any human being can bet that this is a trap, and most importantly; somebody is watching us for sure. "He might have been here since last year, be brave!" Opaoul said. My mind found somewhat relief from her words, but still, I am not sure if a thing like this can live that long. Before moving ahead, I gave my new friend a slight push, and it fell and cracked to snow-dust within a second! "See? This thing was just one breeze away from extinction, it must be a trap, we must move quickly" I said. Opaoul can't think of an appealing statement to nullify my finding.

We moved carefully, took slight breaks tree after tree. Opaoul's face has become pale, she is shivering hard. Finally, my eyes have found a green colour submerged inside the snowy ground. We started digging the snow ground with our bare hands, found a corpse of a man, it was his green attire that caused the reflection. We pulled out the corpse and did a small looting on it. The corpse is not decayed a little, still has all his hard-earned flesh intact fully. I took his leather coat and covered Opaoul with it. I have then found some unrecognisable currency notes, a whole bottle of rum, a small chest of gold coins, and one sharp sword that was used in kingly battles.

I took his hat and gloves, continued our pursuit. Again, a heavy piece of milky snow loaf fell on my shoulder, caused tremendous pain. We ran inside another cave, and again found some collectables inside, this time found one round rusty metal shield, a revolver with four bullets inside, two hand grenades, a half bottle of rum, and a frozen loaf of bread. There are more caves ahead of us, but what is more surprising about these caves is the fact that they look like a round circus tent made of stones and covered in snow! They can house four average size people. To erase my suspicion, I made a scratch on the cave-wall with my new sword.

Yes, my suspicions are right, this is not a naturally formed cave, but made by human beings, with mud and nicely shaped stones. We took our newly acquired loot and headed out, used the rusty metal shield as an umbrella for blocking the snowy bricks raining down! Ironically, a piece of sharp ice fell on my biceps and pierced through. Even though the frozen breeze caressing me reduced the bleeding, it wasn't enough to seal the deal fully. Opaoul is worried, starts crying, she fails to tear the jacket that she is wearing, she ran through the snow and searched the nearby caves. She finally found a piece of cotton and wrapped my wound with it.

Even though I am full of rum, Opaoul is starving. Another strange thing about this forest is that I can't find a single animal or bird, the whole place looks like it has never sprouted any form of life! We have finally arrived at a less tree spot, and there are many caves conjoined here. Variety of colours hidden inside this field of snow, and I know what it is and it is exactly what I guessed. My eyes count at least fifty of them, sleeping peacefully inside the freezing ground, with no threat of their flesh getting ripped apart by worm families. They are dressed in heavy duty attires, and each of them has a sharp sword, bow and arrow, flintlock pistol, golden ornaments etc.

Opaoul casually dug the snow field, gently unwrapped a once puffy jacket from one of the corpses, she then clothed me with it. I have noticed many gunshot wounds on the victims lying comfortably in the snow-bed. This place resembles a world war spot! We continued our journey, but the endless snow plain ahead of us looks unending, and Opaoul has started to show signs of heavy starvation enough to make me carry her from then.

Though I have the support of that rum early, I am indeed feeling the pain of starvation inside my guts. We then came across one disturbing scene, two hands seeking help, but not waving. It is a man who was recently shot to death by someone, the dead man is on his way to be fully submerged into the snowy depths, he looks modern, has a smart phone with him. I am now sure that there is someone spying on every traveller passing this cursed forest. I am getting tired carrying Opaoul on my back, and it is dangerous to take rest now. We heard a growling sound far away, became scared and excited at the same time! Suddenly, a bullet hit the tree next to us!

We have taken cover behind a tree, I took the revolver in my hand, I do remember that it has four shots left inside, but not sure if it still works. While carefully looking for the enemy, another bullet flew right across me, missed me by an inch! Luckily, I have found my enemy, dressed in animal skin, tightly holding a double barrel gun, backup bow and arrows hanging on his back along with a small pouch, brown skin, face covered with snow. He kept coming closer to us after firing each shot. I missed two shots but hit my target with the third shot. He fell to the ground and is dead! He was shot in his chest, anyway, we started to search him.

We found some cooked meat inside his pouch; it helped to reduce our starvation. Yes, I have doubts about the meat source but there is no other option left for us. I have noticed his strong palm; sure, he was a hard worker. Why did he try to kill us? I am confused! Anyway, we started to move again and reached a weird spot. No trees there but numerous corpses submerged in the snowy ground. I forgot to mention some peculiar things about the corpses found in this strange winter forest. These corpses are massive in size, with huge muscles. While observing the newly found field of corpses, I found a few broken vials lying inside the snowy ground.

Opaoul mentioned that the vials are normally used to carry around toxic and disgusting substances, and she predicted that some people would have taken body samples from the corpses. She changed my attention to one broken syringe lying inside the snow, and I picked it to further analyse the thing. The syringe has a damaged needle, and it has a red coloured substance inside. Opaoul continues her hobby of exploring the made-up caves while I am still thinking about the whole dramatic events happening around me. Face ripped off, trapped me in a war field, framed me as an international terrorist. I am hopeless.

We continued our frozen journey, no sign of help anywhere. We finally met an animal here. Not just an animal, but one big sturdy thing with —white fur, black ears, blue eyes, shark-like teeth and a snowy beard around its jawline, puffy tail, and the most unique legs that look like human hands —a fox, I guess! It is standing still, waiting for something or maybe it is a statue. Out of nowhere, Opaoul threw a snowball at it, and still, it doesn't move. "Such a nice sculpture!" I thought, but as expected; the thing shook its head and charged at us. I took my 'one shot left' revolver and offered the final shot into the fox's head, but it is invincible to the shot!

The fox took advantage of my stymied position, almost slapped my head off with one swish movement of its massive hand. Luckily, I am still conscious, and it continues slapping me with its hands, and for sure its hands look exactly like human hands! One extra feature is the creamy colour of it. I am getting tired moving around, saw

Opaoul making a ditch by digging the snow field with a tiny shovel she found inside one of the caves. I know what she is thinking, I hit the fox on its head with the metal revolver, then shoulder speared it aggressively into the ditch made by my sweet little girl. Opaoul started filling the hole, while I keep hitting the thing on its head to keep it down. Finally, we have defeated the wild beast together.

Animal noises are heard from here and there, and we must move very carefully now, by hiding behind the trees and hiding inside the made-up caves. Opaoul looks very happy and she is enjoying her time playing with the snow and exploring every cave out there. "Father! Come look here" Opaoul said loudly. I am shocked to hear her call me father, she then came up to me and grabbed my hand, pulled me aggressively into a cave. I am shocked! Inside the cave, there is one tunnel leading straight to somewhere. But it is enough to keep us undercover from those pesky animals hovering around. We entered the secret tunnel, it is very hard to walk faster through it, must be careful not to break the ice ceiling above our head.

While walking through the tunnel, I found many cigarette butts scattered all around the circle, made tiny holes on the ceiling with the sword and it helped to get some air inside. After many hours of slow travel, our legs became numb. We took some rest, but it is not possible to take rest when the whole icy structure infiltrates your entire body. Because of the transparent property of ice, we noticed some people roaming around a small structure, can hear their footsteps. I am worried about them standing right above the secret tunnel. Luckily, we went past their camping area and moved quicker, can see a different colour in front. The snow circle started to change, and we entered a sand tunnel, continuation of the snow tunnel. Finally, we have reached the end of the whole tunnel adventure.

As expected, there is a door right above us, but it is jammed! Luckily, the sharp sword can unhinge the door. Sunrays of sun splashed into the tunnel, can see the metal ceiling of a building, and we climbed into the above structure. It is a dilapidated building, again! Full of spider webs, empty rum bottles, broken chairs and other decorations. There is an open window, and it shows a beautiful scene of golden land shining with sun's pride. Yes, it is a desert but has some buildings. Opaoul started playing with the rocking chair, its squeaky noise keeps scaring me! Hordes of bats flew out of the chimney and flew out through the open window.

The bat parade was enough to lure the attention of the entire village, one man holding a shotgun in hand entered the building through the open window, he immediately aimed at us. "Explain yourselves" he ordered. I told him exactly where we are from, he looks not satisfied with my reply, but Opaoul said "He is telling the truth, uncle, we are refugees!" and her sweet reply was enough to calm the gunner nerves of the man. He stopped aiming at us and asked us to follow him, we followed him carefully while analysing the whole setup we are now in. It is one big 'hottest desert wasteland' with no sign of vegetation possible. The man introduced himself as Xenvi and he is serving as a self-proclaimed patrol officer for the place.

"Self-proclaimed?" I asked him. He explained that he was a nurse last week and now works as an officer. Yes, I know he doesn't make any sense, but I don't know how to make him explain. "What are your duties now?" I asked him, and he replied that he has to catch intruders like me and has the right to kill any intruder without questioning. But they have no rights to hurt the inhabitants of this desert place, and none of the inhabitants has done anything like that ever in the history of this place. Me and Opaoul are sweating heavily, and we have finally reached the middle of the town area. "Have fun" the officer man said and left us there. I thought he was escorting us to the ruler of this place.

We stood there bewildered, without any idea what to do. The passerby people offered nothing but a suspicious stare, but they gave a tiny smile to little Opaoul. I am sure that if Opaoul wasn't with me, they would have beaten me to death. I am still waiting for someone to offer us help or atleast give us some food. Opaoul suggested me to keep walking, and we moved slowly through the hot sand ground. Some form of relief entered my heart after seeing a four-wheel Jeep wandering around. Though I waved continuously at the driver, he didn't care. Suddenly, Opaoul is missing! I became panic and started my madman search. Cried her name out loud and peeked inside random buildings, even though the residents threw food at my face many times. The anxiety plus the scorching heat plus the helplessness made me faint...

(Whining noises)

XV

The Lamp and the Calendar

Oh, where am I? What just happened? Am I dead? I can hear the ocean speaking. Yeah, I know what has happened, I was just teasing you guys, hope it worked. Anyway, like I mentioned early, I can hear the rumble of ocean, not sure if it is a freaking speaker. I am inside one ancient looking building, the narrowest one I have ever seen, has numerous steps swirling around to the top of the thing. I promised myself not to climb the steps, because they have no railing. The wooden door is unstable; it is almost open even though it is latched clearly. Through the tiny opening of the door, saw thunder sparks reigning down. The entire building is shaking like one rocking chair, maybe this is a big old ship, I thought.

Suddenly, a bucket full of water rammed through the tiny opening on the door! I caught one fish from that collision. I am starving somehow, I mean, yes human beings need food and water, but now that I am inside my own mind, how am I experiencing thirst and hunger! There is one old kerosene lamp hanging on the wall, and found a sharp knife stabbed into the buttery wall, took the lamp and used its heat to burn up the fish, and ate it fully. After regaining some form of mental and physical energy, I moved slowly to explore where I am, sure that I am near a shore. Took some time to unlatch the door, shocked to see that I am inside one lighthouse thing stranded in the middle of a vast deadly ocean, and the sun is setting slowly. I am wearing an oversized t-shirt and an underwear, completely wet!

The water keeps splashing to my face, I walked back inside the lighthouse. Now that I am alone inside a small building, started to examine the whole scene in front of me. There are four open windows on each side, and each window keeps welcoming salty ocean water straight into the building and my mouth. There are no electric appliances, it makes sense, I know. The kerosene lamp is the only light source. Surprise! There is a calendar hanging on the wall. It is twenty-fourteen, ten years before! It is December seventeen because it is marked with a bright red marker. I must have suffered very much confined to this hellish place, made me count each day.

I checked the sole furniture there is, an old desk, house to every species of termites. I found many half-eaten documents but then I found last month's pay slip. My account was credited with three hundred dollars, payment for one single month, What!! No wonder why I am suffering here alone, filled with boredom. The slip has a date, thirty. Hopefully, the thirtieth day this month might bring me something unknown to cheer for. On further ransacking the desk, I found rotten bread and fungi butter, a photo of me and Susan with two of our children at that time. I wish I was given an opportunity to see her so that I could advise her to restrict my lusty provocations.

There is one instruction manual rolled tightly and jammed into one of the holes inside the desk, and it says that I am entitled to turn on the light by climbing all the way to the top, because the switch is placed there! What! I mean, come on guys, what is this! Why didn't they put this creepy switch on the bottom? Is that too much to ask for? I have sworn myself that I will never climb this horrible thing. Again, I am burdened with the mission of 'doing nothing', am forced to kill time, sad that I can't sleep either because of the water splashing from all directions. The sun has finally set completely, darkness everywhere.

No, there is no moonlight, and I regret my previous decision to not turn on the light. The water keeps splashing all around, and I have started to climb the steps, using all my limbs. While climbing slowly, my eyes caught some strange shadows roaming in the surface. I am not frightened by these paranormal things, but the short stick-size steps (gasps) Why didn't they at least make these steps a little broader! After climbing at least a hundred steps, finally reached the top part, turned on the massive light that illuminated two big holes on the ocean surface. I have tried to get in front of the light and wave to get some attention of the ships, but I haven't seen a ship since I came here.

It appears to me that this whole lighthouse thing is one big prison! I am just one middle aged clown running up and down with no way to escape... No, there is one way to escape, I can just jump into the vast ocean and die. But when I tried to jump off, the invisible wall blocked me (gasps) Luckily, the light operation cabin is safe from the splash of ice-cold water! Finally, I took some rest, but no sleep. I kept thinking about my present life, I must survive the tougher tasks laid in front of me. I am very scared about the dense forest, because of the black T-rex mark on it. If you remember Jessica, you know why I am afraid of that extinct buddy symbol that I saw on her medallion.

Somehow, I have managed to survive the night, the beautiful sunrise greeted me. The ocean looks endless and calm, there isn't one ship! Sadly, my eyes can see a variety of waste floating peacefully with the rhythm of the sea. But the light has turned off itself, even though the switch is still on. I slowly climbed my way back to the surface. The main door is unlatched somehow; a pile of dead fishes and other waste welcomed me. After storing some of the dead fishes, slowly cleaned the entire surface. I have also found scraps of gold, money, plastic cans.

Suddenly, my eyes caught one shiny and odd-looking chest, it is smaller in size, decorated with fake diamonds and gold. I know that it doesn't matter if it has anything valuable. But my curious detective mind is eager to find out what is inside of it. With all my strength, I cannot open the box. There is only one way to open it. I slowly climbed the twisted path of steps again, reached midway, dropped the chest straight to the stony ground, don't know if my attempt is successful, but am sure that if I were to slip off the steps, I would become a creepy sticker. I slowly climbed down to the ground, the small chest has become two pieces, a small cushion is resting near the pieces, and one small bottle of something is pushed tightly into this cushion thing.

Carefully, I took out the bottle, and opened it after a great amount of struggle, I am hoping that it will be one of those vials that offers mysterious powers! The bottle is engraved with some strange language. It has a strong smell, it is just aged wine, and I am happy to have it at this point of boredom. One sip of this magical potion turned me into a giant sleep monster. Soon, a pack of hallucinations set foot inside my mind. Images of war and destruction, the extinction of life, horrible creatures wreaking havoc... I woke up a few hours later, sun has done its course again, darkness everywhere. Strangely, the light is still not working, I strongly believe that I didn't turn it off.

I have decided to get to the top one more time, started climbing the stairs slowly, lost balance at the thirtieth step, I guess, crashed into the watery surface.

(Whining noises)

Strangely, I can see the moon now, even though am lying stomach to ground! Can't move my head or speak, but I feel like being carried to somewhere, the smell of desert sand tickled my nostrils. I am relieved getting back to my consciousness again, but my carriers dropped me into a pile of something... (Whining noises)

I am back inside the dark room, and a whole new load of waste has piled up on my body. Again, the door is unlatched! But morning has arrived, slowly got back to my feet, quickly climbed the steps and reached the top again! The switch is on; the light however is not. I tried turning on and off the switch one more time, and this time the light returned to life. It seems like the light will only turn on after one 'on and off' operation, after it is turned off on its own.

So, I must climb up here repeatedly to ' turn on' this thing, ok no problem! I will stay here for the rest of the month, decided. Luckily, I have brought the good old wine with me. Since then, I stayed on top of the light house, with my toxic companion. I keep wondering why don't they assign one more member into this boring job, I am not talking about females, just one more human being to have a talk at least, is that too much to ask for in this age of crooked minds?

Days passed by, finally, the small bottle of wine has emptied, and I am left with no choice other than to suffer, I hope this month will be over soon. To clarify, I slowly climbed down to take the calendar, a huge pile of filth is staring at me, there is no ground. The disgusting smell made me unconscious.

(Whining noises)

Again, I am back in the desert place, still not able to move my body except my eyes, can hear camel sounds, and can smell desert sand mixed with a disgusting smell of something decayed. I am hoping for my consciousness to transfer to the lighthouse setup, but sadly, endured the decayed desert smell for almost an hour, before getting back to the sea house, again the horrible smell of waste keep drilling my nostrils! What!

I am feeling very much distressed for losing my self-consciousness, we all believe in the fact that there exists one thing in this whole universe, immutable to any force, one's consciousness. But now I have lost it too! Anyway, after cleaning up the pile of waste, my stomach started to cry for food. I am surprised that the old wine kept me out of hunger all these days! Sadly, I have already swept the pile of fishes back into the ocean. The stomach rumble has upgraded to painful cramps, without any hesitation, walked closer to the desk, took out the rotten bread, soaked it in sea water, and took a large bite.

From then, I gave special attention to collect every sea food that was thrown at me by the humble sea: shrimps, smelts, Crabs, Sea bass, Octopus, Lobster, Sea urchin etc. The kerosene lamp has dried out from my aggressive cooking, eagerly waited for the arrival of reinforcement. I am surprised there isn't a toilet inside this structure, yes, the sea is not going to get dirty with my liquid waste, but how can I do my solid waste disposal! I don't want to touch it!

With much difficulty, I moved closer to the door frame, gripped myself to both sides of the door frame, and sat down facing backwards, and deposited my waste into the open sea. One huge tide blasted a tide of water back into the lighthouse, and I am forced to climb all the way to the top. Without the wine, sleep has abandoned me. At midnight, I heard a horn sound, luckily, the ocean is calmer like a sleeping baby, to investigate, slowly crawled down the steps and reached the bottom side. Someone is knocking hard on the door, the lamp is out of fuel, and I am struck in darkness, something grabbed my legs. I stand still, waiting for whatever that is about to happen to me.

Suddenly, the "strong" door is unlatched by someone with the help of a knife. There is a small boat anchored outside, and two men charged into the building, greeted me warmly, my first impression is that they are pranking me, because I have heard about these kinds of pranks before. Give me a minute to remember... Ha, yes, hear me now, this is a story I heard from my wife Susan. Once upon a time... Sorry, just teasing you guys, okay, an old lady named Enrit was living alone in her middle-class house, and one night she heard a knock at the door. When she foolishly opened the door, there were three men standing, they greeted her as their long-lost grandmother. She was suffering from Alzheimer's disease and had no idea about her family; thus, she believed that those three strangers were indeed her grand kids.

They continued to act like they were really her own blood, made her narrate stories, her past life, worst experiences, her jobs. But her disease didn't allow her to answer any of their questions. She then realised her mistake, but it was too late. They murdered her silently and ransacked all her wealth. I am expecting the same, one of them has a machete in his pocket, and another one is holding a sledgehammer. They pushed me aside and started to hammer down a metal rod with a pointy end, stabbed into a small gap around one big stone. After many strikes, the stony ground made a small opening, by gripping hard and pulling aggressively, managed to flip off the stony piece, perfectly used to hide one big treasure under this poor building.

Yes, it is a treasure hiding spot, filled with mesmerizing amount of gold and diamonds, along with some strange bones, old chests, old crowns, tightly closed bottles made of rocks etc. One of the men walked back to their boat, and returned with a handful of collectables, most of them are in golden colour. They started to re-arrange the whole stack with the new additions. "Yokuvo, why didn't you eat your ration this month? It has attracted these pesky little intruders into this cabin!" one of them asked me while holding a yellow colour worm. He threw a small sack in front of me, and it is full of worms and other insects. After an hour of labouring inside the secret cabin, they went out of it and closed the secret door.

They are worried about my weird way of acting, said I fell from the stairs to ease the suspicious tension building around us. One of the men went outside and returned with a bundle of bottles. Gladly, they invited me and offered me the first big sip. When I regained my conscious mind, I am alone. I have noticed that the secret door is not fully closed as it should be. Opened it and took a few of the old looking rum bottles, the strong smell coming out of the bottle is enough to kill my boredom for the next few days... Finally, I heard a ship whistle, and there is one big ship slowly sailing towards me.

The ship continued to make huge waves throughout the ocean, the lighthouse has started to rumble. The ship is anchored next to the building, the crew then threw a giant rope that has a hook at the end, it caught one of the metal rings projecting out of the lighthouse. Suddenly, the lighthouse starts moving away from its original spot, slowly gets into the ship's radius. Officers in uniform are waiting for me to get inside the ship, they did a quick scan throughout my body and clothes, and then started to search the house, found the broken chest and the empty bottles. Luckily, they didn't care to ask me anything about it. Again, I am alone inside the big ship even though it is crowded with people.

I am not allowed to enter the upper decks, must stay near the barricade. I stood there looking at the lighthouse, it took at least two hours for the lighthouse to disappear from my sight. Sadly, none of the people bothered to even offer me a chair. When I asked for water, someone genuinely suggested me to open my mouth wide and catch the sea water splashing around. After a few hours, the ship has reached its destination, a less crowded port. I can see Susan and my two kids waving their hands at me, before leaving the ship, one of the officers ordered me to strictly return after five hours. He then handed me two hundred dollars as my payment for the last month.

Yes, I do remember seeing my previous payment cheque of three hundred plus dollars. He kept staring at my bewildered face and offered the answer I am looking for, the reduction in payment is due to my mistake of not turning on the light one night, and I do remember that night. Quite unfortunate! Anyway, grabbed the two hundred dollars and went out, met Susan and kids. She opened her hands for me to hug her, but my response was very slow, and that made her uncomfortable. To ease the situation, I rubbed my forehead to act like having a headache. Luckily, it worked, Susan escorted me into a small cottage and laid my body on a smooth bed.

XVI
International beauty Contest

Susan: 'Feeling good?'

Me: 'Kind of... How is everything... Dear?'

Susan: 'I miss you dear! Forget this curse, let's get back to our house. Don't mind anyone'

Me: 'You sure about that? We will end up homeless'

Susan: 'What? You were making over five hundred dollars per month before you have yourself trapped inside this thing... what happened dear?'

(What! I don't know what to say, it is a curse to live with no past. I must somehow make her slip out the details regarding my entrapment)

Me: 'How is my trapper? Is he dead?'

Susan: 'Like always, he is living like nothing has happened'

Me: 'Oh, he... Do you believe that the happened thing can be changed or repaired... Always'

(Awkward silence...)

Me: 'How are the kids? Oh, I have something to tell you, we must settle for two kids, because... I had a vision from the sea goddess that if we settle for two, she will make them powerful... How's that!'

(Awkward silence...)

Me: 'I fell from the stairs... The lighthouse'

Susan: 'Oh... Have some tea and bread, here'

(Gives four pieces of bread dipped in butter and a large cup of tea)

Me: 'Umm... For how long I should do this? You know, to complete this curse thing, to get back to you and the kids'

Susan: 'Don't worry about Mark, just abandon your ego'

Me: 'How many marks did I get? I have ego?'

Susan: (laughs) 'Don't open that door dear!' (laughs)

Me: 'Here, take this money with you, take care'

Susan: 'Did you purchase your ration?'

Me: 'No, I am tired, will you please buy it for me?'

Susan: 'Ok. Remember, Mark has gone abroad, he is not spying on you anymore!'

Susan went out to buy me ration, while I took some rest finally on a good comfortable bed. But the kids keep crying without Susan, and then I spotted Susan's phone lying on the desk, luckily, her password is just one to six, no space. Her wallpaper is a photo of our family, and it brought tears to my eyes. I have opened the gallery to find more about our real home. She has photos of a good-looking house, not like the one in which I lived as a pickup driver. She has more photos of our family, and when I searched the video folder, found videos of me fighting someone, I don't know who he is, but he looks strong and tall, one must be a fool to pick a fight with this man for sure. As expected, he defeated me easily and poured a whole bucket of fish over my head.

I am wondering why Susan keeps watching this embarrassing thing. Suddenly, Susan came back from the market and has no reaction for me watching the video clip once again. "You will never change!" she replied in a mocking way. "Where is he living now?" I asked her while pointing my finger at the winner. "Mark has gone abroad, I believe" she said. My five-hour vacation is expiring, kissed Susan and left quickly. The ship has started blowing smoke, screaming hard.

I went inside the ship this time, and it is not just a regular ship, but one big barracks. There are a lot of guns, explosive nukes larger than a house, war machines etc. Surprisingly, most of the weapons are too big for any human being to handle. I took one small revolver from the huge stack of weapons. Apart from the weapons, there are a lot of beautiful sport cars scattered around. Just like I mentioned, these cars are not made for any normal person. I tried to enter one of the cars, but an irritating alarm went off quickly, some guards charged into the barracks and kicked me out. The lighthouse starts to become visible from a distance, and I am starving heavily. Unfortunately, I have left my newly bought ration inside the weapon warehouse, and I dare not to enter there again.

Finally, the ship has reached near the lighthouse, and the officer ordered me to jump out and swim to my den. With no choice left, I jumped into the aggressive ocean, the tides are very strong. I am unable to swim back to the building and am slowly drowning... When I woke up finally, I am back inside the lighthouse! Wet and covered in a pile of waste. Once again, my days of boredom has started, I wonder when I will become free from this mind game thing. I keep thinking about the massive weaponry found inside the ship, it is more than enough to destroy the entire universe! What's up with that! Suddenly, my eyes spot something moving at the top.

When I reached the top, there is no one, but sure that something was dropped off from the top, because of the pattern it created on the surrounding water. I am too tired to investigate the matter further, thus, decided to spend the rest of the day at the top. While taking rest for some time, the scenes have changed again, I am back in the desert accompanied by the irritating whining noises, can feel my face getting burned from the scorching heat. But I am helpless! Can't move a muscle except my eyeballs. I don't understand what is happening to me, what kind of disease I have? I can hear sound of trucks raging through the desert and can see helicopters above. I fear getting stuck in this position, paralysed in the middle of a scorching desert, feeling tremendous amount of pain.

After a few minutes, I can hear footsteps all around me. It is a group of kids, and they are smiling at me, started playing with the hot sand. Soon, they showed their true essence, urinated all over me followed by covering me fully with sand. The disgusting smell of urine plus the melting sand offered me a whole new world of pain. (Whining noises)

Luckily, I am back inside the lighthouse mind life, it is night, and because I can't sleep, keep thinking about my life. Suddenly, I heard someone unlatching the squeaky old door at the bottom. I feel irritated and scared at the same time, I should have taken my rations, it had kerosene and candles. After a few minutes, heard the creaking sound of the wooden desk, sure that I have a visitor waiting, and out of curiosity, took a quick peek down the stairs, but there is nothing but darkness.

"Hey there, I know you are down there, don't play games with me, just get out of here or else I will shoot you!" I said loudly. Again, heard some rumble down there, without hesitation, I took the stolen revolver and fired down the stairs. The shot was not what I expected, the bullet exploded like a mini bomb! The lighthouse took a massive hit. I have patiently waited to find out the damage that I have done to this poor structure. Finally, the sun has arrived, packets of sunrays fell on my skin, quickly jumped up and climbed down the stairs. I can see the mighty damage even before reaching mid-way, the one hundred steps structure has turned into a seventy something structure. The entire building now looks like a chess board. I struggled a lot to get to the bottom.

It is a miracle how this building is still standing. Unfortunately, the secret treasure room door is destroyed, it is filled with sea waste and water, and all the precious stones are scattered across the ground, most of them have already joined the mighty ocean. The squeaky old door is torn to pieces, strangely there is a trail of blood leading to the wooden desk, I can see a big fish tail shivering beside the desk. Through one big hole on the desk, I can see two human eyes staring at me. I took my gun and aimed at the desk, "Please don't shoot me, please sir..." the person said to me. She revealed herself before me. She is unable to stand up, slowly crawled to my side.

Her legs are covered with a big fancy fish tail, looks like a mermaid, expect that I can see her hips. She is starving hard, begged me for food. I gave her some rum, I wish I had the ration bag. She enjoyed the rum; she thanked me and crawled to the destroyed door. The trail of blood is still following her, and she looks severely injured. I told her to wait, and she was expecting me to say that. I dressed her wounds with my salty clothes. Her body is shining brightly. Without the door, water keeps splashing heavily into the building.

Luckily, the aged rum bottles are still there, and they are enough for me and her. She started to eat raw fish, and I keep observing her mysterious appearance. I can remember that my eyes have seen larger versions of mysteries, but this mermaid woman looks real. She has long blonde hair, nicely spread out with the help of a small golden crown, has blue eyes and blood red lips, her arms have shiny green fins. She has a golden breast plate that has rainbow colour stones welded on it, and her hips are adorned with silver-coloured scales. She has become intoxicated and is lying on the ground, water keeps washing her constantly, slowly dragging her back to the sea.

The sun is setting, I am forced to bring her back to a safe spot, thus, I must bring her somehow to the top. Luckily, the fallen rocky steps were made in a lock and load fashion. With great effort, I have rearranged the structure back to its prime, picked her up, she weighed at least seventy pounds, somehow managed to get her to the top. Some of her silver fish scales are stuck in my skin, sure they feel like metal. Turned on the light, I have been doing this routinely since my return from the ship, don't know if it will change my future, but still, I fear the possibility of alteration. Okay, I will explain! If I fail to turn on the light for a few days, my payment will be peanuts, and it will cause my family to hit rock bottom, and if my current life can influence my future, well, can't take risk anymore.

Anyway, time went fast because of the powerful drink we had, after sunrise, she returned to her senses. She gets scared seeing me half naked, lying closer to her because there is no more room. I promised her my innocence and explained my actions. She is still wearing that scared expression and is shivering. She made request for more rum, but my laziness made me settle there for the time being. She started crying and begged me to help her find her family. Even though I told her not to tell me her story, she didn't comply. Come on people, I am done with these depressive narratives! I listened carefully just for the sake of her relief. She started narrating, her name is Senya, was one of the prettiest girls in her college, and was very enthusiastic about the festivals and celebrations, just because she could shine with her prettiness.

She had many male followers, who would literally die for her! No, I am not exaggerating this stuff, and I can see her getting angry when she said that. She started to take pride in her pretty face, started to spend more time and money to make her prettier. As days passed by, her followers count drastically increased, and she received a ton of gifts from them. She started to get frustrated with the number of marriage proposals she was receiving from every type of men, including jobless men, men who never went to school, men who never broke a sweat for anything else etc. She stopped narrating and stared at me angrily, she questioned me about why men do wars for pretty women!

I became silent for a whole minute, but she is still looking at me. I said, most men seek pretty women, and I believe we also want that pride that women experience when we sniff around... Clear? she is not satisfied with my answer, anyway, she continued narrating; because she lost most of her time doing makeup, she went down in her studies like a rollercoaster. Her pride made her choose beauty over everything, she started hunting for beauty contests and modelling, and won so many medals and cash prizes, more importantly, she received many more followers after participating in such events. Finally, she met her demise in the form of an international beauty contest organisation, that approached her with an invitation.

Senya was flattened when she heard the prize money, five hundred thousand dollars! She packed herself and went to the contest located in another country. After a day, she reached the location mentioned in the letter, a stadium, but it was in the middle of nowhere, there weren't any buildings nearby, and she became frightened. She was ordered by some masked people, to lie down on a small metal bed that had straps around it. Even though she tried to run away from there, she was caught and was brought back to the bed. They ripped off her clothes and started their operation, they didn't even give her any anaesthetics during the procedure, she screamed in pain while they stitched the mermaid tail and all the decorations on to her body.

After stitching her up, they inserted one small machine into her mouth, which was designed to help her breathe, because they then threw her into one big water tank. It was an aquarium and was filled with mermaids like her. Senya swam around, sadly none of the other mermaids was in the mood to engage in a conversation with her. She found a variety of fishes swimming inside the giant aquarium that was filled with coral reefs. The giant aquarium was sealed tightly with a celestial themed roof. After a few hours, she started playing with the tiny crabs and urchins, suddenly heard a thud sound, the ceiling was opened partially! Someone dressed in diver suit casually swam his way around the structure, carrying a strong metal fishnet, she thought he was looking for sea urchins, but he dropped his fishnet over a mermaid, and dragged her to the top of the ceiling.

The mermaid caught inside the fish net looked like she was done with her existence. Surprisingly, none of the other mermaids was interested in investigating the incident. She saw through the transparent glass that the diver took out his catch from the fishnet and put the mermaid inside a white box, which was later carried away with a forklift. Senya was frightened, and was not feeling any hunger or thirst, but she found out that the water was bitter and refreshing at the same time. Again, none of her companions offered her any word, they kept lying on the ground, meanwhile, she continued playing with her newly found shell friends. After a day, the diver returned, swam around the aquarium. He was carefully observing each of the mermaids, he even took the effort to roll them over to analyse in detail.

Finally, he went to Senya's side and stood there staring at her. She had no clue what he was doing with his eyes, because of his alien mask. Suddenly, he put his fishnet over her body, it was metallic but not electric or anything fancier like she expected. The diver pulled her up to the ceiling, the strong net made some wear and tear all over her fishy body. She was then dropped inside a white plastic box and was taken away. She felt the movement of the box, and sometimes it fell to the ground, she became unconscious. When she was back to her senses, she was placed on a family sized bed, saw bottles of alcohol sitting on the nearby table. She was expecting something very bad to happen anytime soon.

Senya started observing the premises she was forced into, it was an open room, could see the blue sky and its "trusty" companion clouds... Yes, I know what you guys are thinking, how in the universe can any human being, after suffering a body transmutation, narrate her story like she was doing poetry! No, she was not doing any fancy narration, it was my fault, I apologise, apology accepted? Thank you! Anyway, after a few minutes, an old man entered the room. He was wearing nothing and was very hairy and obese. He poured a big glass of alcohol without adding any water in it, drank it full in one sip, followed by taking another shot, his eyes were sealed on Senya's body. He started to throw alcohol over her body, and then threw himself onto the bed...

Ok, that's enough. He raped her for the next few hours, made her unconscious. When she woke up, she was bleeding between her legs and was in a lot of pain. The man showed up again, and stared at her again, followed by another brutal rape. What! What was that! How could any man do stuff like that! Again, she became unconscious, but when she woke up that time, she was inside a glass tank filled with water, surrounded by weapons. After some time, some male guards entered the warehouse, carried the glass tank out of the warehouse. She realised that she was inside one big ship, her carriers climbed a stairway and finally placed the tank inside the captain's cabin. She could see the vast ocean, no sign of land except the lighthouse!

Yes, it was this lighthouse, and I feel relieved that her painful narration has come to an end. Ok. Anyway, she was thrown into the vast ocean by the captain. Somehow, she managed to reach this lighthouse. Surprisingly, she has never visited my home country! Until this day, I thought that my homeland was the only place that inhabited those devils, but she proved me wrong! Anyway, I narrated my own story to her, and she looks less concerned. She just wants to get back to her family, and we patiently waited for some ships other than the military ship that used to come here every month.

XVII
Shotgun to the Head

She made me promise to take her safely to her family if some friendly ships approached us. We took every single one of the ancient rum bottles to the top of the lighthouse, it is worth the effort, fully settled ourselves on the top. I do remember seeing Senya smiling and cheering for my future endeavours, after drinking a highly toxic bottle. If we were real human beings, we should have been dead drinking like this. We have managed to get past ten plus days, and still no sign of any friendly ship! One day, we heard a big scream! Finally, my three pirate friends have arrived, they are shocked to see the damage.

One of them saw me watching them from the top. They have turned into aggressive animals, raced to the top. My quick thinking made me unplug five of the rocky steps. The three men are literally crying for their losses, they are standing on the sixth step from top, helplessly. Unfortunately, one of them slipped and fell, making the others to rage up even more, took their pistols out and started shooting violently. The big light along with the glass windows scattered. I am getting enraged, finally took my gun out, fired one shot at them, felt immediate regret, not because of them getting killed, but for the sudden destruction of the whole structure!

(Whining noises)

Suddenly, the disgusting urine smell pierced my nostrils. I can't open my eyes, slowly started to get back to my feet, wiped the urine-mixed sand off my body. Finally opened my eyes, I am standing in the middle of nowhere, with burnt scars all over my body. Somehow, I managed to reach the small colony again, but the people are staring at me aggressively. I know that, without Opaoul, I am vulnerable to the people's wrath. They started to question me and pushed me away from their house premises. But still, I can see the interior of their houses through the open windows. The whole area resembles the cocoa civilization inside the Chocolust factory.

I have noticed that the people are looking peculiar and similar, they have long ears, wide grey lips, small eyes that look like they are always closed, imperfect nose that looks like someone beat the perfection out of it, wearing loose shirt that extends all the way to their knees, and have many intentionally drilled up holes throughout the dress, thin muscles etc. Their houses are made of sand, and have numerous holes here and there, no sign of electricity, no furniture except for furniture built with sand, such as sand beds, sand chairs, sand tables etc. Still no sign of Opaoul. Suddenly, a commotion has started.

People ran out of their houses and take stand inside a big circle made of thick rope, there comes a helicopter, its high wind produced a whirlwind using the sandy ground. I am forced to shut my eyes due to the sandstorm, and thus, missed the scenes happening around me. Somehow, I have managed to open my eyes, and there is no sign of the chopper, but the circular meeting has dispersed, and people are walking slowly to their homes, each carrying a sack of something. I dare not to find what is inside the sack but am a little curious to be honest. I keep crying out loud the word Opaoul until my throat dried out.

In search of water, I found a truck that has a large vessel on its back, a shiny metal pipe is attached to the vessel. I know there is water inside the vessel, but I am scared to approach the vehicle. After a few minutes of meditation, I have gained some confidence, slowly walked to the truck. The pipe is dripping water into a small bucket now. I have decided to take the water from the bucket, took a closer look around me and saw angry eyes watching me, waiting for me to make a move. I have abandoned my mission and wandered around with a dried-up throat, started to cough heavily. Finally, an old woman came out of her home and invited me into her house. She then gave me some water; it is salty and has a disgusting taste! She is curiously staring at me.

Me: 'Can I have some food? I am starving'

She: 'Ok sir, please wait ten minutes'

(She takes a sharper knife from the kitchen slab made out of sand, and went near the mysterious sack resting peacefully behind a vessel, she tears the sack and takes a handful of green rice, goes to the kitchen and drops the rice into a pot, lit fire under the hole inside the slab, places the pot on top of the hole)

She: 'What is your name, sir?'

Me: 'I am Larry, thank you for letting me inside your house'

She: 'Do you still have the map with you?'

Me: (Confused) 'What map are you talking about! I was forcefully dropped in a random place, and am looking for a way to reach my homeland'

She: 'I don't want to hear your stories; I am talking about the map that contains this place!'

Me: 'How do... You're one of them? Please don't kill me, I have a family'

She: 'Give me the map!'

Me: 'What if I say one big NO!'

(She goes to the corner and takes a shotgun out of her bag, and aims at me)

She: 'What about now?'

Me: 'Listen Lady, I know you people are in love with young people, but they have...'

(She put the gun inside my mouth and ordered me to hand over the map)

(I gave her the map; she grabbed it quickly and starts reading it. She then goes to the kitchen and pours the rice onto a plate)

She: 'Thank you sir, I am Riya from the Global Investigation Circle, please enjoy your rice'

(I took the plate from her hand, and quickly swallows most of the soup)

Me: 'What is this Global thing you are in? Is it good or evil?'

Riya: 'Neither! But it is called the people's circle, a government organisation, I think!'

Me: (Again Confused) 'Can we stop them?'

Riya: 'No! Do you want sex?'

Me: (throws away the plate) 'Shut your damn mouth lady! You think I am a fool or something?'

Riya: 'Yes'

Me: 'Point taken! Now, please help me get back to my homeland, at least arrange me a vehicle'

Riya: 'The real enemies are not inside your homeland, if you are willing to sacrifice your life, join my cause, the ultimate cause!'

(In a quick move, I took her shotgun and aimed right at her forehead)

Me: 'Give me the MAP!'

Riya: 'Trust me Larry, middle-aged uncle with a stolen face, I know what I am doing and going to do, please cooperate with me!'

Me: 'No! I know who the real enemy is, give me the map!'

Riya: 'Chocolust and the Toy factory? Yes, they are good targets, but I know a better one. Please don't do anything stupid!'

(Drops the shotgun)

Me: 'Who are you? What is wrong with those people? Why are they targeting young people? Spreading violence...'

Riya: 'Calm down Sir, let me explain you my findings. As a member of the government crime investigation department, I was thrilled to solve crimes and bring justice to the victims. I have finally met my match after getting involved in one missing case of a young lady. Her mother was on the verge of committing suicide, and I offered her my word. Soon, I found that no other member of my team had any interest in assisting me, and they lectured me about the numerous missing cases registered in the past. I was shocked by their cowardice; we were part of the top-notch crime hunters! And then I found the reason behind that cowardice, it was all because of the GTM, and ironically no one had any information regarding their existence, but still they were scared to move a finger against them'

Me: 'I don't think it is a myth! I believe I have met one of them, not so long ago. Jessica, living in one giant mansion, and she holds'

Riya: 'No need to elaborate, I know their existence. I went searching for them and was caught by them! They took me into a laboratory and scrapped off my pretty younger face, installed an old-wrinkled face, then dropped me... You know... Then took me back to another location, I jumped off the helicopter and crashed into a river next to the Cathpy Island, somehow managed to reach here'

Me: 'So, you believe you can find their hiding spot from this map?'

Riya: 'No, it is unknown to everyone, except its highly precious members. Now, what I have learned from the map thing is, one of the members is ruling the Dense Forest next to the volcanic colony thing!'

Me: 'Do you really think we can capture him?'

Riya: 'No, there is no capturing but killing, we should kill him and gain control of his territory, so that we can get to the secret location of his pesky gang'

Me: 'So basically, you need his power!'

Riya: 'Good thinking, yes, I do. I mean, who doesn't want power? Everyone loves power and will do anything for it. I promise you that I will use this would be power for the betterment of the world. I swear. Now let's find a vehicle and escape here'

We ran outside and sneakily entered a water tank placed on a truck, it is almost empty and has remnants of snow. They are collecting and melting snow from the wintery forest. Riya is preparing for her next move, wrapped a metal chain around her knuckles, sharpened her dagger. I am not convinced by her promise but, am excited to get back to my homeland, which is next to the dense forest she is talking about. After an hour or so, the truck has started moving, the wobbling tank gave us a hard time catching our breath, finally the truck stopped. As expected, I am drowned inside the leftover snow chunks, she climbed out quickly.

After some more struggle, I got back to my feet and started to climb the stairs inside the tank. Suddenly, someone dropped a bucket full of snow into the tank, hit my head, lost balance, fell to the plastic bottom of the tank. The driver heard the sound, took a peek inside the tank, he started blowing his whistle, luckily, Riya knocked him out with a powerful strike to his head. She offered me a hand and helped me get out of the tank; we then climbed into the driver's cabin. Riya has started the engine and off we go. We drove around and entered the wide-open sandy terrains.

Riya explained that she has been living here for over a year now, and she is amazed by the unity of them. Riya keeps talking to me and has no interest in looking at the wide-open desert terrain. She further explained that those desert people have no government or a leader. Legends say that before one hundred years or so, twenty to thirty people were dropped into this place by a helicopter, and they were forced to adapt to this mighty hot place. After years of suffering and deaths, they managed to build a civilization on this wretched land, a civilization built with trust and friendship, without any form of leadership and deity worship. Riya was in a battered position when she reached here and thus, they welcomed her into their small family.

When it comes to food and water, they receive weekly supplies by one anonymous helicopter, and because of the impossibility of agriculture, they are forced to rely on that. For water, they are forced to drink water by melting the unhygienic snow puddled around the boundary of the wintery forest thing. Riya reveals that when she first drank the water, she became mad and livid. I am puzzled by her mentioning that, as you guys know, I drank the ice water early and it had no effect on me. I asked her about the effects of the water in the long run; she doesn't know the answer.

Riya keeps talking about the desert village and slipped one major information. It is about the funeral stuff existing here, when someone die here, the others must report it to the guards at the wintery forest border that I didn't know exists there. They will take the body away and no one knows what they will do with it. Suddenly, our vehicle hit a sand wall and both of us crashed into the hot sand. Black smoke from the engine encircled us, almost suffocating us. Riya offered me an apology immediately, but who wants an apology! We are stranded in a freakish desert, with no sign of land anywhere nearby. She started to study the map again and consoled me. She assured that we are almost near the destination.

Luckily, Riya didn't forget to bring a bottle of ice water from the water tank inside our broken vehicle. "Why are you obsessed with power? I mean, we are all human beings, born to die, we live and learn, play many games and survive each day, there is nothing to prove to anybody. At the end of the day, it is all about just living the life till it ends" I said. She started to laugh and gave me an insulting reply, "That was one big load of philosophical blunder! You have proven yourself worthy of being a 'dad joker'. Even if I don't want power, there is always someone who craves for it, and he will replace me, if I didn't take it. I don't care about death now; I was always tied to the margin sidewalk and endured a lot of humiliation at the hands of people who only had the slightest amount of power! Now it is my turn, this is the opportunity of a lifetime"

Sun has set, darkness everywhere. The hot sand has finally cooled down; we positioned ourselves for a short nap. Riya is still deep inside her thoughts; she admits that she is scared about her upcoming fight. She made it clear that she must defeat the GTM member in a melee fight to earn the badge. I told her about Jessica, another member of the G thing. Surprisingly, Riya is not intimidated by my horrific description, she takes out a red vial from her pocket, she explained that she is keeping the red vial for that fight, and she is sure it will be enough to defeat any living thing. She revealed that she stole the vial from the laboratory she was once held hostage.

The slightly cool atmosphere is not enough to let us enter the relaxing realm, and there is no moon to offer us any form of light, it is complete darkness! We don't know where to go, we are waiting for the slightest sunrays. We have decided to exchange stories to pass time. I told her my sad story, no reaction. Riya started narrating her life, "I was the third and last child of my parents, and we were a middle-class family. My parents and my neighbours were very strict; I didn't have any freedom except to go to school and study. Compared to my two elder brothers, I was very much confined to my room alone. No one cared to listen to my problems, my happiness or anything about me. They denied my request to buy me a phone, though my brothers had two phones each! I decided to study all day long, and my hard work paid off! I have become part of the government's power, slipped into the reality, was kidnapped, carved the life out of me..."

Riya's short narration has ended. We fell asleep. Because of the hump and bump style of the desert, I was rolled around the terrain. Suddenly, my hands became wet! I stabbed my hand inside the water source near me, confirmed the presence of an underground water source.

XVIII
Walls of Trouble

Yes, there is water underneath this mysterious desert, can't see what is hiding inside the water. Darkness makes it look like a puddle of tar. When I dipped my head into it, I saw bright land. In the morning, the first thing I can see is Riya dipping her head inside the water. "I saw a monster down there!" she said, followed by a big laughter. She then started drinking water from the puddle and commented that it is very refreshing. Suddenly, she has disappeared. I jumped into the puddle (splash) I am shocked.

The golden sandy surface and the ceiling are shining; they are the only light source here. Suddenly, the strangest realisation occurred to me, I am not gasping for air! This water is not much liquefied as it should be. The gentle thickness of the water gives space around my face to breathe smoothly. Riya is nowhere to be found, and I swam to the surface to find the ruins of an ancient castle or church. Riya is down there, ransacking the ancient ruins. She picked up a handful of the glowing sand, and it is very tempting to look at.

Suddenly, something hit my left hand, and there is a needle wound on my hand now. Riya looks bewildered, she saw something passed through quickly, in the next moment, she also received the invisible enemy's treatment, wound appears on her right leg. What's more interesting is that no blood is getting spilled out of our wounds. Whoooah! Something just went past my eyes; I am getting uncomfortable. Riya advised me to swim fast, we swam hastily, but when I took a peek back, I saw a cluster of blades following us. Luckily, we have found the exact time to move away. We swam down to the surface filled with ancient stuff, can see the blades hovering above us. Looks like they have no interest to chase us down the ground, and thus we have decided to walk.

It is very hard to walk on the pile of bricks and woods scattered around the surface. With each step, our feet keep getting stuck inside the brick gaps. Finally, we have decided to find something to cover ourselves, to swim safely. We started to roll down the bricks, sea weeds to find something valuable hiding under. We found a good metal door, but when I flipped it over, there are some human dead bodies lying inside of it. Surprisingly, these bodies are not decayed the slightest, still have the stab wounds. We moved to the next area, rolled over the giant stones with equal effort, uncovered one metal box, enough to cover us both.

We opened the box and closed it in a fury! Well, am not surprised, this was how the ancients lived, according to the texts. Can you guys guess what we have discovered inside the box? Ok, I will give a hint; it was one of the crowd-full festivals back then, it involved happy spectators, wooden platform, eighteen plus content, bloodshed... Yes, the guillotine punishment. The box we have opened is full of the prizes received by the guillotine. On further searching, we have found heavy swords, ancient bottles of rum, torture devices etc.

Finally, we have found what we were searching for! It is a big turtle shell. We picked it up and it can provide cover for us both, and with the shell, we swam up and waited for the sharp things. In a minute, thud sounds encircled our shell, and it is vibrating a lot. We swam forward casually and drew near a tree standing proudly in the middle of this magic water body. We rested on its surface, analysed the turtle shell and found the things that were hunting us for some time, they are stuck into the shell. Such fascinating things they are, look exactly like a knife without the handle part, have two beady eyes, sharp nose and fins on top. I wonder where their mouths are! Whatever, Riya started to pluck them out and put them into an animal skin pouch that she found early.

Meanwhile, I keep observing the lonely tree near us. Surprisingly, this tree extends all the way to the top of this water source. It looks like a Bunyan tree and has many branches sticking out from its mighty body. I can see a speck of sky through the small opening on the magic sand ceiling. I swam to the top and tried to penetrate myself through the tiny hole between the sand and the tree, but it isn't big enough to pass my body. With a bit of struggle, punched my head out through the hole and there lies the wide sandy desert, the scorching sun's rays blinded my eyes quickly. After closing my eyes tightly for a few minutes, slowly opened it. Hopeless desert lies in front.

WHAT!!! When I took a quick peek at the sky, I saw something strange on top. Because of the scorching sun, I can't take a good look at what I saw moments before. To get more clarity regarding the matter, I started taking short peeks at the sky, did it ten times, believe I have the full picture. The tree extends all the way to the sky, but what is more interesting about this special tree is that it has one wooden platform at the top. And another thing is that this tree doesn't look like a natural one, it is wider than any tree I have ever seen. The heat rays started to mark its sign on my neck, swam back to meet Riya.

On my way down, I checked the leaves of the suspicious tree's branch. They are made of steel! When I reached the surface, I took one of the blade fish out of Riya's pouch, hit the tree with it, the hidden metal rods and concrete unveiled themselves. Turns out that the tree structure is painted with thick brown paint. Suddenly, I found a hidden red button, pressed it, two concrete doors of the tree have opened sideways, one big ivory colour room welcomed us, the magic water rushed into the space. We swam inside and pressed a button inside. We are literally inside an aquarium, and it is now moving up fast.

Within a minute, we reached the top of the tree, and the ceiling has opened. The floor of the elevator alone has started to rise, eventually it pulled us out along with the magic water. We made it to our feet, and realised that the whole platform is one helipad, without the railing. My heart leaped out, but Riya looks brave enough to take a peek down. After a few minutes, the sun turned angrier as he thought we were challenging him or something. I pressed the button on the edge, and the floor starts to drop down slowly. Before jumping into the elevator floor, took a good look around while holding on to Riya. Suddenly, a ball of water hit my face, slammed me to the edge, luckily, Riya pulled me over, thanks to her bold confidence.

We leaped into the elevator and went down. Ok, please wait while I recollect what I saw during my short glimpse. Mmm... The desert is very vast than I thought, couldn't find a mark of the wintery forest, but did see what lies in front of us, a big mountain and tall grass. But what is confusing my mind is the thing I saw just for a fraction of a second! I saw it standing on top of the mountain, it looked like a mountain! Had trees over its back. And what on earth was that water ball? Hallucination? Anyway, I dropped the subject to the memory bin, put on the turtle shell and continued our adventure.

After some time, night has arrived. We are taking shelter in one sunken ship, somehow, this rusty ship has something that can produce light. We searched for the light source, completely unnecessary. Anyway, we found the reason; a flock of strange looking fishes having a glowing skin. What I meant by calling them strange was that they have human eyes, black hair instead of fins, even have a beard, fleshy lips, and they are in the shape of alphabet 'T', big head that is glowing brighter every time they make a move. Riya scared them off, making the whole ship brighter as daylight.

I am amazed by these fishes, tried to catch one... uhhh... the plan backfired, can you guys guess what happened? Turns out that these pesky 'light house buddies' have inbuilt defensive mechanism to counter predators and kidnappers like me. When I touched one of them, it exploded, its sharp teeth and bones shot into our bodies... I fainted. When I woke up, it is morning. Surprisingly, I am not inside one of my mind adventures! Riya is applying some form of plant mixture on my wounds. She mentions that she found some medicines inside the captain's cabin. Riya then escorted me to the captain's cabin to see something, it is the dead captain's body, he is holding a gun and must have killed himself.

But the crazy part is that his face has a smile. We have decided to investigate the ship further. This is a big ship, but the collision impact has caused it to shrink down to almost ten percent of its original size. We started ransacking each of the rooms, it is always interesting to get involved in these treasure hunt activities, even though there is nothing to do with what we might find. As expected, the rooms are filled with valuable items, pile of ancient currencies, different colour pearls, dead bodies of pet animals, laptops and modems, and finally everyone's trusty favourite - weapons. We returned to the captain's cabin to take our turtle shell, I noticed the year of making the ship engraved on the ship's wheel, two thousand five!

We left the ship, and as we swam safely with the turtle shell, out of nowhere, I am dragged down to the ground. Riya saved me by severing the thing with the blade fish we caught earlier. Great thinking by her, but no time to offer congrats because more of those pesky things start chasing us. Riya handed me some of her weapons, and we fought them till we are tired. Again, one of them grabbed Riya, dragged her down to the surface, but my quick reflex helped her break free before she touched the ground. Fiyuuhhh! Ok, now that we have escaped them, I must clear all your doubts. First, those things are not something you can imagine in your mind for sure!

Those things look exactly like flower vase placed upside down, with wiggling cactus legs protruding out of its vase head. Its head is one slimy jelly, orange colour, and is glowing dimly, and it will stop glowing if we stab something on its jelly head. I believe I mentioned them grabbing us, but that is not the case, they don't need to grab us, they use their jelly heads to touch our feet or any body part. Yes, their jelly heads have some sticky properties. Another thing is that if we touch the ground, there is no escape. The floor is lava, Kidding! it is sticky. The ground has some yellow sticky substance lying on, and this area looks like home to those jelly buddies. We can also see some human beings lying dead on the surface, stuck inside the yellow sticky substance, it has covered the bodies like a spider's web.

Sadly, there is one man standing dead. Of course he is not decayed a bit, poor thing! We carefully swam forward and finally reached a non-sticky surface. We started walking through the surface to avoid the flower vase things, and thus, we found a circle on the ground. We can see a golden light emitting out of the circle. When she stepped on the circle, she disappeared. I swam into the circle, dropped into a sandy cave directly under the circle, believe it or not, we are not wet. That circle is like a portal to enter this cave structure that has not a single drop of water inside! This is a catacomb to be precise; it has different pathways leading to somewhere. One peculiar thing is the glowing sand around us that keeps emitting golden rays.

Normally, these types of catacombs were built for burying or storing dead bodies, but I can't find any hints regarding this place housing the dead. What we did find are some unpolished lumps of gold and attractive stones. I do remember a time in my life, when I was obsessed with these types of things, where did I drop that obsession? I felt tremendous amount of joy when I found a ten-dollar bill on the ground, but I am not feeling such desires now! Even though billions of dollars' worth items staring at me and nothing restraining me from taking a handful of them, still am not feeling any craving... I guess am over that period of life, the period in which we dream for unlimited wealth to do the unimaginable things in our life. I can't believe am over that kind of thinking!

I mean, what's the point of accumulating unlimited wealth on a planet that houses the unimaginable evils! Rich, not rich, it does not matter. Hell is everywhere! (gasps) Anyway, I must help Riya now, she is trying to find something. She then started to dig the sandy ground with her bare hands. After digging a two feet hole, she ordered me to switch position, I took her post and started digging the same spot. I am getting tired; she is not telling me what is in her mind. We continued digging the hole to almost my height, and finally, we found darkness creeping out of the hole.

Riya jumped into the hole and joined me. We scooped away the remaining brightness around us, fell into a void. There is nothing to see, and we are free falling to somewhere. Finally, we are dropped into the magic water again, but still dark. Again, I asked her the same question about the digging operation, and she angrily replied that she just wanted to escape from the catacomb trap. Umm... Ok... Yes, that was a trap indeed, because we couldn't jump back into the mysterious circular entrance due to the absence of water and a ladder thing. Yes, we tried to pile up the sand to create a mount, but that sand was not friendly, it was like a pile of beads!

Riya is getting furious with my long-standing thoughts, not trying to help find an exit. While running my hands around the walls surrounding us, felt a lever. I pulled it up and bright light rushed into the room. We are inside a room half filled with blue liquid; it is very cold. We have no interest to investigate this, luckily, I found a door on the other side. We slowly walked to it and pulled down the lever to open the door. The door opened slowly but we can't get in because the way is blocked by glowing sand. After a few hours, we managed to dig our way through it. We are back inside the catacombs again!

Riya has become furious; we are also starved and dehydrated. Suddenly, I noticed a strange thing lying on the ground, covered in the glowing sand. I carefully took it out of the ground; it is a rifle! Riya found a grenade covered in sand. Again, I am struck by the mysterious air, started digging the walls this time. Yes, found the thing I was looking for! Can you guys guess what it is? Wait, I will give a hint, if there is a gun there will be this thing also. The answer is Food... We found some plastic containers filled with dry aged food packets. Riya starts opening each packet with the blade fish. Luckily, there are some plastic bottles of water.

We poured the water into the dry food package to revive it somehow, and it succeeded. We filled our stomachs and took some rest before wandering again. Few hours later, I woke up, I am still inside the catacombs. Riya is not lazy like me as she has already uncovered the entire wall. It turns out that the wall is not a wall, but a shelf made of thick melted iron! It has many storage rooms for things human beings need for survival. There are packets of dried food, bottled water, weapons, magazines, gloves, high dose medicine pills ranging from one week to one-year cool down time, ammos, radios and mobiles. Unfortunately, there is no signal!

We are excited about this setup, started to uncover every single sand wall standing mysteriously. We are possessed by a treasure hunt spirit. After some time, we have uncovered thousands of plastic containers and surprisingly found a jar of glowing sand! What! I am not willing to slide this topic away with a quick verdict of stupidity. I opened the jar of sand, dropped my finger into it and took a taste. Salt! It is salt... I ran to Remy's side, she has found something unique, it's a bracelet that has alphabets (gasps)

From then, we started to spend our time lavishly by eating the delicious meals packed by some organisation. I keep wondering what the purpose behind this crazy setup was. Anyway, days passed or I feel like that, because we are unable to recognise day and night now. The glowing sand salt surrounding us interrupts our sleep. We have used large quantity of the sand for seasoning the meat packets. It is quite fascinating to watch how the dried meat comes to life after pouring the bottled water. We have consumed only one wall of food, and there is plenty to feed us. Both of us have become obese, luckily, I am not gifted with good genetics, I will still look thinner even if I eat the world.

Things are not in favour of Riya; she has become very obese. We are now confronted with the dangerous question, is it necessary to escape this place? She looks confident, she doesn't even want to move! I have no other choice than to agree her because there isn't a way to escape this structure. After a few more days, I guess, both of us are getting fatter than ever. To add insult to injury, we have dug out jars of wine, chocolate flavour. We consumed several jars of it and enjoyed peaceful sleep. Days went by, we are relying only on the sweet wine jars since we found them.

Again, Riya is getting very obese to the point that she can't move freely. Her legs are getting swollen and darker, small dark patches here and there around her face, and I know where she is going with these symptoms. Sparks of memory blasted into my memory. One of my friend's fathers died from this, I mean, he was fond of sweets, ate them joyously. His family let him eat them because it was one of the few events that made him a bit happy. No, I am not saying that my friend's father was pathetic! He was a government employee, and had to work six days per week, had to put all his life into his job, he once mentioned that he couldn't take a day off because of his evil superior officer.

He was forced to find happiness in those little things, and they didn't want to spoil his small happy moments, eventually, he turned into 'one sweet sack' collectively known as diabetic! He became obese, didn't have time to hit some cardio either, His feet became swollen and burst, infected... Surgery, amputation, kidney fail blah blah blah! Sorry guys, I am getting frustrated. My point is, health is wealth! I have decided to ask her one sarcastic question. She became angry with my mocking question, "Did you swallow the red vial!" Luckily, my mockery helped her to recollect her dreams of beating the mighty leader.

XIX

Tiny toads Dance

We have restarted our search to find an escape and reached near the end of the catacombs. There is the water circle above us, but don't know how to jump up there. I have an idea to stack up the food containers to form a makeshift stairway leading to hell... Sorry, I got carried away. We have started digging the walls to unravel the food boxes, but surprisingly, Riya found a red switch on the wall, she pressed it, suddenly, a hidden podium started to rise. Few minutes after, the podium sealed the circle opening but, after some seconds, it started to descend. One of us must run onto the podium after hitting the switch, obviously, I hit the switch and ran fast onto the podium, and it took us back into the magic water ocean. Luckily, we found another turtle shell near the reef, can see many shell-fish shells there, strangely, they all look very big! Even though I wanted to use the broken sea urchin shell, Riya opposed my idea...

Night has arrived; we have decided not to travel at night. We slept inside the turtle shell placed upside down. The whole area has transformed into a blank canvas except one small spot. Something is glowing down there, and we went down to check, found one narrow cylindrical bazooka thing stabbed into one iron hinge, the middle section of this thing is the glowing part. Dark violet and black colour liquid mixed with white strips are floating inside the middle part. I do remember seeing something like this cylinder...

yes, it was at the wintery forest, guess I forgot to tell you guys, sorry! The part where this cylinder is connected, extends to one large metal structure, which I can't see but feel. Must wait for morning to analyse it further...

Morning has arrived, resumed my investigation of the cylindrical bazooka thing, where is it plugged into. It is a submarine, but of course dilapidated and rusty. Can't open the jammed door! Riya is not interested in analysing it further; we resumed our swimming journey...

Finally, we have arrived at one of the most dangerous looking areas, am literally shaking. The ground disappeared, darkness staring at us. There is no other way to escape this horrible stare. My curious mind has started playing with me by invoking wild fantasies of mythical creatures lurking in the darkness. Riya calms my nerves, we started to swim forward, but the horrible darkness keeps dragging us into the depths. All I can remember is me getting whirlwind-ed into the hellish depths. I am feeling weightless, can see the mighty teeth of a sea monster ready to swallow me! Lost my mind...

(Whining noises)

(Wolves howling) Hmm... Where am I? What is this place? A truck! Oh, I see what's happening. I woke up inside one of my minds within a mind play, how fascinating. But how is this even possible! I mean, I was killed by that giant sea monster, how am I still able to play with my dead mind? Does mind not die or something? Anyway, I went out of the truck and realised that the truck is parked near a cliff. Memories of me being a truck driver rushed into my mind within my mind. I walked to the backside of the truck, but the door is locked with a password. I searched the driver's cabin, found a map and some instructions written on it.

Mission APCL

Key: 6081

Do not open the cargo storage!

Avoid going through rough roads

Never park the vehicle under sunlight for too long

Avoid going above 80 km/hr

Don't drive continuously as it can build up engine and fraction heat

Reach the port before 15:00 Monday

Best Regards

I have decided to type the passcode. Yes, I know it is dangerous to do so, and they must be spying me with hidden dirty angled camera. I mean, the world is getting infested with these cameras, so why not? But maybe they are not that creepy. You see, as the power increases, monitoring decreases. With power, they built structures of fear inside people's minds. I have decided to open the door because I am just a mind hologram, types the passcode, heard a crack sound. The door is opened slightly! I jumped inside, and it is filled with stacks of bazookas... Oh yes, I found one of these on the top of the mechanical submarine underwater.

In the corner, I found one heavy duty top loading washing machine, it is light weighted. To study it further, I took it out of the truck and placed it on the ground, out of nowhere, four sharp pillars shot from its bottom, drilled its way into the earth. There are three buttons on its body: Fire, Abort, Detach. I clicked the fire button, nothing happened! Just kidding guys, I went inside the truck and took one of the bazooka things, slowly made my way back to the machine, opened its mouth, pushed the bazooka deep... Yes, I know what I am doing, it is dangerous to launch this thing. Anyway, I pressed the fire button, expecting a fireworks show.

A timer has activated and started to count down from thirty seconds. My good instincts are screaming inside me to press the abort button, meanwhile, my bad instincts are cheering me to take a deep breath, relax and enjoy the upcoming show. Looks like the flow of time has slowed down, twenty seconds remaining, I am experiencing a break-down inside my mind to press abort, but still, I controlled myself. Ten seconds left, my mind has started to show brutal scenes of war from the movies I watched in the past. Surprisingly, this is the first time am finding out that I used to watch films in my past. Ok, let me clarify that, ever since I lost my memories, I received the opportunity to travel back to the mind-line to re-experience them, but it was my middle-aged self, inside my young body...

(Boom!) The timer has expired! The bazooka was shot into the sky and exploded right away; it is raining down things shaped like a tarot card. It is night, can't see clearly. I put the washing machine thing back into the truck, went inside the driver cabin, took some rest till the sun returned for its next shift! After contemplating on my sad and pity life for hours, the sun started to spread its lovely blessings. The screen next to the steering wheel shows it is Monday, and it means that I must get to the port before 15:00. I slowly drove my way down the steep curved mountain roads. Luckily, the truck screen offered me commands about the directions I should follow.

By maintaining the required speed and other suggestions, finally reached the port thirty minutes before the deadline. There is one red colour parking spot reserved for my vehicle, labelled as APCL. I don't know why, but the red colour always gets me troubled with bad thoughts. I went to the nearby food stall, surprisingly, the shop owner greeted me by calling my name! That is... Larry, yes. Even I am confused. "What's up, man? How are you?" I asked him, but he just grinned at me and went back to his bread making business. Defeated! I went outside but noticed the TV on the wall showing the shocking incident that happened last night.

"Strange virus spreads around the nayvun valley this morning, traffic through this route has been strictly prohibited till an announcement is made"

Oh! It's the valley that I spent last night, maybe I have caught the virus too. The media evils started to show images of brutality; most of the victims have turned into a burned-up image, and no one is approaching them to give treatment. "Let them rot and die there while we watch you suffer, enjoying a chocolate dipped donut!" This should be the channel's motto. Why do they show this stuff if they can't help them, they must be enjoying the scenes from a distance. I mean, that place is already locked down by the authority, and has spread vital instructions regarding the hazard, then why? One live death tracker is in the corner of the screen, and it has just hit the four-digit mark. The time has hit 15:10, and I ran back to the truck, but it's not there.

I found the truck near one big ship, and it is in a line of trucks to enter the big ship. There are no securities or any scanners nearby, the trucks are slowly entering the ship. I have decided to enter the truck, sneaked my way behind it, typed the passcode, and entered the truck's cargo container. It is amazing how fearless these power holders are, they don't need any type of protection. I can feel the truck climbing the steep bridge between the ship and the port. The truck's container is filled with a dark violet glow, emitting from the stack of bazookas, and it is very scary to watch the creepy movements happening inside the bazooka thing as it has an uncovered middle section.

It looks like a dark aquarium filled with an entire civilization of tiny toads, and they are dancing around happily. I took a short nap, woke up to the loud thud sound of the doors opening. One man entered the truck, he completely ignored my presence, starts unloading the washing machines and the bazookas. After some time, he left me, I slowly climbed down the truck. I am now in an island! There is a crowd of people standing, I joined them. All of them look scared, no speaking. An angry guard is approaching us, and he looks horrible. He is holding a sharp spear and looks very strong.

Within a few minutes, he dispersed the crowd by assigning groups of people to different areas, by pointing his sharp spear. No one dared to question him, and my group is assigned to the kitchen! And there is one big pantry awaiting us, full of every food item available on earth, and not available on earth. There aren't any guards controlling the building, but still we have started to prepare various dishes. I am confused why are they being so dedicated to work here. I have taken the task of finishing the dishes with different food sprinklers, have perfected at least five hundred dishes, and then an alarm went off.

My group leaves the kitchen and gets inside the tiny cottages next to the kitchen building. I went out of the building to see a spacecraft landing on the island, and it starts picking up the stack of bazookas, many more in number compared to the small stack that was in the truck I drove. I keep thinking about where is the invisible wall that blocked me from dangerous scenes, it must have left me. Suddenly, I noticed several carts of food slowly pushed to somewhere. I followed them, a sign board caught my attention! 'IEEOIO'. Name of this island? I am excited. Well, I forgot to mention that I have found one of the special maps when I searched my pockets. In the map, this island has a T-rex mark. One of them is here! Finally, the food carts have entered a stadium. I can't see what is lurking inside the stadium, and the man holding the spear is standing beside the open entrance, made me reconsider my decision to enter the stadium. But still, I can see the top of his head, he has long golden hair.

Sounds of violent chewing and crunching has started to fill the entire Island. Unfortunately, this noise has made us vulnerable to hungry pirates, they are coming. I sprinted back into the kitchen, guess they won't ransack the kitchen, they are after gold and silver, not after the real valuable things! The hungry pirate ships charged into the island. An alarm went off. The pirates have jumped out of their ship, armed with swords and pistols... No, I have mistaken them, sorry. They are holding advanced weapons! We are always fond of stereotyping others.

The mighty man holding the spear charged into the pirate gang, he managed to kill several pirates before getting cut from every angle. He succumbed to his victorious death! "The Pirates of the Northeast, hereby make known that this island now belongs to us, and all of you must worship us" said one of the pirates. They have started celebrating... What? Have they any idea about... One big sword, at least hundred metres long, made of marble stone, hit the shore where the pirates were dancing and drinking.

I couldn't see the impact due to the mighty shockwave. Suddenly, people started to group up and walked to the giant sword, they slowly lifted it. With ten thousand hands working on it, finally, they picked it up. They slowly carried the sword to the stadium, one giant hand slipped out of the stadium, the hand looks like two lengthy and sturdy stones connected by a golden lever, except its fleshy palm, picked up the sword and took it back inside the stadium. The group has started to cheer.

I am standing confused but now there is an opportunity to enter the stadium because, the spear man has died! I went closer to the entrance, hid behind the wall, and started taking careful peeks at the thing inside there. (Whining noises)

"Get up Man! Get up! I woke up to find that I am resting in the upside-down turtle shell, and Riya is still hurting me to wake me up. It occurred to me that she is taking advantage of my silent body that still has the drum beating inside, but does it have any relevance really? I mean, she is squeezing my muscles very hard, and her hands just shifted to below my waist. I jerked up quickly; she stopped her search and enquired me what happened. She explained that, during my unconscious time, I was blabbering about ghosts and monsters, and my eyes were moving to all directions. Riya has happy news to share!

Riya is happy that she has found an exit. We swam to the exit while covering ourselves with the turtle shell. I am not sure if this small opening can help us escape into the outer world, but it is the dead end, we swam into the opening!

XX

Go big or go Home

We swam out of the small surface of water, and the turtle shell is still with us. We are inside the forest, but there are no trees but tall grass that look like trees, thick and sturdy. Riya is bleeding from her hands; she wrapped the grass around her wounds. We dropped the turtle shell and walked forward. After walking a mile through the overgrown grass, our bodies are covered in green slime and fragments of rainbow-coloured metals. Suddenly, we are stopped by one weird looking panda thing! Size of an adult dog, has tiny hands and legs, looks cute with its cat like face. It is staring at us aggressively, and sure it is not friendly. We are waiting patiently for its first move!

After some time, it breathed in all the nearby air, turned himself a giant balloon that has the size of a bull, jumped up to the sky and fell onto my body. I fell to the ground, and it kept bouncing on my body for a few minutes. To be honest, I didn't experience any pain because it has little weight, but what is a bit concerning is its constant dipping of itself into the surroundings, and with all those debris collected from the ground, it then paints us with that. I have started to experience itchiness and blister formation on my skin. Remy is enjoying the scene, but she has also noticed the danger it is doing. Plus, it has started to hit me with its tiny hands, feels like getting a massage! After covering me with all that dirt, it changed its focus to Remy, she escaped its jump, but soon it caught her.

She is covering her face; I pushed it away. Remy got up and took some of the piercing fishes out of her pocket, handed me one. The balloon thing returned, and threw itself over me again, but when it landed on top of me, I held the fish on top of my chest, and the thing landed on the fish, drops of blood splashed all over my chest, and it has disappeared. We went back to take the turtle shell, held it on top of us and resumed walking. The shell has the length enough to reach our waistline. I am standing in the front, can see through two tiny holes on the shell, and am giving instructions to her about the path. Our new transformation has helped us scare away many strange animals roaming around the place.

We are in the range of an active volcano, and I can hear its boiling sound. We have decided to move away from its range, but it has erupted quickly, unleashing a trail of light blue coloured liquid all over the plains. But the strange thing is that the volcano didn't blast out its contents but, simply poured it out. We dropped the turtle shell upside down on the ground and climbed inside it to escape the boiling liquid flowing through the plains. The blue liquid has very strong chemical smell, and it is not that thick like the orange lava cream thing. I have noticed that the blue liquid surfed around the grass trees, through the path between the overgrown grass fields. We rolled our shell back and picked it up again, went through the grass to avoid the chemical contents.

We rammed ourselves through the grass using the turtle shell. Now that we have some relief, I started to check the turtle shell closely, found fingernail markings and thick blood stains on it. Anyway, few hours passed, and we are getting starved. With no option left, we have decided to eat the grass enveloping us. Surprisingly, these things look attractive and delicious, have thick stem, strong green colour, and am sure that there is a mystery liquid rattling inside of it. I picked one after good effort, and shared it, tasted like aloe vera, but has some intoxicating properties. We are unable to walk any longer, again dropped the turtle shell upside down, laid inside for a couple of hours sleep.

(Whining noises)

When I woke up after some time, I am inside a ship! What the! That story didn't end? Come on Brain, have mercy on me! Ok, whatever, I will just play along with you... Anyway, I am inside a cabin, can see the roaring ocean outside the window. Strange, I must say, I am on a royal bed, that has golden colour bedsheet and pillows. After racing my eyes throughout the room, found some portraits of people having that eyepatch badge of pirates hanging on the wooden wall, a rack of swords and pistols, chests of gold coins, a chandelier adorned with scallop shells, and finally a feasting table full of boiled meat and fresh fruits with the clichéd deer horn candle standing in the middle of it. The ocean water keeps splashing the windows, and in the next moment, someone entered the cabin.

It is a woman, she is young and is wearing a golden coat, she looks pretty and scary at the same time! She greeted me warmly, introduced herself as the captain of this ship; Brute, and she explained to me that they have rescued me. I am wearing a life jacket, and she mentioned that I was floating above the ocean water when they found me. The mermaid woman, oh I forgot her name, she must have put the jacket on me. What is more confusing to me is the captain's statement about me being their slave till I repay them with thanks points. Ok, I didn't get it right first, what she meant is that she wants me to help her crew and show my gratitude for rescuing me. I have agreed happily, what else should I do in the middle of a rumbling ocean! She admits herself that she is one debut captain, and she needs help with the map.

She added that she was an orphan and was kidnapped by a prostitute company, when she was a child. After many years, she found her way out and successfully killed the original captain of this ship and put her name on his ship. It came to my notice that she wants my help as she knows that I am a lighthouse expert, and she has the big map that my original self has. She wants me to show one luxury area for plundering, and after searching the map, I have found a GTM leader camping miles away from us, and strangely, he is located at the middle of the ocean.

Me: 'Tell me about the firepower this ship has'

Captain: 'We have eighty cannons, ten mortars, three hundred barrels of gunpowder and oil, hundred and fifty plus pistols and shotguns, thousands of swords etc.'

Me: 'That's not enough! We must visit the blacksmith shop quickly'

Captain: 'How dare you shame my ship! What kind of prize are you referring to? Is it worth the ammunition?'

Me: 'You can have this entire ocean to your name; that's the prize I am talking about! I hope there won't be any invisible wall around it'

Captain: 'You crazy or something?'

(Goes out and gives command to her crew)

Captain: 'Ok, we are heading to the blacksmith shop, be quick with your plan!'

I don't know what is happening inside my mind within my mind, yes, I have a second mind, and it is devoid of fear. I just want to lead a battle against one of the powerful beings on earth, with the power of one hundred plus cannon balls. The ship has reached the shore; the captain has started to equip the ship with the mighty upgrades that I suggested her. Meanwhile, I have started wandering the shore, which is the same place I was dropped in every month. I started to search for my family, went to the building Susan took me the last time I visited her, before the destruction of the lighthouse. There is me standing with Susan and my kids, but it is not actually me! See, I am seeing a man who looks like me, but he has the original Larry's face, he is staying with my wife and kids, caressing them.

I am not feeling jealous, am way over such stuff now! I went inside a saloon, looked in the mirror. Yep! It is not me; I am someone else. I am wearing a new face, different from the one that the authority planted over my face during my terrorist activities. I went out and started to spy on me and my family, some tragedy has befallen them, a group of soldiers came out from a jeep and arrested me, not me, the other me. Oh, this might be confusing to you guys, from now on, I will be calling this other me as 'Y', the soldiers arrested Y and threw him into the back seat. Susan is crying hard, and she is running after the vehicle, she fell to the ground, tired. I walked up to her and introduced myself as Y's friend.

Susan has accepted my lie; we went to the police station in Y's truck. Susan explained that Y's arrest is because of his involvement in the lighthouse destruction, and he will be sentenced to death if they fail to pay the ransom of five hundred thousand dollars. When we entered the station, the officers offered me their gratitude, and addressed me as 'Sir', I am surprised and suspicious. They called me Bobby, offered salutes, they are eager to hear my commands. I gave them orders for patrolling the children's park, and they all went out immediately. In the meantime, I have unlocked Y and made him reunite with Susan. It is me staring at me moment, a once in a lifetime moment for sure! Y might be thinking that I am trying to win his wife or something.

I have decided to enter the station locker room, looted all the valuable items in there labelled as evidence. It must be worth a lot of money, gifted all of it to Y and Susan, offered my wishes and sent them away in a good-condition car that was parked outside the station building. But they don't want to leave without me, and in the next minute, I am inside the car. Before leaving the station premises, we stole every piece of guns, grenades and explosives from the station and went straight to the harbour. Ship 'Brute' has grown bigger and sturdy with the new upgrades, and we all went inside it, made sail to our target. Y has the fire still burning in him, and he is ready to risk anything for our upcoming fight.

After sailing for some time, blood treasures started to pop up here and there. Ok, let me elaborate that, the sea is full of wooden chests, barrels of wine, dead half-eaten human bodies, and numerous gems and gold coins! Yes, I know these gems have no ability to float around, but I don't know, you must believe what you see with your eyes, right? We caught every chest floating around, and they are filled with pearls and rubies, along with ancient monuments and most importantly fine aged rum. We are slowly becoming the richest people on earth, may be. Anyway, skeletons of broken ships greeted us warmly. The prize that awaits us, the island, there it is, make sail fellas!

We can see something huge sleeping there, shot all cannons at once, it is nothing but a mountain! We roamed around the island with our massive warship but can't find him anywhere. With fire burning in our hearts and with a crew that lives by the proverb 'Go Big or Go Home' raging up every second, we landed on the island, armed with multiple weapons. Me, Y, Susan and the Captain led the crew from the front. The island is full of trees and has many herbivorous animals. And the most interesting thing is that there are precious gems and stones scattered across the sand. He is nowhere to be found, but Susan heard someone snoring inside a cave near the mountain there.

We all surrounded the cave and started throwing explosives into the cave, in a moment, one big man having the size of a bear came out. He is bleeding and is missing one arm. He looks surrendered, but we don't want to give him mercy. All of us fired every round of bullets into his massive body, and he fell to the ground, formed a massive pool of blood. We started celebrating, cooked food, took every treasure back into the ship, the captain planted the Ship's flag on top of the dead leader's body. We have officially become super rich, went happily to our native place. Y and Susan invited me to their house, and we happily lived after... What an exciting story! What do you guys really think about that story? Boring, right? Why are we always fond of bad things? Why can't we just enjoy the small happy moments in our lives that always slide away unnoticed? urghhhh...

I am sorry guys, I am still resting inside the captain's cabin, and I am still looking like the original me, the 'me me'. The ship will soon reach the blacksmith port, as the captain mentioned earlier. Once again, I am sorry guys! I believe every human being does that, imagining their life in the most beautiful way; winning every task laid in front of them, taking care of the helpless ones, spreading love and hero vibes, getting the things we always wanted— We can achieve everything inside our mind, and I just wanted that. The fun fact is that I was dreaming inside my mind within a mind! Finally, we have arrived at the destined port. The captain assigned me to have a talk with the harbour master.

Him: 'This ship is already equipped with the firepower required to destroy any ship out there; did I miss something?'

Me: 'No, sir. This is not about defeating ships, we are going to fight an abomination, get it?'

Him: 'I need to speak with your Captain, mister Genius'

Me: 'Hey, look here man, I am tired of your (beep) don't speak to me like I am stupid. just imagine if one big mountain came to life, grown arms and legs, and started attacking our ship, I am talking about that, get me?'

Him: 'Sir, please sit down for a moment'

I sat on a metal box casually, waited for the man's return. He is talking with the captain, he returned quickly. His response was "Have all these punks gone mad!". Anyway, the works will take about two to three hours to finish, I retreated to my cabin and took a small nap... (Whining noises) Yes, I woke up inside the turtle shell, Remy is already shaking my body to wake me up, and we resumed our grass journey.

XXI

Greed is never Good

After a few hours, we have finally reached the end of the grass trees, and in front of us is one deserted wasteland! Yes, I know I have been using the term 'Wasteland' very often, but this is one perfect use of the term for sure. What lies in front of us is a vast land that has dark sand and cracks all over it, no form of vegetation. We continued our journey with our big old shell friend, moved carefully. With each step, dark green liquid keeps bursting out of the cracks on the ground. Within a few minutes, our legs are covered in that liquid, we couldn't do anything to avoid it. In a minute, my feet have turned sturdy as a rock but still can feel them and feels no pain. After walking a few more miles, finally we saw something other than the wasteland thing.

Sorry if I have made you a little bit more excited, it is nothing but a big lump of mud! Don't judge me fast... It has hammer head horns! And made only slight movements. We walked slowly, but the thing started moving left and right, blocking our way. In a fraction of a second, it charged at us, we tried to block its hit by lowering the turtle shell. (Boom!) The turtle shell has broken down to pieces. I am lying flat on the ground; Remy is near me. I can feel pain all around my body, raised myself up on one elbow, can see the thing standing in distance. It is really a piece of mud having four stony legs and an unpolished tombstone shaped head on top of its neck.

It is ready to charge again, but for some reason, is still waiting. Remy has started to get back to her feet slowly, and the thing broke its calm nerve, charged at her. Remy starts running around; her parkour skills have indeed come to the rescue. After running some time, she learned the drill, laid herself flat on the ground. As expected, the thing made its stop and started its observation again. She advised me to crawl along, and we did crawl some distance, but the filthy liquid popping out of the ground cracks hit us hard. My hands turned sturdy as a rock after getting dipped in the liquid, made it easy for crawling. My hands have turned into dark grey colour and very heavy. The mud animal followed us along, and now it has company of its friends, watching us from a distance.

Our crawling journey came to an end after one of the small volcanoes has erupted, its contents charged at us. With no choice left, we got up and ran fast as we could, the mud things are after us, and we ran into a land full of small volcanoes. The volcanoes are spitting out their contents slowly! We ran through them, and after some time, Remy stopped her run, she starts taking control of her breathing. I thought she was giving up, but I keep running because I have my biggest mission to compete. Finally, my respiratory system has failed and put an end to my run. I kneeled and started taking heavy breaths while staring at the boiling liquid at my feet that now has the colour of a rainbow.

I turned back to see what happened, was expecting the tombstone headers to hit me straight into another dimension. Surprisingly, they are nowhere near me, and Remy is casually walking towards me. "I guess they don't like walking through this slime" she said. Our legs have already turned into rocks, and thus, there is no problem walking here. I am surprised to see such small volcanoes; they are only the size of a manhole! Again, my curious mind made me investigate further, found that they are not nature's creation but, sturdy metal pipes. Not surprised! Anyway, we walked forward and entered a field of strange plants. These plants are two feet long, blue colour stem with yellowish leaves shaped like a human hand.

Thin stem with some kind of glowing thing moving inside. And finally, the fruit they produced is one can-shaped orange colour thing, which is squishy and smells like gasoline. Remy wants me to take a bite of it but am not ready for that. Instead, I picked one and threw it to the distant muddy terrains, resting peacefully. It exploded on impact, a huge blast is heard, dark foamy liquid blasted into the sky and slowly rained down. The strong disturbing smell made us vomit and cough hard. Huge blisters started to form on our skin, and they popped immediately.

We laid on the muddy field, crawled our way through the terrain that is making a strange sound, and the surface is boiling somehow, so we changed our path and moved into the plant's neighbourhood. The plants have sturdy roots and small prickles here and there. Suddenly, one big splash of water hit my face, water filled my nose, mouth and ears, tasted bitter and salty, but has no colour, luckily. Remy is stunned; she thought that maybe the splash was from the squishy evil fruit hanging above us. I am not convinced by that thought. In less than a minute, another splash came. Remy's face this time, we raised our heads up and observed the place, nothing suspicious, there is only the pity looking terrain, and a mountain.

We moved slowly, but the water balls keep beating our face, and we lost our balance eventually. There is no way to counter them, stuck in the middle of a deserted land with two feet long plants for cover, is not a good place to be in. The water balls keep hitting us no matter how many sneaky techniques we used. What is more irritating is that they keep hitting my head, and soon, I lost my consciousness. (Whining noises) When I woke up, I have become excited. Captain did notice my excitement; she is not feeling the same! Even though, I have some imaginary expectations regarding the target, I haven't found any hints connecting my expectations.

There are no ships, no islands, not even a scrap of wood floating anywhere near our ship, and we are, according to the map, getting closer to our target. Captain is sweating heavily. Finally, we found a massive island, technically speaking, it is not an island, but one big wooden platform, floating casually on the water, filled with sand

and has trees standing on it. There are some people standing on it, they are cooking food, can see the pile of all fishes waiting to get cooked. Our ship is surrounded by hungry crocodiles, and they have started to hit the ship hard. Still, no sign of our target. With less patience left, I took one pistol from the weapon box and fired at the sky.

Yes, we finally caught his attention, the wooden island started rocking fast, a giant figure emerged from the ground, maybe he was sleeping, he stands tall among the trees with a happy smile blossomed on his face. Captain takes a few steps back and she looks stuck. Meanwhile, I am observing the physical features of our prize. He is almost tall as an elephant, cream coloured skin, has glazing blue shells covering his arms, chest, and neck. Below waist, he is not human. Yes, he has one, two... eight Octopus tentacles as his legs, covered in seaweed. He is wearing a helmet made of huge sea urchin shell, and it suits him well with the black pearl necklace pridefully hanging around his neck. But I must tell you guys, he looks very cute, the sharp eyebrows, light blue eyes with thick eyelashes, flawless skin with blood red lips, might be real blood, who knows!

Now I am wondering what he is waiting for, and why are we waiting for? I mean, I have observed him for at least ten minutes, it is time for the action! Who will make the first move? That is the question now. He looks very thrilled and is waving at us to bring him what we prepared for him. Our captain looks like a piece of ice, she gave me a pity look, which I don't know how to translate. I walked to her and advised her to command the mortars, but her response was not what I expected "You crazy son of... (beep sound) ... Get us out of here you... (more beep sounds) ..." she said fiercely. Why is she yelling at me? What did I do? This is what she asked for. She fainted! I have taken control of the ship now.

: "MORTARS READY... FIRE IN 3,2,1...FIREEEEE"

Twenty mortar shells fired into the sky, can see the flames encircling each volley, the shells grouped up above the enemy's wooden platform, and went down fast, followed by one shocking turn of event, it was a spectacular scene to watch for sure. He jumped up high and collected every single one of the shots in mid-air, threw them all into the seawater. Surprisingly, he intentionally missed our ship, those shots could have easily turned our ship obsolete. The slow mortar shells are to be blamed here, I guess.

: "BRAVE WARRIORS, LOAD EVERY BROADSIDE CANNON WITH MORE POWDER... AIM AT HIM... FIRE IN 3 2 ONE FIREEEEE"

In the next moment, three cluster of burning cannon balls, crashed into the target, and he had less time to react. Our shots hit every single piece of obstacles inside the wooden island. The cooking pots scattered to pieces, the pile of sea creatures splashed back into the sea, the proud trees dropped dead, and they are on fire, sand mountains levelled, but the wooden platform survived somehow. Ok, I know I am going away from the matter, he looks angry, sadly, the cannon fireballs could not penetrate his thick shell skin but destroyed his fancy sea urchin helmet, and he is bleeding from his nose slightly.

: "RELOA..."

He took one big jump and landed on our ship, almost slamming us down into the blue hell. There is one giant man standing in front of us now, and we can't shoot inside the ship. There is no escape, with crocodiles circling the ship and the beast standing in front, it is sure that we will die soon. As a last resort move, the crew has gathered with swords and pistols, started attacking the beast. Now that he is facing away from me, I can see his back, full of spikes, and on each of the spikes, human skulls are placed, decorations to show his devilish attitude. He picked up some of our crew members, including me and then jumped back to his wooden island, but he applied more force during that jump, and the ship crumbled into two pieces, giving a feast to the hungry crocodiles.

He then dropped us on the island, and returned to his usual business, sleep. I am sad that our Captain was not one of the Beast's picks! Anyway, the crew started to rearrange the injured island like it is their home. What else to do by them? They don't have families to look after, just some free souls. I am not interested in rebuilding this hell, I went to the cooking area, ate a platter of delicious sea food mix, followed by a short nap on the sandy ground to make return to the volcanic place... (Whining noises) Yep, I woke up there. It is night, and luckily, the water balls firing has stopped. Remy mentioned that she was waiting for me to get back to consciousness. We moved slowly through the field, the dark fruits are glowing brightly, can see movements inside them.

We have reached the field's end, can see the mountain clearly. Because of the absence of moon and the glowing fruit, we can't see where we are heading to. Yes, I know we are going to the mountain but am not sure if there were some monsters hiding nearby, and Remy also mentioned the possibility of finding a bear trap nearby. Well, the thing is that it is not just a mountain, but has something going inside it, there is light emitting out of the mountain holes. I think those holes are for ventilation. We moved slowly through the darkness, suddenly, Remy felt something hard standing near her, she walked back to my side. We stayed still for the next few minutes and continued walking more carefully and slowly. Again, we are scared by the hard thing hiding inside the darkness.

Suddenly, I have an epiphany; if we can't see them, they can't. And if they were able to see through darkness, we would be resting in our graves! With my newly gained confidence, felt the hard thing standing in front of us, it is shaped like a chair, a flat rock attached into a solid rectangular box of earth. We walked forward and realised that the whole area is filled with these types of chairs. As we slowly moved our way through these chairs, morning has arrived shortly, and finally we can see where we really are. Yep, it is a field full of chairs made of stone and earth. After an hour, we have managed to find our way through it and reached near the big mountain. It looks like one great mountain wall covering the entire place, climbing it will be challenging.

There are many holes on the mountain, can see colourful fumes coming out of those holes, definitely a dangerous game to play. Riya knows that there will be another way, she is sure that this mountain is not just a massive mud, she points to the helipad constructed near the left-hand side of the mountain. She then proposed a plan to infiltrate the secret mountain thing. Her plan is to enter the structure through one of the ventilation holes, and thus, we started to observe the interval points at which the fumes are expelled out. We then started to climb the mountain, surprised to find cottages on it. Well, not like buildings built on top of earth, but carved into the mountain, and they are covered with slanted concrete walls, decorated with artificial grass and rocks.

The mountain is full of these cottages, people in uniform are sleeping inside some of them, also noticed an open weapon wardrobe inside them. We crawled slowly to the top of the mountain, can see the water cannons placed around the top. The cannons are made of transparent material; they are not firing now. We moved closer to the first ventilation hole; it has the size of a truck wheel and has no coverings luckily! Unfortunately, Riya's calculations failed, the smoke hit her face, she started to shake and vomit violently, grabbed my throat, her muscles enlarged, skin turned to blood red colour. She has grown twice her original size, destroyed the ventilation hole completely with her powerful punch, and dropped into it.

I have decided to follow and assist her! The alarms went off, and with difficulty, I have managed to climb my way down to the surface. It is a laboratory! They have caught her with an electric net, locked us in an empty cage.

XXII

Super villain eating Grass

Few hours passed, they are casually doing their work, some are sleeping on the chairs. Remy has become unconscious and is shaking violently due to the heavy electric supply she ate. With nothing to do and no one to talk to, I have jumpstarted my investigation mind. I can see a lot of computers, mechanical hands doing work, liquids boiling inside beakers... There they are; a pile of the dark squishy fruits that we have seen at the field. Anyway, those things are leaking out heavily, but the crazy part is that each of its drops is slowly flying down to the ground.

There is a stack of missiles sitting in a corner, and they look like the ones I have seen underwater, and inside the wintery forest, I can see the glowing violet colour liquid moving inside the middle part of them. I am getting frustrated; all I can see is these kinds of toxic things! Life has become one big lump of negativity, no happiness, everyone looks worried and depressed, no matter how much they have achieved or won. What is the need to build these toxic things? Just like these materials, we are also making toxicity inside our minds, uhhhh... am getting tired!

But what is that weird clip showing on the plasma Television. It says, "Congratulations ARHE Legends" followed by a few bullet points that I am unable to read. What's more disturbing is the video followed by the stupid bullet points decorated with firecracker animations. The video looks simple, I must explain it in detail (clears throat) It starts with a robbery scene, I must remind you guys that all the characters shown in this clip are animated ones, video of someone raping a woman, video of someone murdering an old man, more clips of horror. Each of the clips is less than a second, and after showing these creepy shorts, it then shows the outer space, with balls here and there. Then shows a group of people wearing a crown, the symbol of power.

They sent a cylindrical thing into a ball. The thing has wings like an angel, and it hits the ball hard, starts sprinkling something out of it in the form of glittering stars. Those stars touch the cartoonish characters and start transforming them. The thirty seconds video clip ends with a "Make it happen" quote. Is that really a cartoon skit? Riya woke up, and after a few minutes, a man wearing multiple badges across his uniform enters the cabin and gives us a salute. "My friends are going to love this feast" he said. What!

The man walked to the corner and pressed one red button, then he took a seat on top of a box and starts watching us like he was watching a movie. Few seconds later, one secret door inside the cage has opened, and came hundreds of zombies, they all look same, terrifying and disgusting. I just don't know what to call these things other than zombies. No, they don't look like the stereotypical zombie image that we often see in video games and creepy movies. Ok, let me describe one for you guys, mmm... As always, he looks like humans, but has four arms, has porcupine spikes on top of his hands, has cannon balls stuck inside his hand, his long-overgrown hair makes it hard to see his face, has no dress but his hair covers the stuff, more importantly, has puffy wings. I can hear their growling noise; they are slowly walking towards us.

Riya has finally decided to take the red vial. She drank it full, transformed into a wild beast, now looks like a mythic monster.

She charged into the mass of zombies and destroyed them within seconds, the entire room has turned into a blood pool, with a pile of flesh in the middle. Beast Riya kept throwing chaos inside the big laboratory until the lab people pumped out some toxic smoke, she grabbed me and blasted the strong concrete ceiling. She jumped out and ran faster through the overgrown grass, while carrying me on her shoulders. She has the speed of at least one hundred kilometres per hour. When I regained my consciousness back, am resting on a sand bed near a small stream. Riya is analysing the map, and she told me to get ready quickly because the red vial only has twelve hours of power duration. She again yanked me up on her shoulder, and continues running...

We have finally arrived at the final step; Riya is still inside the toxic vial effect. She has less than ten hours before the effect wears off, must fight the boss before that happens. There is nothing but a land full of thick green bushes, no trees, no rocks, no mountains. Riya has no time to waste, and we started walking through the bushes. There is no form of life, and it is quite concerning. Walking through the bushes is very intimidating and hard, the ground is full of sturdy roots. We have managed to get past at least a few miles.

Riya is getting nervous; she has only eight hours left. We are done with wandering through these unending bush land, there must be something that we are missing. I have tried to search under the bush roots, but they are very thick. Suddenly, I heard some noises coming from the underground! Riya became furious, she did a thunderous jump, the bush land cracked a little. Out of nowhere, a large spear shot through the bushy ground, hit her thighs. Thanks to the vial's power, the spear was unable to penetrate her flesh. She picked it up; it is one wooden spear with a sharp rock tied to both ends.

Riya did a few more jumps, a big portion of the sturdy ground crashed down. She caught me, we landed on the underground! No, it is not underground, we are surrounded by a flock of people, they look identical, wearing no clothes, instead, they have covered up themselves with brown mud. There is a pile of bodies under Riya's feet, she must have crushed them during her superhero landing. I can see the frightened look on each of their eyes. She produced a big roar; we are alone again! Oh, I forgot to explain where we are exactly, we are not technically undergrounded, we are surrounded by a thousand plus trees, the grass bushes are their leaves.

We walked forward. Remy is getting nervous. As we walked for over an hour, the gap between the trees has increased, but still the sky is not visible. These trees have numerous branches on top of them; it looks like a web of twigs up there. Suddenly, a few big cigarette butts scattered around there caught our attention, each has the size of a log. Remy starts practicing her moves. We walked further, came across a large pool of water, filled with plants and snakes. We walked around it, and found a giant bed, made of sturdy wood, and a leaf mattress.

It is really intimidating to imagine how many branches these trees have on top of them. Remy continued her practice by lifting the fallen trees, she looks confident now. In the meantime, the identical people are roaming around like they are on a mission. They are not responding to my questions. Remy has forgotten how many hours she has, she is busy changing her exercises. From push-ups to punching the ground harder, she is getting more aggressive than ever. Finally, I made her stop and we restarted our venture. I like the natural appearance of everything I have seen inside this forest. I am now excited to see the king of the jungle, his appearance. We walked forward, luckily, these mythical trees hold water inside their flesh, helped us quench our thirst. Suddenly, my eyes caught a mighty chair, on closer observation, found bones, shells, gold medallions sticking out here and there.

Suddenly, I saw an artistic drawing carved on the upper portion of the chair, a giant monster and many worshippers surrounding him. Remy didn't allow me to inspect the chair further; she is getting very nervous. We hasten forward, she carried me on her shoulder for extra weight and to help me relax, she kept punching the air while running. I am enjoying the ride, calmed her a bit with my words. Again, we are stopped by another scene, the colony of those identical people.

But there are no buildings, but numerous furniture scattered around. By furniture, I mean, mud beds, unpolished wooden tables and chairs, vessels and plates made of rocks and logs. There are a lot of children running around, these children alone makeup two-third of the whole population here. Many of the adults are relaxing on the beds. Meanwhile, some of them are cooking meat now, the delicious aroma keeps striking my nostrils. Along with the aroma, one disturbing thought has entered my pesky mind. Can you guys guess what I am brewing inside my mind? Well, I haven't seen any animals roaming around this forest, yet! So, from where these people collect the meat for cooking. If it is from what I think it is from, I am going to lose my good mind.

Finally, they sensed our presence, they are not scared anymore. With smile, they gave us a wooden plate filled with small portions of crushed boneless red meat and a wooden bottle filled with cold water. We ate it all, gave a salute for their heart-warming service. If you are wondering, I am still sitting on Remy's shoulders, can feel her fast-beating heart with my feet. She starts running again... Suddenly, she stopped, I don't know what happened but am sure there is a solid reason. "What happened, dear?" I asked her. "I HEARD THE NOISE OF A CREATURE AGGRESSIVELY EATING, NOT TOO FAR AWAY!" she said in a super villain tone. She put me down, and we slowly walked forward. I can see a glimpse of something big sitting on the ground, a few miles away.

The creature is covered in mud, but has overgrown hair on top of its head, almost covered in leaves and dirt. The most absurd thing is the overgrown tree growing out of its back, which is also covered in thick mud. We can see it making some movements, looks like it is enjoying a feast. Riya advised me to remain silent, meanwhile, she is shaking in fear. She is surprised to see me standing here like I was here for a picnic, she appreciated my bravery, and then I have realised that this is not any mind adventure, I can be killed for real here! I am a little bit scared now. We carefully took each step and has moved closer to it.

We are stymied, Remy is planning something inside her head, meanwhile I am comparing him with Jessica, another GTM member. He is much bigger than Jessica, bigger than a mammoth! His characteristics are mesmerizing: burning red eyes, beautiful grass bushes growing all over his dirt covered skin, metal footwear, no moustache but a long beard covered in mud that resembles an upside down ant tower, a crown made of brown colour bones, two earrings made of fresh fruits, and a necklace adorned with herbal plants also covered with mud, can see mighty veins bulging out of his exposed skin, a Mudman.

The refreshing aroma poured from his herbs necklace filled the premises. Remy started to panic, and she doesn't know how to make the first move, so, I threw a rock at him, it caught his attention. "WHO ARE YOU? WHY INTERRUPT ME?" he asked Remy, I guess he didn't see me. "I Want... Ur Crown... Challenges You... Sir" Remy said somehow. I hid behind a nearby tree, and prayed for Remy to defeat him, even though it feels impossible. The Mudman jumped up, we lost balance and fell to the ground, he saw me but ignored completely. The Mudman waited for Remy to get back to her feet. She charged at him and offered brutal blows with her big fist, he absorbed the blows, he looks hurt.

Finally, Remy became tired and he pushed her away, her non-stop punches have made him lose some of the thick mud plates grabbing onto his body, revealed the black medallion at the end of his herbs necklace. I screamed at Remy to grab the necklace, with no idea left in her mind, she went for the necklace. But he made his second move, with inches away from grabbing the medallion, he caught her and violently shook her, followed my ripping her in half and stomping her deep into the muddy ground, engraved her easily. His bloody eyes then turned at me, I ran as fast as I could, stopped only after draining the last drop of my energy. I don't know how much distance I have covered, but sure that he is nowhere to be found.

XXIII
Two hundred thousand Sin!

Luckily, I found a tree with a hole, drank plenty of water from it, replenished fully. After that, I walked forward, took the map out and realised that there is one river stream connecting my homeland, must get there but don't know how much distance I have to travel. Thoughts of Remy sprang back to my mind, I feel sorry for her fate, it was me who made her pick that dangerous undertaking, otherwise she would have lived happily in that desert. Anyway, I slowly made my way, can hear growling noises and rumbling of footsteps. I quickly turned back; made sure he is not following me. Yeah, why does he want to follow me? I am just like a cat to him. But what is making that irritating noise all over the place, found my answer in the distance. It looks like a farm, but there are no boundaries or cages for the animals, they are roaming freely, and somehow, they are not trying to run away from that area.

When I reached closer to the open farm, have noticed something weird about the whole animals wandering around there, they are abominations! Ok, I will explain further. Chickens with the body of a bull, have horns, four legs and a tail as well. Deer with two heads and thin legs. Big Buffaloes with huge humps on their back. Ducks with long neck. Rabbits with a shell and big horns. And finally, the most mesmerizing thing I have ever seen in my entire life, Zebras with a golden moustache around their faces. That's not the only feature, these Zebras don't have their usual black and white strip style markings on their body, instead, each of these Zebras is adorned with a variety of drawings on their body!

I can see drawings of —a pastoral setting, mountains, sunset scenery, a Zebra drawing, a Car, the Solar system, modern skyscraper, world map, drawing of someone etc. The most beautiful drawing being a family picture of the entire animal kingdom. These Zebras are bigger and aggressive than the normal ones. Anyway, it is clear that there is a mad scientist behind all this nonsense. I made my way through the farm, luckily, the animals don't care about me interrupting their habitat. I must mention that I am relieved of my previous assumption about the source of the meat question I had while inside the identical people colony. Suddenly, the ear sweetening voice of a river stream entered my ear canal. I have become over excited and ran straight, ended up in an open laboratory setup! There are some white coat people walking around the tables. I have entered the open lab premises; they don't care about my presence. I have no interest to watch them experimenting, found a way to exit the table filled area, but my eyes caught a document lying on the table next to me, it has only five pages and has good looking figures. I have decided to investigate the document.

ARHE

Operation Arms: sector 107

Greetings Scientists,

It is hereby makes known to all of you genius people that the purpose of your camp is to develop the V5T11 Serum required for the upcoming experiment. Must ensure that your project is free from any mistake. For trials, visit our honourable GTM King of Sector 107, he will provide you with subjects. For additional support, map of sector 107 with the supply points is given below.

(Special Map of Sector 107)

(Pictures of the honourable King)

(Pictures of People living inside the dense forest)

Without finding any valuable information, I closed the document and slowly walked away from the scene. Yes, there is a river marked in the special map, and I should walk west, but I am in the middle of nowhere and have no compass with me. Unfortunately, my left hand hit one of the beakers filled with smoky liquid, and it scattered all over the ground! The glass shattering sound didn't alert the others, but the uncontrollable smoke blasted out of the ground betrayed me. In a minute, a swarm of scientists gathered around me, and surprisingly, one of the scientists welcomed me. I asked him about the river, and he advised me to walk straight, but before leaving the place, he suggested me to try some of their newly found energy drink.

It is now that I noticed the massive weaponry lying around a tree. I know what kind of mistake I have done! I should have snuck my way out of this place, instead I brought myself into this situation. Again, it is because of my curiosity thing that forced me to interact with these maniacs. Anyway, now I must drink this mysterious blue coloured drink, it definitely looks like a poison thing, and the whole liquid keeps whirl winding around the bottle constantly. They are not enjoying my slow response, their attitude changes completely, one of them takes out a pistol and aims at me. With death staring at me, I drank the liquid slowly, felt like swallowing snow. They started to observe me, after a minute, nothing happened. They returned to their science business, forget my existence there!

I took one sealed bottle of water and sprinted to reach the river stream, and finally it is in reach of my eyes. I started to experience something weird happening inside my body. I fell to the muddy ground and felt excruciating pain streaming all over my body. I can feel my skin getting harder, heartbeat increased rapidly, my whole body is shivering. I can hardly crawl because of the immense weight I can feel in my legs, as if a kettlebell was attached to my feet. I can sense that I will lose my consciousness anytime soon, I crawled slowly with great effort to reach the riverbank. My vision started to get blurry, luckily, I found a Canoe tied to a willow, untied it and rolled myself into it, and with the motion of water, the Canoe moved slowly, flowing to whatever location it loves to go. Finally, I lost my consciousness...

(Whining noises)

I woke up... Oh, what the! Sorry guys, I am again back inside one of my realistic flashback lives! Anyway, what do I have here? Let me check quick, wait! Is it night? Why is it dark? Can't see anything, am I blind? Am I wearing a blindfold? Let me check my face, no blindfold, can feel my eyeballs, where am I? What is going on? Am I stuck in some over smart geek's dimension thing? What! I just heard something, can you please repeat what you just said. "You are inside the artificial programme for developing an artificial world, full of limitless possibilities and happiness" a female robotic voice said. I asked her what I have to do to escape from at least the darkness swallowing me right now.

The voice explained that I must complete the tasks assigned to me to complete the contract. "What tasks?" I asked. In the next second, a digital dialogue box opened in front of me, displayed on an invisible screen. There are some bullet points written inside the dialogue box.

Build a highly facilitated conference room, worth fifty thousand luxury points

Build a mysterious forest, with numerous animals to hunt, worth thirty thousand primitive points

Build one big town, with all desire fulfilling activities, worth two hundred thousand sin points

The list goes on... I don't know what to do, suddenly, my eyes caught attention of some hefty numbers displayed on one side, Luxury (75,000), Primitive (45,000), Sin (250,000), Cosmo (750,000) etc. I have decided to select the first mission because there is nothing else to do. Ok, to build a conference room it is, I need bricks! Out of nowhere, a huge pile of red bricks, more than enough to build the tallest building on earth, appeared in front of me. Now that there is light around me, I am shocked to see my attire, metal wires spiralled around my whole body! Anyway, back to the mission, I have noticed that the luxury points number has lowered down to 64,500. Without further due, I started arranging the bricks to build a large square structure in the middle of the dark canvas, the bricks are interlock designed, but I am frustrated after taking the tenth brick.

"I can't do this! I need more working hands" I said. Suddenly, fifteen hands are attached to my body in a straight line down the shoulders. It is frightening! But I think I have the whole idea behind this, this platform works on voice commands. "Undo last command" I said, all my extra hands have disappeared. For the first time in my life, I am experiencing some form of bliss. I don't know why, maybe because of my newly found power. I mean, this is the kind of power that drives every human being to do brutal things. From now on, I am not going to move a muscle, I will control everything with my powerful voice.

: "MAKE A CONFERENCE HALL WITH THESE BRICKS"

Suddenly, the huge pile of bricks turned themselves into a massive building. But the problem now is, the building is one big dome with no ventilation or windows.

: "INSERT SOME WINDOWS, AIR CONDITIONERS, A BIG ROUND TABLE, FEW CHAIRS, MICROPHONES, LIGHTS"

In a fraction of a second, the brick dome transformed itself into a big hall with the additions ordered by me. The luxury points decreased to 5,000. For the remaining points, I ordered a beautiful garden around the building. Finally, a clink sound is heard! The scenes have shifted away from me, I am now back inside a round chamber full of mirrors, and I am sitting on a pedestal made of sturdy glass. I went out of the chamber, and realised that I am inside a big building that has numerous chambers like the one I was sitting in. Each chamber has the person's name and photo pasted on the door, but my chamber is labelled as Febin's, though it is my photo pasted under the name. Another thing is that each chamber is painted in four colours: Brass, Gold, Silver, Red. My chamber is

Brass.

After wandering around for an hour, I saw a man lying on the floor. I thought he was dead, but he is not, he is crying and cursing himself for signing the contract of some sort. I helped him back to his feet and tried my best to console him with some existential questions and answers. Surprisingly, my trick has worked perfectly, he stopped crying, introduced himself as Vipin. He then started his own unhappy narration, uhh... I am done with listening to these dystopian stories! The world has become a sad story! Anyway, Vipin explained to me that he was a clerk in a private company, was leading a routine life of going to work six days per week, resting on the seventh day. He has a wife and two boys.

Vipin was unhappy with his life; thus, he chose to sign the contract of this madness that I was also signed but have no clue of when that happened. I asked him to talk more about this contract. According to him, this project is some kind of futuristic video game concept, and we are all hired to create the surroundings required for the game. No, I don't believe in his assumption but continued listening. He made sure that today is his seventieth day here, and he wants to quit, but it is not possible. I don't think I have been here for that much period! But my long-grown beard, stache and nails say the opposite. He admits that the sole reason he signed the contract was because of the six-digit payment offered by the company, and now he has no hope of escaping from here to collect his reward.

He mentioned that he has completed a total of twenty-one missions assigned to him, his last missions were —create a new species worth 300,000 Bio points, build an amusement park worth 780,000 Jolly points, create Hell worth 500,000 Crime points and finally build a mansion worth of 25,000,00 Luxury points. It is clear that he received good projects compared to mine, he then went back to his chamber to complete more tasks. There are no guards to control us, it is up to us to decide whether to enter our chambers or not. Anyway, I have decided to take a closer look around my new workplace, and the whole building looks identical, it has hundreds of round chambers and nothing else.

I am wondering about the most obvious thought that would pop up inside anyone's mind, when faced with a situation like I am trapped in. Can you guys guess it? Food! Yes, there aren't any laterals either, but no food closes that matter pretty much easily. I believe am standing outside for at least ten hours now, was observing the photos pasted on each of the chambers, took short naps around, felt unusual hunger, and I am left with no choice other than to enter my chamber. The moment I entered my chamber; my hunger has disappeared. The mind inside my mind! What! (Laughs) After a few minutes, I was transferred into a dark canvas with nothing in sight. Again, I have started my voice command orchestra.

: "SHOW TASK NUMBER TWO!"

The digital dialogue box opens; it shows that I must create a hunting ground worth 45,000 primitive points.

: "MAKE A FOREST WITH TREES, RIVERS, SMALL MOUNTAINS INSIDE IT"

In the next moment, appeared a mighty forest full of identical trees, with an umbrella shaped top. Twenty thousand primitive points are debited from my account. I slowly walked into the forest; this is one beautiful piece of land. The most fun part is that it is easier to describe this artificial power forest, because of its identical speciality. Luckily, the trees have blue colour fruits, and it tasted like a mixed juice made with every fruit available on earth. The computer graphics are excellent; each bite produced a crunchy sound with its juice dripping out into my clothes. I have noticed that every tree, rock, river, grass etc. Looks the same.

The rocks look polished and shiny, there are caves with room for three people, the mountains just have the length of a normal tree, it is fun to climb on top of them. Looking from the top, I can see the entire forest that has a radius of ten miles at least. The treetops look like the trees in the dense forest. Time for the next command.

: "SPAWN SOME GUNS, BOWS, SLINGS ALONG WITH SOME ANIMALS"

What happened next is just mesmerizing to watch, the entire mountain where I am standing has turned into a barracks, no I am not talking about the mountain turning into a giant building, what I meant was that a variety of guns have spawned and are stabbed into the mountain ground, just pick them up and shoot anyone you want. Surprisingly, my command did not spawn any animals! I noticed that my primitive points decreased to ten thousand. I think maybe my use of the umbrella term has confused the computer and my points; thus, I have decided to pinpoint each victim into my newly built platform.

: "SPAWN EQUAL NUMBER OF DEERS, BUFFALOES, BIRDS, ZEBRAS, RABBITS"

And there they are, I have counted five deer with my first stare. Heard a clink sound again, indicating that I have completed the task. My points decreased to two thousand, and then I thought something crazier. Can you guys guess what it is? Well, it is a quite simple trick our mind does when we are given a surplus amount of something, we take it for granted and do something crazier with it, right! I took one rifle out of the ground and said,

: "SPAWN A TIGER"

I am expecting a beasty voice, but there isn't. The primitive points decreased to two hundred, sure that he is here somewhere. I climbed down the mountain, ran through the forest to find my prey. Finally, I found him enjoying a deer he just caught, his face is covered with blood. No, I am not scared. He can't kill me or injure me. I regret my decision to spawn the Buffaloes and the Zebras because they are just enjoying the grassy ground, not fit for the hunting ground. And I think that a hunting ground should be an arena to show one's power, and with numerous weapons scattered across the forest, humans will have a fighting chance with anything put in front of them. I took more guns out of the ground and then made my command.

: "REPLACE ALL ANIMALS INSIDE THIS FOREST WITH CHEETAHS AND PANTHERS"

I can't hear the rage. I climbed the mountain again and observed the forest carefully. Aha! There he is, I have found one bad boy running around looking for something to hunt. There is a battle going on with two of them, and some of them are just casually taking a nap. Suddenly, I saw two eyes staring at me from behind a tree. Even though I am not scared, his aggressive stare sprinkled some fear in my heart, tightened my grip, aimed at him and fired a shot. As expected, I missed! My shot has alarmed every hungry fellow. They have circled me, and it is the scariest image anyone can think of! They slowly advanced towards me, ready to bite their favourite body part off me.

: "ELIMINA AHHHHHHH......

Ahhh... Oh, I am back inside the chamber... That was one brutal experience, I don't want to remember it anymore, please get this memory out of my mind, Computer! COMPUTER!!! Why does it keeps coming back to my mind? I guess I have to suffer more... I have experienced pain from every scratch and bite they made on my hologram body, and because of my invincible condition, I have suffered even more. I went out of the chamber and took a walk, but still, the painful memory keeps kicking back into my head. I kept punching the metal ground to calm myself, laid on the ground helplessly.

(Whining noises)

XXIV
Stand at Ease

I can now see the full moon on the sky, playing with the shiny stars. I can hear the smooth sound of water flowing at a constant pace. Once again, I am back inside my real body! I can only move my eyeballs. Luckily, I am lying in a seated position and can see what lies ahead of me, by slightly lowering my eyeballs. Nothing but one big pool of water. There is no wind, and the water is calmer. Out of nowhere, fishes start jumping over the Canoe like playing a hula-hoop. I am starving hard; wish I was inside the AI chamber thing. Birds are circling me, one of them sat on my chest and started to dig down into my chest meat, but my newly acquired toxic shell armour is no joke, he gave up after his beak broke. He starts crying for his lost and flew away from me along with his fellows.

The Canoe gained some movement from the wind, and after a few hours of staring at the moon, finally my eyes caught some dark structures standing in distance. It is an island (Whining noises) Suddenly, my mind starts shaking, I woke up inside the AI chamber warehouse thing, Vipin is shaking me violently, he thought I was dead. Luckily, he has brought some interesting news regarding the whole situation that I am in. He is freed, he has completed his job, and his bank account is credited with three million dollars. I am shocked to hear the payment info, maybe I can also win that much money. Vipin explained that his contract was for five million points, he revealed a secret trick for completing the contract; just pick the task that has the highest point value!

Vipin is walked out of the building by two guards, the mighty doors are opened, I can see a grove of overgrown bamboo trees spread across the surroundings, sure that this building is placed in the middle of a forest. The doors closed quickly, I went back to my chamber, cleared my mind within my mind, went back to the dark canvas. Luckily, my last task is labelled as successfully completed!

: "SHOW MY CONTRACT"

The dialogue box opens a bright page that has my duplicate name and my own photo placed on top of the page. I am assigned to collect only two million points and will be rewarded with five hundred thousand dollars. I am thrilled but noticed a statement written under the title 'NB', it states that I can't quit myself, and in the case of my death, the company has no responsibility, and no payment will be processed. It looks suspicious, and I feel like a fool for signing a contract like this just for the sake of money! Anyway, I have decided to try my best to stack up my points just for the sake of my family. It is frustrating how much I have to endure myself for my family's well-being!

: "SHOW THE MOST EXPENSIVE TASK, WORTH TWO MILLION POINTS"

The dialogue box opens; it shows a task worth of two million points. The task is to build a paradise land capable of fulfilling every aspect of human mind! Ok, what to do next? What kind of things can fulfil the human mind? My first thought was a pub, and my second thought...

: "SPAWN A MASSIVE PUB AND THE BIGGEST BROTHEL"

In a minute, a beautiful looking pub is standing in front of me, ten times bigger than a cricket stadium. And next to it stands a brothel, twice bigger than a football stadium. I know I am using more sport metaphors; I don't know what to use instead. Quickly, I noticed that there is another column in the corner below the points column, and it is the 'Happy meter', currently at Zero. Anyway, I went inside the Pub, there is no one inside, but has numerous alcohol bottles displayed on the wall shelf. There are red coloured seats and beds everywhere, twenty metal poles for some pretty dancers. Surprisingly, there are trees planted inside, decorated with lights. I poured myself a glass from the finest looking whisky bottle, enjoyed the soft music playing by some hidden speakers inside the ceiling. The blood red ambience is something special, found the love symbol imprinted on every seat.

The pub has many rooms. I just noticed that I have already spent five hundred thousand Happy points! Now it's time to enter men's favourite building, it looks very odd compared to the pub, has a big picture of a lady wearing only innerwear, painted on the top of the building. It is not the only photo there, the windows, doors, carpets, pillars etc. have pornographic images printed on them. Has numerous rooms with a variety of posters pasted on each door. I have no intention to check what is inside the rooms, and left the brothel quickly, for sure this building can house thousands of people. I am worried about what to add next, still have to place some things worth one and a half million points!

: "SPAWN AN AMUSEMENT PARK WITH SKY HIGH TREES, MOUNTAINS, ROLLERCOASTERS ALL AROUND, POOLS... BUGGEE JUMP, RACETRACK... MOVIE THEATRE"

My Happy points went down to one million points, and there is a wide area of amusement, filled with the things I asked the computer boss. I can feel and smell each component it has built within a few seconds of time, by just using some made up points! But the most concerning factor is that my Happy meter is still showing 'Zero'. What? I have created everything that can raise the happiness of any human being, and still I am getting mocked by the board. I am ready to announce my new command.

: "SPAWN A CHURCH, A BAKERY AND A RESTAURANT, SMOOTH ROADS, CAR FACTORY, LABORATORY"

I have two hundred thousand happy points left, and shockingly, I am still left with zero on the happy meter thing. I am confused about myself, feels like I am trapped in this horrible task. I need help from a person, and I guess the computer can give me someone to make a discussion.

: "SPAWN A FRIEND"

A ding sound is heard, indicating that there is someone spawn inside my new world. I went searching for him, kept saying "Hey there!" aloud, but no response received. Anyway, I have decided to explore the new buildings, starting with the amusement park. I walked across the sidewalk, reached the entrance decorated with figures of funny cartoon characters. I can see fat trees, middle sized mountains, racetracks, and most importantly, the rollercoaster that runs all around the massive park. I jumped into the empty rollercoaster thing; it can carry at least a hundred people. The problem now is that there is a need of another person to press the engine start button, which is located far away from the ride.

Each time I pressed the button and ran fast as I could, I failed to enter the ride in time. I can't give up, tried repeatedly, finally jumped into the end section, wrapped the seatbelts around me and grabbed onto a metal bar. Faster than I expected, and it rode around the entire park. Suddenly, I saw a man running outside the park, he looks bewildered for sure. Unfortunately, the rollercoaster has no intention to stop anytime soon. However, the view from the coaster is amazing, I have seen a massive pool of water, variety of other rides, food courts, giant figurines of animals etc. I am enjoying my new world very much, then what's the matter with the happy meter thing? It still shows Zero! Finally, my coaster journey has come to an end.

I went out of the park, started searching for the man, went to the church next, normal-sized, has an odd-looking door that has a variety of decorations, no, this is not some decorations, but a carved portrait of an apocalypse scene. I don't want to ruin my mind by a detailed study of it. Anyway, I have entered the church, dozens of benches and desks welcomed me in, the massive hall is filled with flowers, the sweet smell of newly polished wood struck my nostrils hard. The atmosphere is peaceful; the holy text is placed on a pedestal. Unlit candles stared at me restlessly, and the ceiling is full of different colour glasses that filter out every evil seed from the yellow rays of sun. Surprisingly, there is no statue or any picture of the almighty.

Enough of the spiritual exploration. I went out and walked into the bakery to have some gluttonous refreshments. The bakery is in the shape of a Cocoa bean, and this shape is enough to give me the worst flashbacks possible. (Whining noises) Suddenly, my mind has started to crumble down, and my newly built fortress has disappeared, I am back inside darkness again. I have lost all my progression... No, I haven't! I have just returned to my canoe life, stuck inside a canoe, incapacitated. The moon is nowhere to be found, can hear the rumbling noise of thunderstorm. The canoe is motionless, and the lightnings have started to strike the ground! Suddenly, my eyes caught the sight of one distant land, and with each lightning blast, my eyes received more clarity.

Some of the lightnings have caused the trees of the distant land to burn up and illuminate the place. Now I can see what is in front, it is a jungle and in some miraculous way, the fire has subdued. Some of the lightning bolts hit the water, am shivering hard, closed my eyes tight. (Whining noises) I am back inside the AI world, entered the bakery. Sadly, it is empty! The restaurant is also empty. Though, I must tell you guys that there are ingredients available inside the storeroom to make any delicious meal. Luckily, I haven't felt hunger since I entered the chamber. Suddenly, I noticed a light blinking inside the massive brothel building, not surprised. I went there to see my new friend. The light show is still going on, he is in serious search of something! I went inside the building and started searching for him. He is moving very fast; he keeps opening and closing the doors, while ignoring my manly voice. Finally, he takes some rest on a random sofa.

Me: 'Hello, sir'

Him: 'Larry! What are you doing here my boy? Did you sign the contract? where are those pretty ladies?'

Me: 'Who are you, sir? I don't remember seeing you!'

Him: 'What! You forgot your brother-in-law, how shameful!'

Me: 'Alan? You look like someone else; Do I look the same?'

Him: 'What? You look the same. What happened to my face? Do you have a mirror?'

Me: 'GIVE ME A MIRROR!'

Him: 'Hello... Are you crazy! There is no one...

(I give him the mirror)

Him: 'Oh my! What did they do to me? My face... I look pretty, the best contract I have ever signed, Woo hoo!'

Me: 'Ah, sorry to break the illusion, you will be back to your aged body later, we are inside a computer programme!'

Alan: 'Yeah, whatever... SHOW ME SOME PRETTY LADIES'

Me: 'Oh, they may be out of stock, try something new'

Alan: 'GIVE ME SOME FINE AGED WHISKY'

Me: 'Again, out of stock, I guess, try something new'

Alan: 'Nah, I am good. Let's just study these buildings, there will be some people hiding behind'

Me: 'No need to worry, we are alone here, there is no other person'

Alan: 'What a horrible assumption!' (laughs) 'Let's check'

It occurred to me that there is no point in explaining facts to these kinds of people! No, I was not talking about him alone, there exist numerous people who are themselves volunteered for these kinds of positions. They won't listen to any advice, suggestions, facts, not even universal truths! They just stick with their idiotic beliefs, take everything for granted, even if the thing causes harmful problems to them.

Alan: 'To whom are you blabbering? Come fast, let's check'

Me: 'Yes, coming.... The contract you mentioned, what was it? I signed it blindly, what exactly is our task here?'

Alan: (Laughs) 'Same here, boy, I don't recollect it either, what is the need of that!'

Me: 'What made you sign this contract, Brother?'

Alan: 'Well, I had nothing else to do, that's why, I guess... What about you my boy, Susan dead?

I am getting angry with his disrespectful replies, anyway I have decided to suppress my anger, because there is no way to make these kinds of people good or something, it's a sad and helpless fact that every human being must cooperate with! Suddenly, I have started to experience lack of breath and swelling in my throat, stumbled to the carpet, meanwhile, Alan is still searching for his prizes. My eyes are getting enlarged, ears and nose feel like something has been stuffed inside of it! (Whining noises) Again, I am back to my Canoe life, huge water drops keep pounding down my body, and my open mouth is filled with rainwater, I can feel it's bitter taste but cannot move my lips or close them. I can see my poor flat stomach vibrating.

Luckily, one strong thunder strike did severe damage to the surrounding water, the force caused the Canoe to jerk heavily, and it helped to change my position on the Canoe to a downward dog position on the wooden ground, the plank seat helped my body to get stuck on it, thus, my face was not crushed. Water blasted out of my mouth like opening a dam, I have regained control of my breathing, while stuck on the wooden plank helplessly! Can feel the rapid momentum gained by the Canoe, and within a few minutes, it hit something and stopped moving completely, the impact has caused me to vomit blood. I can't see where the Canoe has taken me because of my blind position, I am just hoping that the Canoe has taken me to my homeland.

After an hour of hanging on the plank, the Whining noises returned. I am back inside the AI playground, the brothel to be precise. Alan is nowhere to be found, and I am exhausted from the traumatic events, went to the Pub. I can see the lights inside the pub; it is very bright in there. As expected, Alan is having his best time with the whiskey's, he has already drunk half of the shelf, he proudly announced his devilish drinking capacity, and he is also worried about emptying the entire stock, started to cry. "I am a failure... I signed this contract especially to meet new people... even though I knew I was entering a computer world... And still... Where are people? I need communication, I need Care, Love..." Alan said, and then stormed out of the room, and he is walking to the brothel, again! I am feeling immense pity for him.

: "ERASE MY FRIEND"

In the next moment, he has disappeared. Ok, wait... Please don't judge me guys, I know I have the power to fulfil his desires, just give me a minute to process something...

: "SPAWN FIVE HUNDRED YOUNG MEN AND WOMEN"

Dust filled gust swallowed me, can hear the commotion, chattering, celebrations. Finally, the gust has decided to take some rest, and now I can see the eyes staring at me, awaiting orders. But what makes them stand there disciplined and await my orders? I have only asked for a crowd. Whatever the reason is, it is always great to see one disciplined crowd. Surprisingly, I can see them really struggling to stand there still, their eyes are trying to move but they can't. I am confused about the crowd I just spawned; are they dummies? Then I thought, maybe they are just showing how much slavish they are because, to be a slave is what they need to do here since they have already abandoned their real appearance.

: "SPAWN A WATCH"

I started the timer and waited one solid hour. But nothing happened, they are still standing and waiting for something to happen. Sure, that they are not dummies, because I touched some of them and even made a small cut on a man, he started bleeding, hot red blood oozed out of the cut. Don't worry guys, I have healed him right after with my power. They are indeed waiting for my orders; I am amazed by my new power. I wish I could live here for the rest of my life. No wonder why those power-hungry maniacs are getting corrupted. Again, I am confused why Alan was able to wander around without my commands, was that because he is my brother-in-law or something? Anyway, I have decided to break the ice.

: "EVERYBODY ATTENTION!"

(Crowd does the action)

: "EVERYBODY STAND-AT-EASE"

(Crowd does the action)

: "EVERYBODY SAY MY NAME OUTLOUD, AND CHEER ME"

(Crowd praises the name Larry)

: "EVERYBODY PERFORM A HANDSTAND!"

(Crowd performs the action, but most of them fall back and forth, resulting in one powerful rumble all around, soon they are back to their normal position)

: "EVERYBODY START BUILDING A SANDCASTLE"

Crowd starts to collect sand, creates massive gusts of sand all around the premises, they have started to build a sandy foundation with the water collected from the Pub's tank. With two thousand hands working on the same structure, the structure keeps expanding fast, but without a captain's guidance, the sand abomination keeps crumbling down. Meanwhile, hundreds of hands are still working on the foundation. Somehow, I am enjoying the scenes, I know for sure that I am doing unethical stuff, but am sure they are signed up for this, and I don't want to become a friendly leader, because it can create more friends for me here, that will result in an increase of power bearers, and that will increase the struggles of these poor people! After an hour of working with the sand, they have managed to build an apartment without a ceiling.

I have ordered them to stop and have decided to assign them various tasks to perform at each building. But the most difficult thing is that how should I assign people to the brothel? To break the ice, I asked them to volunteer themselves for this post first. Surprisingly, a good number of men and women opted for the post, reducing my job pressure. I have noticed that my Happy points went down to less than fifty thousand, and I am not done with my spawning spree! After assigning tasks to all, I went to the Pub to have a drink, sat quietly while enjoying my drink. Quickly, I thought about Alan, asked the computer to re-spawn my friend, Alan. He spawned in front of me, and before I can greet him, he ran out of the building and is again headed to the brothel, I guess. I hope he might find his match there this time.

Finally, I can see movements on the happy meter, now it stands at twenty percent and is constantly changing. I have figured out how this thing works; all I have to do is to make things that will make my friend and other people happy. I keep thinking about what is missing here... Yes, I must change the wasteland like appearance of this place.

: "TRANSFORM THIS DUSTY LAND INTO A MEADOW, FULL OF TREES, PLANTS, STREAMS"

One big dialogue box opened followed by an Err sound. The dialogue box shows that I don't have enough Happy points to make the things I asked for. I must eliminate one or two buildings to create my favourite scenery; I have decided to study each building to find out which is the less crowded place. As expected, the brothel and the pub are shining bright. The Church is filled with women, and when it comes to the bakery and restaurant, I can see some people. But what shocked me is that there is no one inside the amusement park! What? I have spawned a thousand young handsome athletic men and women, and they don't want to enter the park! Maybe AI treats youngsters differently, the only possible explanation I can think.

I went to the Pub to have a drink; the building is overcrowded. Surprisingly, my entry has made a stir among them, most of them left the main sofa, and the debut bartender gave me an eye-catching cocktail. It tastes much better than the one I made before in here myself, can feel my muscles getting frozen and shrunk, it was just a figure of speech, sorry! Anyway, while I am enjoying my cocktail, one pretty woman keeps staring at me, others are minding their business, but this one lady, I don't like her stare. She then gets up and slowly walks towards my seat.

XXV
Live long and Prosper

She didn't hesitate to sit beside me, the crowd became silent, I can see other people looking at us with excitement. The excitement to watch me unleash my full power on her, but I think she is not trying to show off, and if she is, I must teach her a lesson for her disrespecting me, my power.

She: 'Boy, don't you recognise me?'

Me: (Spawns a mirror) 'Here, take a look at this...

She: 'Oh God! Who am I? What happened to me? Am I dead? Is this the afterlife they were lecturing about?'

Me: 'No, you're not dead, technically, who are you?'

She: 'You don't remember your neighbour, son?'

Me: 'Who does really! Don't you just say your face has changed? Why are you asking stupid questions?'

She: 'Sorry dear, don't you remember Delia?'

Me: 'Delia who?'

She: 'Delia, the prostitute living next to your wretched house, don't you know, it is me who helped your wife to get a good career in being a whore'

Me: 'How dare you insult my wife!'

: "TURN THIS DELIA WOMAN INTO A STATUE"

In the next second, a pedestal formed under her feet, and she turned into a structure made of wax. Her face looks scared and in extreme pain. The people inside the pub are in shock, they ran out of the building, screaming in fear.

Me: 'Eat the pain, lady. This is what you get for disrespecting power!'

I can see her eyes producing tears, sure she can hear me. To add more drama into the situation, I have taken a baseball bat from the playing area, slowly walked to statue Delia. Even though I have no plan to hit her with it, I am feeling the need to hit her for some weird reason. I started throwing threats at her, and sure she is not enjoying my wrath. The bartenders, hiding behind the table, stormed out of the building.

Me: 'Stop there! Come and make me a drink or I will...

They returned fast and started to make a cocktail for me with their shaky hands. I am feeling bad about my unhealthy way of ruling.

: "UNDO MY LAST COMMAND"

Delia transforms back to her human form. She checks herself thoroughly.

Delia: 'Sorry Sir, don't hurt me anymore. I will just get back to the brothel'

Me: 'Wait! Tell me what's in your contract, and how did you end up here?'

Delia: 'What contract are you talking about, Sir? I believe I was kidnapped by some people, they took me to somewhere, dropped me into an empty pod like I was a pebble, the pod was full of lights and computer screens, boom! I woke up here with thousands of people'

Me: 'Oh! That's terrible, that's all they did? Just took you out of your house and dropped inside an empty pod thing!'

Delia: 'Yeah, it did hurt, but it's okay, sir, am concerned about them keeping my word'

Me: 'Uhmm... What "word" are you talking about?'

Delia: 'You know, what would one 'eighty-year-old disease packed immobile being' ask for?'

Me: 'You put yourself into this thing, didn't you?'

Delia: 'All I signed was one paycheck of five hundred dollars, and they promised me to free me from my rusty old body, I agreed thinking that it was all a prank of some sort, luckily, it wasn't a prank' (chuckles)

Me: 'Ok, enough talk, now get back to Work!'

Delia walks towards the brothel, and I am once again engaged in my thoughts on transforming my new home. However, I did find the answer to my previous thought, why the amusement park was lonely!

: "ERASE THE AMUSEMENT PARK, SPAWN A MEADOW, WITH TREES, RIVERS, MOUNTAINS'

Wow! The horrible wasteland image of this place is transformed into a beautiful land filled with greenery, puffy trees full of fruits, small mountains. I fell to the grassy land, relaxing and better than any bed. I raised myself up on one elbow and observed my fellow people. I can see more than hundred men and women taking advantage of the beautiful scenery, and what's even great is the eighty percent level gained by the Happy meter. It keeps increasing, I returned to my normal sleeping position, closed my eyes and took deep breaths to enjoy the fresh wind filled with fragrances of different flowers and wood shavings (Whining noises) Suddenly, the refreshing aroma turned into decayed fish smell. I opened my eyes... Yes, that has happened again uhhh... I am back inside my Canoe life, and still no change in my position, stuck on the plank with eyes staring at the wooden bottom of the Canoe, filled with water and dead fishes, the disgusting smell keeps stabbing my nostrils.

It is morning, I can feel my body getting burned up by the Sun. I can hear bird noises. What is worrying me now are the human voices nearby. They are a little far away, not sure how far, but I can hear their voices slightly, sure that they are discussing about my body. Still, I am unable to move a muscle except my eyes, they have started throwing rocks at me. I am getting scared about them burying me alive, but it is very unlikely, right? I mean, why do they care burying me? It is a lot of work, and why waste it on me! After a minute, I can hear one of their footsteps getting closer to me, he jumped into the Canoe, rocking the entire thing, I am feeling like getting ripped in half by the wooden plank with each movement it makes.

The man touched my butt, and I am getting strange thoughts about his intention and his gang's. He is searching all my pockets, basically looting a dead body that is alive! He proudly announced his loot to the gang members; he has taken the map as well! After looting my entire body, he gave me a farewell slap on my back, and it hurt a lot, not to mention my almost ripped stomach. After hanging on it for an hour or so (Whining noises) again, I am back inside the computer world, resting peacefully on the grass. I am filled with rage for the gang that disrespected my body, if I get a chance to meet them here, you people cannot imagine what I will do to them. I have noticed the Happy meter getting up to ninety percent now, I am left with ten thousand Happy points only!

: "MAKE RAIN A REGULAR FRIEND OF THIS PLACE"

Creamy clouds blocked the blue sky and turned into drops of ice-cold water, with each drop splashed onto my AI generated body, I can still feel the smooth effect it offers if I were in my physical form. I can see people celebrating, dancing and singing. The Happy meter finally reached the hundred percent followed by a cling sound. The dialogue box appeared.

"Congrats Larry, congrats for your greatest achievement, your bank account has been credited with five hundred thousand dollars, live long and prosper"

The chamber turned dark, I went out of it and there are four guards waiting outside my chamber. They are wearing fully covered knight helmets, and they escorted me to the outside jungle. After getting me out, the guards retreated into the facility and closed the entrance. I am now stranded in a jungle again! But this jungle is one strange thing, full of red colour bamboo trees with red leaves, and the ground is filled with dried bamboo leaves. I don't know which way to follow, and there are no pathways either. Is this how someone treats a man who did them the greatest good! Anyway, I roamed around the jungle like a ghost, I am getting frustrated with the walking, and to ease some tension, rammed myself into a red bamboo bush, the heavy impact broke some of the bamboo sticks.

I was expecting some refreshing drinks from them, but they are filled with flesh and blood! Not surprised, I mean, what to expect from a horrible place like this, especially inside my mind. What is this place? Why did they lie to me about my winnings? They could have easily threatened me to do the things instead, right? So, is there a way I must follow to reach the other end, safe end, home may be! Ok... I have walked for an hour or so, finally saw something other than the blood red bamboos, it is an entrance slash exit to the jungle thing. One man, wearing a tight red colour uniform approached me, he ordered me to take a seat inside the wooden cabin there. Before entering the building, I noticed different colour liquids stored in vials, and there is Vipin along with some others lying on the bed, unconscious. Yes, it is what you think it is!

I crawled underneath the half-designed gate and ran as fast as I can through the wide-open road, sad that there are no buildings near this evil place. I keep looking back to see any vehicle coming, but it is not my day, I guess! I can see the massive wall of the bamboo forest, noticed that it has guns attached, and they are moving slightly. I sat on my knees, raised both of my hands and waited helplessly. Something hit my stomach, it is one harpoon like projectile but, has a glass cylinder filled with some gluey olive-green liquid, at the other end of the projectile. I fell to the ground, everything turned blank...

(Whining noises)

I woke up, again! Hanging stomach first on the wooden Canoe plank. I have regained my muscle controls, still can't make myself retreat to my normal human posture. It looks like my stomach is stuck on the wooden plank, anyway, after many struggles, rolled back and fell back first to the wooden surface of the Canoe. I checked my stomach; it is badly wounded with blood oozing out of the sides. One big red rash is across my stomach, and I am feeling a good amount of pain throughout my body. I have decided to rest here till some form of help arrives, but the merciless sun rays forced me to think again. I checked my body to find the map but realised that the beggar gang stole it. The only thing they didn't take is the vial of water, am not in a condition to upset my stomach at all.

After resting inside the Canoe for a day, I am feeling a slight relief in my injured stomach. I slowly got back to my feet with the help of a wooden stick; the canoe is stuck between two big rocks. I rolled out of it and walked slowly into the mini forest. I am feeling relieved finally getting back to my homeland. Suddenly, a gunshot is heard, accompanied by the flapping sounds made by a flock of birds. I am unable to walk quickly through the rough terrain... I fainted after eating a random mushroom found under one giant oak tree, I was tempted by the blazing red colour. This forest is full of hunters, and they have caught me. I am now inside a makeshift cage made with sticks and vines; a dead deer is lying next to me, and it is staring at me nonstop.

I have realised that I am naked. Even though I pleaded my throat out, they are engaged in more killings and stuffing the corpses into the cage that I am in. I am starving hard, just like the tiger slowly approaching the cage. It started to pull the dead animals out of the cage, and because of me being a big size lunch, the tiger focused all its attention on me, almost broke the cage but the hunters arrived in time to save their prizes. They killed the tiger with many rounds of bullets, all seven of them started celebrating by drinking alcohol, poured some of it on my body as well, and it helped me ease my stomach pain. Something strange happened when they used the vial of water that they have stolen from my pocket, to dilute alcohol. Some of them started to vomit blood and huge blisters started to form all around their body, most of them popped quickly.

They are all dead. With the help of a random knife dragged into the cage, I am freed. I have started to wander through the mini forest. I am happy seeing a normal forest that has unique trees, rocks, animals etc. Luckily, there aren't any predators now, and even if there is one, I have two shotguns taken from the dead hunters. Luckily, I found one mini truck parked there. I entered the truck and drove my way through the forest, reached the main road. I don't know which way to go to reach my house or Zeiwo's farmhouse hideout. Picked a random side, roared through the road, while police sirens are following me. I tried my best to evade, but luck is not in my favour this time, was caught and arrested! Wonder why? How can they let go a man who does not have an ID, cash, clothes, not even his real face!

They have taken me to the station, and there my eyes found one 'long time no see' ally, he is just casually chilling outside the station ground, looks rustier, my pickup truck! They put me in a lonely cell, and it turns out that they know who I am and my face. After a few hours, the superior officer has arrived, he kicked his way into the cell, I didn't know the cell was never locked all this time, my bad! "Here we meet again, mister David, never thought we would catch you this easily, what happened, my friend!" he asked me. Just like you guys are thinking now, I don't know what he was referring to, sure he is mocking me, right? Anyway, I remained silent, hoping that he will continue the scene, but he went out and joined the other officers drinking alcohol. And once again, the cell is not locked properly.

After some time, they are all drunk and passed out, meanwhile, I sneaked out of the prison, entered the pickup truck, luckily the keys inside, started the engine and hit the road again. Now I know where to go, because I have observed the map pasted on the police station wall. I am driving to my home first, but mid-way, I saw a suspicious car following me, I am panicked, start searching the truck, the three vials are the only weapons available. With no other option, drank the white liquid fully in one sip, and starts waiting for the mysterious transformation. Ahhh... Ahhh... My head... Brain pop... Uhhh... Don't know... I stopped the vehicle to the side, and my suspicious kidnappers didn't bother stopping their vehicle to get me. But I am still feeling excruciating pain inside my head, can hear every noise in high frequency, intolerable!

Somehow, I have managed to get to my neighbourhood. I believe I have never mentioned anything about my "dearest" neighbours. They are perfect people, who love to toy with our poverty. Throwing expensive cigar butts into our compound was their greatest hobby. Anyway, I offered my greetings to one of our closest neighbours, Vivek, but he stands there bewildered, then the strange thing happened!

["Who the freak is this guy? Do I know him? Was he the bartender last night? Oh, wait, was this the disgusting truck that old man used to drive around? I believe so. This might be his son"]

What you just read was a soliloquy of this man, and I was able to hear that! At the same time, my head is still in pain.

He: 'Hey man, how are you? Where is your father? Haven't seen him for a long time now?'

"He's fine, thanks" I said and walked to my house. I realised my mistake! I forgot who I am and where my family really is. I am David and my family lives happily inside Zeiwo's farmhouse hideout, I must write that down for future reference... Ok, got it. Entered my house premises, and what to expect after taking a long vacation is clear here. Empty alcohol bottles, decayed meat and bones, pile of cigar butts, construction wastes etc. And on top of all that, I found bullet butts scattered all around, also found holes across the house walls. I went back to my truck, drove to Zeiwo's hideout... The farm is no more, it is filled with small to big cottages, and there is one gate and a group of security people.

One of them announced "School is that way, my boy" I said I want to meet Zeiwo but they keep repeating the old school jokes. Finally, I am arrested for infiltrating the field. They dragged me into the main building, and my head is getting burdened with different thoughts of the people around here.

["Who is this boy?" "Lost mama's hands?" "Fine young man, I should help him, don't want to make a scene" "Oh, he might steal my girl, must get him out of here" "How can I escape here? I don't want to fight a war" "why everyone keeps looking at me" "He looks weak, why hire him?" "Is this holiday season, how much unfair life really is" "what is all this fuss? Did they find me fake sleeping?" "Why am I not handsome like him, life is unfair" "I wish to be alone" "Oh, he is molesting her, somebody please help her, I wish I was not lazy"

"I wish I were younger like him" "Please, let him be single" "Are they going to kill him?" "He has a pickup truck; I must escape in it and restart my life" "What is this place? What have I done? I want to study" "I guess she might be alone there, must take advantage" "Why am I still unemployed?"]

Finally, they presented me to Zeiwo. She is also thinking about the old school jokes, but she fails to come up with a good full joke. "Please don't use that joke on me! Am Larry, detective Oginfinn" I said. Spent an hour of explaining my real identity.

Zeiwo has mentioned that she and her team have already collected every weapon from the dilapidated Pub. After going through all of that, I went to the cottage where Susan and the kids are staying. Surprisingly, they are staying inside the farmhouse and are given a spacious room, air conditioned, newly painted. Knocked on the door, heard someone approaching the door from the other side, but they waited a minute before opening the door. It is Susan...

XXVI
Pearl has a shy Friend

["What a young handsome man! I wish he was my boyfriend. Please God, let him be single, and don't bring back Larry ever again, let me enjoy some good life finally"]

Yes, that was exactly what she is thinking now! And am not surprised she thought that way, I mean, why not? I am meeting her after a very long time, all because of my unnecessary actions. I should have limited myself to my family like most people do! Thank God, my four kids are in good health. Susan is still checking me out in a weird way, difficult to control my laughter nerves. Does face still holds the ultimate power of attractiveness? I guess so!

Me: 'Are you Susan?'

Susan: 'Yes sir, come inside, I made coffee for you'

Me: 'Oh, no thank you. Larry?'

Susan: 'Is he dead?'

["Please say he is no more, or passed away, or murdered, or jailed, or dead"]

She is literally holding her hands, praying.

Me: 'Sorry, he is no more, died in a shipwreck'

["Thank God, now please make him like me, as a reward for all of my sacrifices"]

Susan: 'Are you single? Under thirty?'

Me: 'Yes. I am Larry's friend... Friend's son, my father sent me here to look after Larry's kids!"

["Come inside and undress yourself young man, let mama see what you got! Naughty girl likes you very much"]

Things escalated quickly and am getting scared. I am not acting like the most gentlemanly person, and I am not scared about revealing my identity to her. But the thing that I am worried about is my mocking features; with a young handsome face and a soggy wrinkled body that has no form of hormone power left, I guess. If she finds out the truth, both of us will be embarrassed to the point, higher than the Mount Everest.

["What is he thinking? Is he drunk or something? What's there to see looking at the ceiling. Is he sick? Definitely not. Maybe I should offer him a welcome kiss to his young lips"]

(Susan leans forward to kiss me, and I move a step back)

Me: 'I am sick! Can I have some water? And a bed to take some rest, and some peace. I don't want you to get sick from me, that will make me feel bad a lot'

["Oh, don't worry dear, I have no problem with dying for you. I can't wait"]

Me: (I took out my phone) 'Oh, ok, I will be there in a minute. I must go, Zeiwo is calling me and I must see her now. Take care dear'

Susan: 'I didn't hear any bell, and you are sick! stay here, take some rest with us'

Me: (I took out my phone) 'Yes, I am coming. Don't send guards, be there in a minute, I swear!'

Without waiting to hear Susan's response, ran out of the farmhouse, took some explosives from the makeshift barracks, entered the pickup truck and left there. I have arrived at the building, my old detective office, and it is still in control of the Chocolust brand. There are two guards standing inside, and there is an automatic rifle aiming at the entrance. First, I took a frag grenade and threw it to the side of the wall (Boom!) That wall now has a big hole. The guards are alerted! They ran outside and started looking for the cause. Meanwhile, I have already thrown four smoke grenades into the compound, causing the entire area to suffocate. I sneakily went inside the building through the destroyed wall. Luckily, the automatic rifle is unable to shoot me due to the wall blocking the aim. The guards walked out of the compound to find the intruder who just went inside, smart guards! I started my search for the hidden compartment, has found it after a few minutes. Ran out without looking anywhere, drove to the farmhouse.

I have reached Zeiwo's hideout, took one small cottage to myself alone, made some coffee in case. And finally, started to read... (reads the document) "The guards put blindfold around my face, and I was taken to somewhere, someone kept caressing me softly, was expecting some form of sexual assault anytime soon, but nothing happened. The vehicle was stopped, and I stepped out of it. Someone led me to a fully air-conditioned place, and then the person carried me into a bedroom, slowly placed me on the bed. I was expecting an assault anytime soon.

The person hugged me tightly, and I realised that it was a woman! Felt her soft skin, long hair and big breasts. I was relieved, but she kept touching me in a sexual way. Finally, she removed my tight blindfold, I was mesmerized! She was beautiful like an angel, and her skin was smooth and bright, long black hair, blue eyes, red lips etc. But one unique thing about her was that she was very tall and had big thighs and arms. She was sitting naked! "What do you want from me?" I asked her in a silent tone. She laughed and walked to the shelf side. "You, I want love, care, affection and in return you can enjoy the taste of pure power that I possess, my name is Margaret" she said.

I didn't understand what she really meant, but it turned out that she did mean it, every word she said, and I started to experience the amplified version of power, I can eat anything at any time without costing a penny! I can travel around the universe, I can kill anyone without wrestling with the law, but it was frustrating to engage in love making with Margaret, she had no idea about what to do, and she did appear very shy during that time. She was very furious to her enemies, mastered in ripping apart flesh and bones, torturing the mind, demolishing anything she hated for no other reason. But she never acted angry towards me, and I realised that I had authority over Margaret. Yes, I tried to make her stop doing violence, but her reply was, "I was tortured by many in my childhood, was raped twice by my caretaker neighbours. I must satisfy my bloodlust, don't bring this matter up anymore"

Is that a good reason to kill random people just because you were tortured in the past? Absolutely Not! Well, I didn't have the nerves to tell her my opinion. Anyway, the most shocking thing happened two weeks later, she made me press her medallion hanging around her neck. Within a minute, a jet plane came to pick us, we entered it and it took off to outer space, landed on a random planet. One parallel universe! And in the middle of the place, there is a mega mansion, where I was not given permission to enter. I waited outside, spied through a window peep hole and saw a man burning in flames. I couldn't see what was happening inside, and who was that man, why did he receive such punishment? After getting back to earth, Margaret's mansion, I asked her about the whole parallel setup, and she didn't care to answer my question, instead we engaged in non-stop sexual activities.

After that horrible night, I was very angry. I was done with my acting! Was tired of her sexual assaults. I decided to put an end to her domination, and I knew that she would destroy me if I didn't satisfy her lust. I decided to kill her! Hired assassins with my newly gained power, and it turned out that a lot of power-hungry people were plotting against her. I collaborated with one group and planned to ambush her alone, and for that I had to escort her out of her mansion and get her to one random place. Using my acting skills, I tricked her into going out with me. and escorted her into the middle of the ambush wheel. I heard several gunshots; I laid down and watched the show. One of the ambushers leaped forward and swung his mighty sword made of laser beam at her.

He was unable to penetrate a violet screen appeared in front of her, her medallion was glowing bright, I saw the bullets getting deflected after hitting the violet screen. It was a shield, projected out of the medallion. Suddenly, the medallion shot a thick laser beam that went through the man's chest. She was standing silent and still and finally made her first move. Well, it was complicated to explain, everything happened in a second! All I could see was shattered ground, I believe she disappeared in that second, and I did hear people screaming in pain in that same second, returned to where she was standing in that exact second. I could see blood bathed bodies all around the surroundings. All my confusions were cleared when she picked me up and accelerated herself over one thousand miles per second, reached the mansion in the next second!

Somehow, she didn't suspect me. Again, we engaged in sexual activities. I was over my breaking point and decided to make a stand. I noticed that whenever she tried to assault me, she was not wearing her medallion. I decided to take advantage of that, and the next time she forced herself on top of me, I stabbed her neck with a sharp knife that I hid inside my underwear. Blood started to blast out of her thick neck; she shouldn't have befriended me! Rest in Hell, dear Margaret. I slowly walked to the table and picked the medallion. Strangely, the medallion had no strings around, but when I placed it on top of my chest, two metal strings shot out from both ends and wrapped around my neck. Suddenly, I had the feeling that my veins turned berserk. There was no time to think, the group might have been alerted, I decided to bury the thing inside the forest" (Document ends)

(DRAWING OF THE AREA)

Oh, I know this place. I am excited to unravel the prize as soon as possible, but Zeiwo insisted that everyone should stay in the hideout till the end of the war. And war preparations are done. Am getting sidelined for having a baby face, but Zeiwo made me the leader of the missile unit. And again, the members are not interested in following my guidelines, they just walked carelessly. We have arrived at our first target, the Chocolust factory. There are workers walking around the factory still, and I proposed my team to fire at one nearby tree to make the workers know about the upcoming terror, allowing them to escape. But they ignored my command

and shot ten shells into the main entrance, destroyed two-third of the factory. I am not happy with their merciless and revengeful approach. I know they are holding onto painful memories but is that enough to justify what they did now! Surprisingly, Zeiwo does support the team. She and her infantry team charged inside and made a pile of bullet butts in the centre, causing complete destruction.

Next, we went to the Toy factory thing, and just like last time; my team shot ten plus shells straight into the entrance. Again, Zeiwo and team charged inside to finish them. After all that explosions and smoke, we returned to our hideout. "I hereby make known that we have eliminated the greatest evils existed in our country, let's celebrate our victory. Cheers" Zeiwo delivered her speech. Well, I am also happy. Yes, I know what you guys are thinking; what about Jessica and the whole GTM things? Well, I don't think they are interested in silly human trafficking business, they should be after some unimaginable evil missions. People who possess luxurious amount of power, never see human beings worthy of an opponent to fight with. Honestly, am still feeling incomplete, I went out, woke up my truck and drove to the location mentioned in Pearl's documents.

Zeiwo is unaware of the greatest evils there is, and I want to meet them. I have finally arrived at the forest where the ruin of the ancient shrine is, the rough path is not friendly to my old buddy, started walking, and reached the location within two hours' time. For some reason, I am excited! According to Pearl's map, she placed the medallion near one of the lion statues. Yes, I can see two monkey sized roaring lion statues, half submerged inside the ground. I am very eager to go and dug my prize out, but the problem is that the whole area is now under control of some pirates! I can see the skull and two bones image flag on top of one of the makeshift warehouse structures. Blood thirsty pirates are patrolling the area, and they are holding shotguns. I am a fool to not bring any weapon with me, wait... There is something...

I went back to the truck, opened the secret door on the passenger seat, took the red vial and drank it. I became unconscious and fell to the ground. I woke up and realised that I have become a bodybuilder. I can assure you guys that my brand-new muscles are not for show, I can feel the intense rage effect boiling inside my brain and passing through every nerve channel. I can't wait to unleash myself, ran into the pirates' camp, they have already heard my thunderous footsteps. The fight has started; shotgun bullets scattered all around me, I jumped sky high and landed on top of the makeshift pirate camp, crashing the entire structure down to the abyss, and the shockwave damage was enough to bury them all underground.

Unfortunately, my powerful landing has resulted in changing the entire structure of this place, the lion statues are nowhere to be found! Without wasting more time, started to dig here and there rapidly, have found several bodies of the pirates, decayed animal carcasses, buried treasure chests, weapons, trees, barrels of something, skeletons, and finally found the medallion. It looks very shiny and beautiful, but the thing started to shoot laser beams from all its sides, caused severe damage to the trees and rocks, but I am unharmed. The strange thing is that it has generated a rapid amount of heat energy around it, forced me to drop it. Once again, I picked it up and placed it on my chest, and it shot cables from both sides around my neck, tight! ... I can't breathe! I ran fast to reach the truck, slowly rolled under the truck before losing my mind...

XXVII
Kindest person Award

I woke up after ten long hours! Luckily, I still have my memory, and I have changed into my normal body profile, still have pearl's documents and the medallion shaped like one black pear hanging around my neck. I don't know why I am still holding onto Pearl's documents. The medallion has an image of a T-rex dinosaur, carved out and filled up with gold. I can see reinforcement guards entering the restricted and demolished area, rolled out of the truck, and sneakily entered it. Unfortunately, the thing doesn't start, not even make a noise. After trying my luck for seven more times, exited the truck and ran through the wretched plains and finally reached the main road, sneakily entered an empty garbage truck resting on the roadside. The truck started to move...

The truck must have covered at least a hundred kilometres now. Finally, my phone came back to life, informed detective Susan about my location. The strong disgusting smell of the truck gave me a hard time. When the truck finally came to a stop, I jumped out of it and ran to the nearest building there. It is an abandoned school, infested with vegetation. It is getting darker, entered the mini forest school playground, pressed the dinosaur button on the necklace. I waited for a minute, heard a jet engine. The jet plane made its landing near my side and opened its door. There is no one inside, and it is just a self-driving jet plane. I went inside, the door closed, and it took off into the sky! Straight into the clouds, I closed my eyes and tightly grabbed onto the seatbelt.

I am inside the private jet for an hour, and it has already entered the outer space. Finally, the self-driving thing finally made its stop on top of a bright piece of land, sure that this is another planet! The jet opened its doors automatically, but I am not ready to exit. I am so done with exploring's and wandering's, and sure this place is not anyone's cup of tea. Suddenly, the necklace started to glow, within a minute, two boys have come near the jet, they are wearing a metal collar around their neck and are naked completely. They can't talk because their mouths are tight shut with a metal mask! They waved their hands forward, and I followed their wave commands.

We are walking the main road; pile of uneven cut gold bricks adorned both sides of the road. Along with the gold, there are a ton of bullets and artillery shells spread across the pathway! The scariest things are the giant nukes loaded into the firing stations, and it can fire at any moment. I can see a bright light shining from the distance, and it is not coming from any light source, but from the reflection of the shiniest stones I have ever seen, and all the buildings here are made of these stones. The two boys finally escorted me into a big arch, happily the full form of this whole powerhouse is written on this arch.

It says, "Golden T-rex Market", my young bodyguards finally left me alone. The temperature is moderate, and my eyes are fixed on the numerous pearls and diamonds spread across the pathway, a handful of this land will grant me a fortune for ages! Suddenly, the strange looking buildings surrounding me started to shoot projectiles into the sky, and they crashed into different asteroid pieces. I am sure this is not Earth or any natural planet; this curiosity drove me into a tall building that has a huge telescopic head! There is no one guarding the building, and when I entered it, I was teleported straight into the top of the thing. Through the giant telescope, I started to observe the crazy place.

Yes, I was right! I am literally standing on an artificial planet that is floating on space with the help of crazy physics. I can see

Earth, the Sun, the Moon and other planets. Suddenly, I noticed a huge fire blazing on the northern part of the Earth, I believe that is one of the hidden spots available only in the special map! There is a big building standing in the middle of this made-up platform slash planet thing. Surprisingly, I can't spot any human being other than the two naked boys resting beside a building made of gold. Yes, I know this is a little bit exaggerating to hear, but it is what it is, and I have doubts that these gold things maybe just golden paint.

I have entered the big golden building, it has a name 'WEAPONS', this is like a museum setup and has a lot of things placed on the display. Test tubes, the bazooka things, toy watches, spray cans, pill containers, harpoons, armours, robots, and of course different types of weapons as well. But the most confusing thing I found here is the stack of books, freshly printed. I picked one of them carefully out of the stack, and it is a dictionary! The cover page shows a man flying with magical looking wings, made of steel, I guess. 'The dictionary of the new world: edition one' written below the flying man.

I opened it, looks exactly like our standard dictionary... Oh, wait! This is not like the ones we read. I am sorry guys, I have this problem of judging a book by its cover thing, guess most of us do. Whatever, I started flipping the pages aggressively, it is in alphabetical order, but the description is what makes it unique. Hear me; word Job – work for the leader, sacrifice yourself for the leader, make him proud. Word Genius – dedicate your whole life to making new inventions, as ordered by the leader. Word Marriage – the union of two bodies, making a new body, enlarging the work force of the leader's army. I forgot to mention that every page ends with the phrase 'Hail Sir FLAMBUST'

Ok, I think I know what this book is for, kind of. They just want this book to educate the new human beings taking birth after their deadly mission of Destruction (laughs hard) what kind of buffoons are these people! I mean, how can a new human being read this book? These explanations are made with other words that the person might learn after going through the whole book. Without any image to signify each word, this is just oil mixed with water setup. I stood there for some time, enjoying the book. Hear this, Word Leader – the person responsible for your birth, who holds power over the entire Universe, holds the right to insist any rule on to his children, Hail Sir FLAMBUST. To be honest, this is the first time I have experienced the famous proverb... Oh, I forgot it, you know the proverb praising 'reading', that. I flipped to the back cover page that has a biography of Sir FLAMBUST.

Sir FLAMBUST

(Figure: a picture of a mighty man, who has platinum coloured hair and beard, orange to reddish skin, blue eyes, and has flames drawn around the photo frame for scary effect)

Sir FLAMBUST, the great leader of the Universe, entering his 867th year of unbeaten reign. The most kind, charming, and strongest living being. Weighing 2500 pounds of TR56 infused muscle tissues, with inbuilt self-fuel production mechanics, and fifteen feet tall, winner of Universe heavy weight champion. And winner of awards such as Great leader award, Kindest person award, Intellect Carnage prize etc. The mastermind behind the missions titled 'Job for Slaves' 'Health is Wealth' 'One for One: not for damned' 'More than Animals' 'Pride Ourselves' 'Independence Mayhem' 'Under Omnipotence' 'Money not be Happy' 'Apocalypse: rise of new borns'

I went out of the building, walked for an hour. Fragrance of sweet flowers rushed into my nostrils, and there is a sunflower farm. What is more fascinating about this farm is that there are different colours of sunflowers: red, black, brown, orange, blue, violet, white, pink, green etc. In addition to the variety of colours, each sunflower has a glowing aura. Sadly, some of the sunflowers are missing most of their head, how can someone destroy such a beautiful flower? There are eight small cottages spread across the farm. I went inside one of the cottages, it is dark inside, nothing to see. Suddenly, I am standing in the wintery forest setting, I can feel the freezing snow under my feet. When I looked back, there is no cottage behind me, and as you guys think now, how am I supposed to exit here?

I am scared. I can't endure this anymore. Anyway, I walked straight for an hour, still no sign of any building except the caves. On my way, I found a familiar hat slammed into the snow, it was Opaoul's, now I am sure that this is how people travel in the future. Fast and cost efficient! But how am I going to exit this place? After wandering here and there for almost ten plus hours, I found a dagger inside a random cave. You know what am thinking? Yes, it is exactly what am thinking. With force, pulled the dagger to my chest, but the T-rex necklace jerked me hard with one powerful zap of electric current, made me drop the dagger before killing myself.

I fell to the snowy floor, helpless, saw a broken blue sunflower piece submerged inside the snow. I dug it out and held it in my hands, it makes a strong aroma of toxicity. I can feel death just by holding it, I don't know why I am thinking like this. No, you guys have mistaken me! I am not feeling such because I am narrating this, it is just beyond that. Let's say, we do some actions that are dangerous and we know it, but we still do it, and most of the time we would get in trouble. For example, if we live life as taken for granted, we will end up talentless and broke (cries) ... This is such kind of feeling, the feeling of danger, toxic. Whatever, I took a bite, it tastes salty and sweet combined, grinded it down into my acid ocean. Everything turns blank!

I moved around with hands reaching forward, and finally finds a doorknob, opens the door, am back inside the sunflower farm. Am not interested in observing the farm further, returned to the entrance. Now it all makes sense, now it all makes sense! There is one caution board planted near the entrance,

[Must grab one of the toxic flowers before entering the fast travel cottages; and to return, you need to eat a portion of the flower and wait for a minute]

I am getting very tired due to dehydration, searched for a good-looking building. There stands a mighty building, with the name board 'ARHE LAB'. I went inside the laboratory without thinking a second time, and the T-rex symbol necklace gave me instant entry. I believe they have no idea about the real T-rex members. I asked one scientist dude for some water. Soon, some of the scientists gathered around me, and offered a small platter full of pills. "Here sir, this will quench your thirst" they said collectively. Took a white squishy pill and dropped it into my mouth, it popped instantly, mmm... I can feel one bucket-full of water rushing its way down to my stomach, fresh ice-cold water, mmmm... Best feeling ever. I thanked them for such an invention, their expression just changed into shock. Maybe they didn't expect me to like it. Anyway, I started to move around the facility to try other inventions.

I have come across different type of pills, stacked up for distribution. Luckily, one of the scientists is with me, helping me with my questions. He explained to me that some of the pills have cool down period of one day up to a year! And he added that the pills are essential to the new civilization of life. I don't understand but I did shake my head to make me not look like a fool in the house. However, he offered me a pill to satisfy my appetite, this one is orange colour, not squishy, but very crunchy, and has no cool down period. I carefully placed the pill in my mouth, and slowly crushed it, feels like eating chalk powder. I made it into a paste with my saliva, and slowly surfed it down my throat, mmm... Roasted lamb with baked potatoes and roasted beans... Sweet chocolate lava cake to end one delicious meal!

I am amazed by the things I just experienced, marvellous! Continued the journey, and finally found the bazooka like thing, but this one is very big compared to the ones I saw inside the truck, the wintery forest, the magic waterbody etc. And there are a bunch of these big bazookas loaded on to one machine. He noticed my bewildered look, but I know that can raise suspicion if I ask him about this bazooka thing. After a good amount of thinking, asked him, "What's the radius of this thing now? Did you guys increase it?". He looks bewildered now. "I am sorry sir, we haven't received any command to increase the radius, as it will decrease the spread of TD9, and that may result in a few groups getting escaped" he said.

I believe I have learned something. I must extract data from him regarding this TD9 thing, without him knowing that I have no idea about anything. "If so, make this TD9 more powerful" I said. As expected, he looks confused; "I am afraid it is not possible, sir" he said, the look on his face shows perfectly how much he hates me throwing out dumb science blunders. He is waiting for my new question, meanwhile, I am just looking at random things to avoid his attention. Sweats started to form around my forehead, and I am feeling tense and restless, because I can't use the famous excuse of hot temperature, because the room is almost frozen. How embarrassing will it be if one of the powerful leaders sweats like a coward!

I carefully wiped the sweats, and started thinking about one solid tricky question... "Is there any possibility of this mission becoming a failure?" I asked him. Again, he stands confused, and this time he looks like he knows my disguise. I couldn't keep up my fake acting skills, my face turned back to its real expression, worried! He noticed it quickly and grabbed my collar. "You thief..." his last words. You guys are now confused, aren't you? Yes, he is no more. The moment he grabbed my collar, the T-rex necklace shot one powerful blast of laser, that went through his head and hit the laboratory wall, drilled a hole through the sturdy concrete wall also. The scientists are terrified. They started screaming and kneeled around me.

I am fuelled with fierce confidence and asked them, "I want a detailed description about the progress of this mission, Right NOW!" I can see them getting bathed in sweat and fear. One middle aged scientist came forward and started to narrate the whole mission, while the others stayed on their kneel position. "Sir, the mission Apocalypse is designed to create more advanced human beings, and this is the fifth year, we will be able to launch it next year" he said. Not the answer I am looking for. I have a feeling that there is no use to ask any of them regarding the matter, because they will never provide me a spoon feed description of this horrible mission they are working on.

I ordered them to produce a report on the mission, and they handed me a hundred-page length thesis. I walked into the leader's cabin there. The front page has the mission Apocalypse title along with the ARHE signature and badge next to it. I flipped to the first heading, Overview- mission Apocalypse is designed to create advanced human beings capable of withstanding high level mental and physical struggles, required to conquer the unconquered universe. I flipped through different chapters, finally, my eyes caught a chapter that has the bazooka figure in it.

The bazooka thing is named as 'TD9 Container' and on further reading, found out that the thing, after it explodes, spreads TD9 virus around a smaller radius, and it is one of the most crucial steps for the reincarnation protocol. At the end of the page, there is one Nota bene section, it says, "Must be set to one kilometre radius" Anyway, I flipped to the section 'TD9', hoping that it will give me the answers am looking for. (Laughs) Sorry guys, it is hard to not laugh looking at this figure. This TD thing looks like an ant-like version of a toad, but thinner and has one lengthy stomach, has two hyphen eyes, dot nose and a wide mouth. TD9 also known as 'The destroyer power 9' was created to make the reincarnation process happen. "When launched into the atmosphere, these creatures slowly find their hosts. It will take at least seven hours to begin the reincarnation process, ends within ninety plus days, the host will be dead twelve hours after getting infected"— What!! What is this? The host, ninety days, infection... I flipped to the section titled 'Duration' and it mentions that the whole mission must be completed within the next one hundred years, and it is easy to make changes to the program using the 'Ultimatum device' at any point of time during the mission.

I am getting tired of reading this massive document. I know there exist people who love to read hundred pages within an hour, sure am not one of them. I prefer watching videos of someone describing the matter. I couldn't understand anything from the short videos and the scientist's narration, but this written document helped me understand the things. Reading matters guys! Anyway, flipped again and landed on the section titled 'Ultimatum device', a bracelet thing drawn in the middle, and it looks like a watch, oh yes,

I remember seeing a collection of these things inside the weapon museum where they keep those funny dictionaries... No, it's not a watch for sure, but one wrist strap that has eight square blocks with alphabets A to H written on each of the blocks. The description says that it is a device used for time travel stuff.

By clicking on each of the blocks, scientists and workers can get to that particular time frame. Block 'E' is the boiling point, and it is there most of the objectives are assigned, all mistakes and errors must be corrected in here. Changes done to each block will reflect in H block, the final block. This section also ends with one Nota bene, although the device was designed to travel between each block, after entering a block, the person must wait for a year or get killed before leaving one selected block. The main headquarters will be in the H block. Only the GTM leader SIR 'FLAMBUST' has the rights to stop the mission.

Ok, so the main leader has the power to stop the mission, and that is not going to happen. And I just remember my conversation with that dead scientist, he also mentioned about the possibility of the bazooka bombs failure, if their radius is increased. I have regained my power attitude and called the main leader of the lab, ordered him to increase the radius to twice its original radius. He was reluctant at first, but my scary attitude made him settle to increase 0.5, and he added that if the radius needs to be altered longer, it requires consent from Mr FLAMBUST, and I don't want to get into such trouble anymore.

This is getting interesting; I am happy that I am understanding some kind of science. Let me tell you what I have learned from reading some parts of the document; mission Apocalypse designed by the GTM leader, to erase humanity and give birth to a new sturdy human race. How simple is that! (irritating alarm sound) Where is that noise coming from? It's coming from the necklace thing, and it is beeping bright as well. "Come to the mansion immediately" a robotic voice inside the necklace said out loud. I dropped the document, ran outside, and hasted forward. The slaves are looking at me in amazement, maybe it's their first time seeing a leader running around. I am stopped by one weird looking building, again! Forgot about the robotic voice completely.

I went inside the building, it is designed like a big eye that has multiple lenses, and a lot of cannon trunks placed around the top like eyebrows. Inside the building, there are numerous screens showing a variety of activities happening around earth. All these footages include a crowd, and surprisingly, I can see Zeiwo's farmhouse and its surrounding cottages. It is live! I have realised that Zeiwo and her team have been included in watchlist after we destroyed the factories. I have tried to use my power to release them from the list, but it requires Sir FLAMBUST's approval. I have decided to ask him to spare my team. The robotic voice from the necklace issued a final warning to enter the mansion in five minutes.

I went outside, sprinted to enter the mansion, can see jets flying over and landing on a vast area of land. There is a big mansion standing inside that vast land that is filled with jets and small people, and the GTM leaders are casually entering the mansion, surprisingly, I just noticed a few small people also entering the mansion. Suddenly, one huge spark of confidence blasted into my nervous system, all because of knowing that there exist some normal leaders, and what does it mean? Well, it means that I won't be caught when I enter the mansion with the stolen power. I mean, there will always be some people in every industry, who are just smaller than normal human beings, but they can do extraordinary stuff. Today, I will be one of them! With my newly gained confidence, I marched my way into the mansion's entrance.

Luckily, there is one self-moving aisle going through the centre of the mansion. The naked workers bowed seeing me, meanwhile, I keep wondering why these workers are naked? Surprisingly, they look well and healthy. I believe I have bored you guys with many descriptions of these mansions, so am not going to do that this time. Keep in mind that this mansion was built in an "ancient sacred place" theme. I am shocked to see a second entrance ahead, and the first entrance is just a dining area for the leaders, already filled with delicious looking food, to be served by workers who are wearing a golden dress!

I went inside the big hall, almost big as a country! I have finally realised my mistake, there are no small sized leaders, all the smaller people that I saw entering here stopped inside the dining hall area. The giant leaders have started laughing at me while sitting on their mythical thrones but, made no effort to hurt me physically. They must be sitting there for a meeting, and I just interrupted them, I guess. I can see a fireball at the other end of the long hall. The self-moving aisle has increased its speed, am getting closer to the final boss of the Universe. Within a few minutes, I am going to meet the most powerful human being in the universe. I am excited and am getting weird fantasies of dethroning the leader's leader. If that were to happen, I would have to live in fear of someone dethroning me, right?

But I am sure that I will enjoy the position whatever, I mean, who would not want to enjoy such a life within one's shortest life span on Earth? I have reached mid-way, can see Jessica staring at me. The fireball at the end is actually one giant human being. He is the leader, and he is burning in fire, but still his body is visible through the flames surrounding him. His skin looks red in colour, and he is very muscular like every member in this evil club. His eyes, ears, nose, mouth etc. look similar to human beings, except his hair, made of silver metallic bands that extend all the way to his chin. But the concerning factor is the flames surrounding him, now that I am getting closer to him, I can see grey colour oil dripping down his body, and these drops catch the fire and keep burning for some time, and then other batch of oil takes the heat.

He turned his attention to me who has just accepted his own fate and thus appeared brave. He jumped up from the seat, has no feet but blowtorch valves attached to both legs, helping him move smoothly around. He is wearing a skirt of heavy metal plates welded onto a thick chain wrapped around his waist. Happy that he has some manners! I can see a shiny golden medallion welded on to his chest, and it has a golden T-rex image protruding out of the medallion. He just picked up his sword back from a pedestal, and the sword also caught the fire slowly when his flaming oil dripped onto it. It is mesmerizing to watch the tiny drops of oil getting dropped to the ground that catch the fire mid-way, and upon hitting the floor, explode into fragments of fire! He turned back and started questioning me,

Him: 'Go back, never come back again!'

I am not listening to his questions, because am disturbed by looking at his back, there is one big factory running on. I can see the metal pipes, smoke, wheel with teeth's rotating, rattling chains... (Sizzling sound) Aahhh... I screamed hard, he just flicked his sword at me, and it splashed the burning oils into my skin, causing third degree burns over my body, and my dress is filled with holes. I said "Please have mercy on the people of Earth, stop mission Apo..."

Him: 'GO AWAY YOU LITTLE CREEP!'

I ran back the aisle, but it keeps moving towards the flaming creature, I used all my energy to sprint through and ran past hundred or so metres. Luckily, Jessica picked me up, took the GTM necklace off my neck and threw me over the open ceiling. I crashed into a pool of blue water.

XXVIII

Bravery meter Theory

The powerful splash made me unconscious, and when I woke up, am inside a hospital bed. It turns out that some of the workers took me here. Finally, the doctor made his visit, he told me that I was here for two weeks now, and I was in a condition of severe brain damage. The doctor added that it is because of the most advanced facilities available in this planet that saved my life.

Me: 'Who are you, sir?'

Doc: 'I am your doctor, who are you to ask?'

Me: 'I was the captain of the gang that battle against the Golden T-rex members, have destroyed some of their buildings'

Doc: (laughs) 'Why are you being so pride, sir? You failed Why take pride in failure? Did you destroy the world? The world belongs to these evils! Live or die, the only option we will ever have'

Me: 'Stop spreading negativity around you coward piece of intellectual overload! Nothing is powerful than people's power! You know it, right?'

Doc: 'Which people, sir? We don't even have unity inside our families either, think about it'

Me: 'Point taken... But my team will destroy these evils, we will fight till we die. My team is waiting for me on earth. You will see!'

Doc: (laughs) 'You can go now; you are medically cleared. Go now and save us' (laughs)

Me: 'Why are you keep mocking us? Don't you have any love for this world?'

Doc: 'Why don't you live like the way the world lets you live? Let them hold on to their dearest power. If you want to dethrone them, it is only because you want their power'

Me: 'You're crazy, they are kidnapping people, and doing cruel stuff to them, fooling commoners, breeding some brutal plan that will erase every earthly being'

Doc: 'Whatever you say, I believe them, as long as there is no news about them bring any good to people. Anyway, best wishes for your mission, sir'

Me: 'How did you end up here, sir?'

Doc: 'Don't worry about that sir, I can't describe it. Farewell'

I went out of the hospital and walked around the place. Since I have lost my stolen necklace, the naked slaves are not offering any respect to me. After walking for a few miles, one luxury car stopped near me, two men jumped out of it and made me unconscious by forcedly injecting one big injection. They dropped me into their car's trunk...

"Wake up David Wake up!" Susan yelled at me. I woke up inside our old house, Susan started kissing me. My four children joined us to celebrate my homecoming. Susan has prepared a delicious meal for us. You guys know what is running inside my mind. I am confused about why they spared me! And how did I end up here? Susan gave me some answers regarding my homecoming, she revealed that I was dropped here in a golden luxurious car, and it drove away immediately. Susan slowly mentioned me about my daughter G1's abdomen surgery, and it is scheduled on tomorrow morning. I can't sleep because of my last journey, and because of the thought of what is about to hit Earth soon.

"Don't worry dear, she will be alright, the doctor promised me that it is just a minor surgery, calm your mind and have a good night sleep" Susan tried to console me. I would have been consoled if I were not involved with the factory evils. I feel pity for myself, I mean, what power I have, to even question these evil people. I should have limited my life to my small family like every human being! Susan has started to snore loudly, and I have somehow managed to waste my sleep time with more of these kinds of negative thoughts. In the morning, we are ready to go to the hospital, the rusty pickup truck is waiting for us. Surprisingly, it has managed to wake up after three to four tries.

We went to the hospital, and I am struck with the need of ten thousand dollars for the surgery. I have decided to drop my fake persona, but when I checked my bank account in my phone, my eyes turned blind! My account has ten billion dollars! First, I thought it was a prank by the devils, but I paid the hospital bill with it. I don't know what is happening, after we went home, I revealed my newly found wealth to Susan. She became very excited and started searching her phone, a few minutes later, my phone has become full of messages of cash withdrawals. Yes, she begged me for my card, and I gave it to her happily.

But I have no problem with her spendthrift, I let her buy whatever she wants to fulfil her life. "David, you are my God, that stupid man left me at the perfect time!" Susan said happily. So, it turns out that money can buy happiness! I keep trying to recollect the final words of the GTM leader, his words were not any famous saying but a challenge for me. So far not so good, Susan has already spent nearly a million dollars now! And honestly, I have also started to take a little slide to the money. My first thought was about buying a good-looking car, but Susan is one fast thinker. "Dearest, please close your eyes and stretch out your hand... Ok, now open your eyes. Happy!"

I knew she bought a car, received a notification from the nearest car showroom. When I opened my eyes, she shocked me completely, it is not a car key but a house key! She has bought a small bungalow near the forest side. Anyway, my guess is also correct, there is a red luxury car resting next to the rusty truck. For some reason, my mind fuelled with rage, I grabbed an axe, dismantled the whole truck with it. A few touches were enough to do most of the work. Susan clapped happily. I took the keys of my new car, and went to

Zeiwo's farmhouse to warn them about the dangers they are in. Yes, I know I should have informed them earlier, but I was drowned in my newly found wealth.

Zeiwo's farmhouse is no longer there. All I can see is one massive hole, in the shape of a sphere, sure some kind of big cannonball hit the place, and vaporised everything within five-to-ten-kilometre radius! I stand there weeping about my loss, you guys believe or not, I have come here with new ideas in mind. Now that I have a billion dollars with me, I can buy highly advanced weapons, and we can have a fighting chance against the FLAMBUST, the one-man army. "Hello sir, how can I help you?" one random man asked me. I can see respect burning in his eyes, for me. He explained to me that this area was hit by a nuke last Friday, and the government has apologized for the matter because they made it clear that the nuke was accidentally fired due to one malfunction. "Do you really believe that?" I asked him, and his reply is what I expected him to say!

"I do sir, and I don't care whether it was an accident or not, am not interested in spending my time with such matters. But am happy to believe that it was an accident" he said and left. I went back to my new home but am still not over with the strange eye contact gave by many people. Susan was waiting for me, she is holding a golden bouquet of flowers, small crowd of ten men and five women are also standing by her side. "CONGRATS DAVID" they said together. Turns out that I have won the award for being the most intelligent man in the world, and I am labelled in magazines and newspapers as the man who invented the Apocalypse vial. I know who is behind all this mockery, but what am most concerned about is the fact that why no one is aware of this vial thing, I mean, the name says it all, right?

When I asked Susan about this, all she had to say was, "it doesn't matter what that thing is, as long as you have created it, my love" Some of the people offered fancy guesses about my new invention; mosquito killing drug, micro bacterial killer, make human being immortal, time travel medicine, grant super powers to humans etc.

Yes, I get it, who can possibly guess what it really is? Like always, too much of something is never good! Is this what called modernity? To kill every living being, and to recreate them accordingly to someone's wishes... I bought myself some time and started contemplating on my life. Lost my name, face, went through hellish ventures, and yet to be transformed into some maniac creature.

My children now look at me like am a stranger, and Susan who holds no gratitude for the sacrifices I did for the betterment of our family, she still thinks that my original self is a good for nothing crap. I am alone in this world! (explosion sound) God! What is that! ... Something just hit the building and shook it whole for a moment. I went out, half of our new mansion is missing! "Bombs everywhere, run..." someone screamed out loud. Susan, the kids and me rushed into the car, speed our way to the nearest police station. "Sorry sir, the armoury department was conducting a nuke test, and some of them hit your house due to some error in deployment, this won't happen again" the officer said. And what is more surprising is what Susan has to offer!

"Thank god, hope they fix that quickly" she said while swiping her sweats off. We went out, entered the car, and realised that we have become homeless. Well, we have lost half of our mansion, and it is dangerous to live on the other half. Whatever, we still have nine plus billion dollars in our account. Susan has bought a resort this time, with one phone call. We went there, and it is a beautiful place. The kids have started playing around happily, and it does put a smile on my face. Successfully passed a day inside the resort, bit afraid, I know what to expect in my life. They spared my life for a reason, to toy with my instinctual fears is their primary goal. Suddenly, my phone received a message; "your account has been credited with 10 billion dollars. Happy spending"

What the... Susan became shocked! To ease the situation, I told her that I have sold a long-held stock on the stock market, and she bought my word. She asked me to donate a few billions to charity for getting some fame, and we did so. Our faces are all over the internet, and on every channel. Second tragedy stroke on the third day, one of my daughters was shot down to death! It was a sniper shot, went through her forehead, she is lying on a blood pool with an innocent smile fading away slowly. Again, we went to the police station. "The resort you are living in is not the safest area, a sniper training camp is about hundred kilometres from there, they should have misfired it. Evacuate the resort, this won't happen again!" Officer replied.

We went to the resort, evacuated it and moved to somewhere Susan knows. She gave me directions and finally reached one big mountain. On top of the mountain, stands an isolated sturdy looking house. With one cheeky smile, she announced that she has bought this house three days ago. Anyway, we buried our dead daughter beside a willow tree. It surprised me why Susan is not feeling any emotion for our dead child? Has wealth turned her into some emotionless scrap! I am sweating heavily with each plane flying above us. My peace has broken; I wonder when it was stable. I guess money can't buy happiness, especially if your life is this much vulnerable to outside forces. One week later, we are still alive, and we are still living at the mountain building. Luckily, the house is filled with enough rations for almost a year, so we don't have to go out.

The view from the mountain is mesmerizing, I can see boss Jessica's grand mansion staring at me from a great distance. Am getting scared each time I go out of the house, feels like am a patch in the circle. Target for anyone! Third tragedy stroke in the evening today, in the form of a massive earthquake. The mountain is literally jumping up and down like it is jump roping. We went out and ran fast through the crumbling ground; we were mixed inside the sand tides and avalanched our way down. I was rolled down like a boulder and finally stopped its course after hitting a concrete wall. I woke up on a hospital bed; Susan is also on a bed beside me. The doctor slowly approached me and revealed that our kids are no more! ... What have I done to deserve this fate... My ki... They...

"Wake up David" Susan is shaking me violently. She has heard the news, and she is weeping hard. After three more days of stay, we are discharged from the hospital. I have decided to buy an apartment this time, suggested by Susan. For fifteen million dollars, we bought one luxurious apartment, and still my account balance has not dropped down a bit. Whatever, we continued living our sad life there, the room services are great. At night, Susan proposed me to have sex! This put me in a strange situation. Well, am not saying that my type two hunger has left me but, I am just a young face on an old suit. "Come on baby, we haven't done it yet, am so lonely! Larry never gave me a good time; he didn't understand the meaning of pleasure. He lasted only seconds!" she said.

I am getting enraged, but an intense amount of fear rushed into my nerves suddenly. I just heard hissing sounds; sure, they are not coming from Susan. There is more! "Jumbo, switch on the lights" lights turned on. Uhhh... There are snakes on the floor! Different sizes, am getting a seizure, fought my way out of it. "What's the matter, dear?" Susan asked, I told her what is making the hiss sound, made sure to not let her watch the ugly scene. I tried to contact the guards, but they are not picking up the phone. We are both shaking in fear and sweating a lot. After a few hours, the hissing is still going on strong but, I am getting suspicious why these snakes aren't attacking us. I picked one up and it is just a rubber toy that has a speaker placed inside its mouth. Susan caught high temperature fever from that event and am getting tired of this whole mockery.

I have decided to hire some guards, hired fifty of them for a salary of ten thousand dollars per month, gave six months payment in advance as well. I don't care about my enemies coming after me but, I can't make Susan fall victim to their plot. Two days passed successfully, I am getting pressure from Susan for not engaging in love making. Finally, I have decided to remove my fake youth face, I mean, to reveal the truth behind my young face. Susan is getting unbearable day after day; she keeps wearing tight and short clothes that is almost suffocating her. At nights, she is totally unrest for not getting any attention from me and finally she lost her cool, grabbed me tightly and pushed me onto the bed. "Am I too old for you, huh! Now shut up and enjoy!" she said and started kissing me aggressively, slowly unbuttoned my pants.

Suddenly, our room is filled with bright light. I can hear a helicopter approaching. The light keeps getting brighter, and my danger reception skills have kicked in. Tightly hugged Susan, rolled out of the bed, hit the floor hard, rolled under the bed. Fraction of a second later, one helicopter charged into our apartment by crashing through the glass wall. Shattered everything on its path, exploded with thunderous sound. Lucky or unlucky, we are still alive, with minor injuries only. We are taken to a hospital, but the ambulance gets stopped on the way. It was a sudden break that shook the whole patient cabin, and it detached from the vehicle. Someone opened the cabin, pulled out my stretcher, stabbed me five times. I don't remember what happened after that, when I woke up, I am inside the hospital, can't believe am still alive, and am not happy at all.

Luckily, Susan is with my side. She has called the police officers into the hospital. "The gang that hijacked the ambulance and stabbed you, were looking for a serial rapist man, and they mistook you for him. Get well soon David" officer said. I know you guys are tired of hearing these kinds of absurd replies but am not. What is hurting me more is that Susan taking those replies seriously. She thanked God for not taking my life and said "Serial rapist, You! That's funny" Anyway, I am discharged after a month. The hospital bill has surpassed over a million dollars! I know it won't be a problem for me, but what if I didn't have the money. I am too scared to imagine that scenario.

Susan has arranged a taxi, and she has decided not to buy buildings anymore. Instead, she suggested me to spend the rest of our lives inside some sacred places. We went to a monastery that has a lot of monks and prophets wandering around. This place is far away from the city, and I am hoping that my enemies will consider me defeated. Who are my enemies for real? Yes, I know what you guys think, the GTM leaders, right? But I don't feel the same just because, why do they need to play with me and my family? I mean, they have already setup one crazy mission to eliminate the entire species, and I am sure that they don't consider me as a worthy opponent to play games with! Whatever, we have started to live among the monks and sages. For the first time in my life, I have started to feel peace and happiness.

Almost two weeks have passed, we have transformed ourselves into mini monks. I guess, I understand the meaning of God now. We are living in a universe that is overwhelmed with madness, and the thought of God has become meaningless to most of the people, and I was one of them. But now I feel God around me, it is residing in this beautiful place, the replenishing energy this place offers, is from God. I feel pity for the people worshipping the GTM leader as their supreme. And I am distressed about the thought of the evil GTM leader destroying this beautiful place through his mission. But am hoping that, after some billions of years, someone will eliminate these GTM freaks and reinstate peace and prosperity back inside the universe.

Three weeks have passed, and my birthday has arrived. I am not sure it is the exact date, but Susan is sure about it. She has arranged some celebrations for me. I don't remember when the last time I celebrated my birthday. I can see something big wrapped up in front of the monastery entrance, I am not surprised but sad that Susan has restarted her spending spree! Most of the monks wished me the clichéd wish, "Live long and prosper". I guess they don't know much about me. They just wished me to not hurt my feelings, what else can someone say about a man they don't know that much. Anyway, Susan unwrapped the gift, my eyes are filled with happy tears. No, it is not some shiny piece of stone worth a billion, it is my good old pickup truck, repaired and painted new. Hope it starts with one twist of the key.

"I am sorry my friend, I was drowned in pride and luxury" I said to the truck. Susan is making tears of her own. We went out for a ride, and it started on the first try. I can still feel the unsafe kind of thought, don't know why I am feeling so, might be because of my past travels in the luxury cars. Anyway, I have decided to offer my truck to the monastery for delivery services. One peaceful month has passed. Another tragedy strokes the first day of the second month of our stay. Susan is no more... I don't know whether it was an accident or not, what happened was we were walking on the sidewalk, and suddenly, one of the huge bells hanging on top of a metal pole fell... Yes, that happened! Now, I have become all alone, and whoever is targeting me, I hereby make known that you have won this match. Now show yourself and take me, take your worthless prize!

I waited for an hour, but nothing. I went out of the monastery, wiped the sacred powder off my forehead and neck, dropped the wooden bracelets, sandals and necklaces, undressed the robes, untied my hair, entered my pickup truck parked outside, started the engine, charged my phone battery using the car battery, raced to the black market, bought five billion dollars' worth of weapons, ammos, chemical salts, military grade vests, one hundred thousand mercenaries and twenty thousand trucks.

I don't care whether these mercenaries are kidnapped victims or not. First, I went to the police station, kidnapped the high-ranking officer, destroyed the whole building with a single shot from an advanced laser scope inbuilt grenade. I tied him to a chair, made several cuts throughout his body, poured the chemical salts all over him constantly! Loud siren screams disturbed the air. He agreed to cooperate with us, and it was the first time I offered him some space to answer. "It was... the corporate gang... you... leader of anti-corporates mob... we don't have the power to fight them sir... we are bound to obey the powers, aren't we?" he said. Dropped him into a crocodile river, and then me and my professional army unleashed a rampage of destruction on the ones who are after me since I landed here from the GTM land.

I am feeling extreme happiness from taking revenge upon my enemies. Honestly, that was very easier than I thought. It turns out that if you have the money, you will automatically get the power running inside your nerves. Now that I am marked as one notorious criminal, my greedy self has activated! You know what it wants, right? It wants the highest power possible. And for that, I must defeat Jessica! I went to the black market again, ransacked every bit of weaponry, including the beefy nukes. Ok, you might be wondering why there aren't any consequences for my invasion upon the second high powered market? Well, it is not what you think it is! You see, these kinds of high-powered structures are not maintained with the power of its members or weaponry, but the emotion of FEAR!

If a power structure has more weapons and mercenaries, it is not that powerful. But here comes the catch! I have just ransacked a power structure that belongs to the category of Fear, and it means that I am left with no choice other than to fight. Me and my army are on the way to Jessica's mega mansion, and I am feeling great amount of confidence from all the giant nukes stored on our weapon trucks. We have just passed Zeiwo's destroyed farmhouse, the whole area has turned into a cliff. My confidence level received a serious hit seeing the horrible scene. I don't know what is happening inside me, definitely not great. We went past the newly built Chocolust factory, and it looks stronger than ever, and now has no armed guards patrolling the place. Again, my bravery received hit, questions started to pop inside my mind about my new endeavour. Whatever, we roared forward. To change view, started to look at the blue sky, found the smoky trails of jets, planes, missiles, nukes. "I can't defeat her! No one can, I am a fool!" I said myself.

I don't want to kill my crew, they all must be saved, Jessica's mansion is only a few miles away! I took a quick peek in the rear-view mirror, can see the trail of trucks following my vehicle, fuelled with rage and fear. Am sure they have no idea about where they are heading to, and I just feel like a lunatic. They have joined me only for the money, and if not paid, they will abandon me. What's up with that! Don't get me? Ok, let me explain; they, me, you, we are all part of humanity, and I guess we are obliged to join hands to keep this precious community alive, right?

(silence)

Sorry guys, it's hard to talk and drive. Ok, so this community thing, we need to keep it alive, but here I have spent billions of corrupt moneys, to recruit a handful of fighters, and they don't care about anything but money! Maybe they have to put food on their family's table, I know that. But we must fight the evils off bit by bit, stop wasting time on fighting silly social media riots and gender wars, or else the real power's will build something to eliminate our entire race, for some fancy reasons. I am losing all my hope in this endeavour. I have hope in the distant future, in which the entire world joins hands and eradicates these destroyers out of the equation.

I slammed the speed pedal full, then took a sharp turn to the left...

Breaking News!!!

Sir David is no more — Vehicle lost control!

Kevtit county: Winner of bravery award, great scientist, great monk, great soldier and the first winner of the award for the kindest person on earth. Sir David is no more, his good soul flew away from our world today, his vehicle lost control and crashed into the mountain valley. He played a major role in eliminating world hunger and saving millions of patients. His new mission 'Apocalypse' will be implemented in less than two years, it was his dream come true mission, and we are bound to honour his dream. His funeral ceremony will be conducted on next Tuesday at the Great Hall. All are welcome.

In memory of Sir David (32)

Heartily condolences from the GTM members